The Poseidon Project

by

E. William Podojil

The Herb Society Mysteries,
Book One

Cover Art by *The Wild Rose Press, Inc.*

The Wild Rose Press, Inc.
PO Box 708
Adams Basin, NY 14410-0708
Visit us at www.thewildrosepress.com

Publishing History
First Edition, 2024
Trade Paperback ISBN 978-1-5092-5684-6
Digital ISBN 978-1-5092-5685-3

The Herb Society Mysteries, Book One
Published in the United States of America

Dedication

To Maureen and Edward Podojil
Thanks for teaching me to dream big, work hard, and
never give up.

Acknowledgements

My father taught me that in order to be successful, I had to surround myself with the best and smartest people.

The Poseidon Project was a coordinated effort with the most amazing team. I want to thank the professional team at Wild Rose Press for all its work in publishing this story. Thank you to Dianne Rich, Editor for believing in my story and making me a better writer and storyteller. Dianne led this process from my first query letter to publication and I can't thank her enough. I hope to work with you on the next novel, Dianne! Finally, I want to thank my friends and family for following me on my journey to write another novel. Most especially, to my husband, Joe for the support, challenges and always being there for me, and to my sons, Nico, Miguel, Eddy and my furry son, Hurley for making me happy, proud and complete.

"Out of suffering have emerged the strongest souls; the most massive characters are seared with scars."

Khalil Gibran

"Thousands have lived without love, not one without water."

W. H. Auden

Chapter 1

Molly Halloran woke up alone, the pillow next to her still indented, a reminder left behind by her husband's head. Daylight crept through the blinds and illuminated their bedroom enough that she could see the southwestern style furniture and artwork decorating their spacious bedroom.

John had left the house at three a.m. for an early flight to Newark that connected to a twelve-hour hop to the United Arab Emirates. He'd been working on this deal for over a year and finally came to an agreement, in principle, to create an investment and ownership structure with Phoenix Equities in the lead position. Molly often accompanied him on trips, but she wasn't interested in flying from one desert halfway around the world to another one. The deal was highly confidential, and he only referred to it as Project Poseidon.

Poseidon was owned by a consortium of investors who had approached Phoenix Equities for financial backing. The negotiations were long and extremely complex. The company needed investment to scale up operations, and when successful, Poseidon technology would help millions of people around the world. John was unusually tight-lipped about this particular project, only mentioning that it was a game changer.

****

Retirement was not what Molly had expected. She

and John had worked hard to build a business, raise a family, and live frugally so one day, they could build their dream home. Her eyes studied the expensive adobe-style plasterwork on the walls of her bedroom. It was an upgrade she had to have. Their architect specified it to add authenticity to their sprawling home, yet it was only a caricature of the real adobe, hand-crafted by natives for shelter against the burning sun. The home's southwestern décor now felt contrived. Their home could grace a magazine cover and was a testament to their years of hard work. But it was sterile and told nothing about their lives or adventures. The patina of age, sweat, and authenticity was hidden beneath a façade of store-bought artwork and furniture.

She sat up in the bed and swung her feet to the floor, careful to check for scorpions that may have scurried into their air-conditioned sanctuary, frantic to escape the desert heat. Despite her athletic figure, her knees and hips cracked and groaned as she stood and walked to the bathroom. Molly pondered whether she should make coffee first or take a shower, laughing to herself at the insignificant magnitude of her decision. The last twelve months had been an adjustment, to put it mildly. Retirement had been the goal, and after a lifetime of working, she wished for unstructured time, no more stress, and the freedom to do whatever she wanted. That included building this house; replacing their old vacation home that used to stand on the property. Her husband inherited it from his parents, and he, Molly, and the kids enjoyed the quirky yet comfortable house where they built two decades of vacation memories. She needed a change, so they tore it down and replaced it with the showplace that now stood in its place.

Be careful what you wish for, made sense to her now. She strode into their palatial bathroom and dropped her robe. The scar where her left breast used to live reminded her of life's fragility. For nearly two decades, she felt revulsion at her disfigurement and changed her clothes in the dark to avoid looking at herself. Now she saw it for what it was, a battle scar from a war in which she had prevailed, at least for now.

Molly reflected on her youth when her body was intact and supple, and the possibilities seemed unlimited. While she was grateful for her health, family, and abundance, something was missing. Her children were grown, and now she was a grandmother to little ones who lived too far away. She stepped into the shower and turned the spigot. Nothing. Soon, the wide showerhead sputtered, and water drizzled on top of her head. It was the desert; what did she expect? When the water finally rained down upon her, she lost herself in a slideshow of memories that played through her mind. Meeting John, Argonne, her adventures with the Herb Society, having her first baby and then two more, teaching, surviving breast cancer, losing her parents, and here she was. A succession of life events that suddenly came crashing to a screeching halt. Her work, her routines, her purpose, and everything that defined her stopped, as if she sprinted full-speed into a fake adobe wall.

She toweled off and got dressed in her cavernous walk-in closet. Why did her dream home feel more like a tomb, embalmed to last forever, but dead inside? Her current life felt like a purgatory between her uncertain future and mourning everything she had been. It was a feeling she would never reveal to anyone. Nobody wanted a sad Molly Halloran.

****

To combat monotony and attempt to stay healthy, Molly began walking, first just a lap around the block to today where she walked several miles each day. Both her parents lived well into their nineties, so she predicted her body and mind had to last at least another twenty years, give or take. Death didn't scare her. Tedium, not having purpose and being irrelevant scared her. Her time outside strengthened her body and allowed for her mind to daydream and wander. Every day, she felt stronger, and she pushed herself a little further. Her body began to crave the movement, and her mind flourished with new opportunities and goals, rejuvenated by activity and fresh air.

Today, she ascended the steepest hill in Ocotillo Ridge, a feat that seemed impossible only a few months ago. Her arms pumped like pistons and sweat beaded her brow as she huffed to the summit. Here she stood proudly, surrounded by a crown of mountains, hundreds of millions of years old. Their craggy, imperfect cliffs still held their infinite beauty, despite their flaws and scars. She thought about her own scars as she inhaled the cool morning air through her nostrils. After counting to ten, she exhaled and wondered what all of this looked like eons ago when it was covered by an ancient sea. Mountains were born out of violence, conflict, and unplanned events that changed everything. Like hers, the mountain ranges were scars, too, changing the landscape forever into something ethereal and beautiful. It was all about perspective and attitude. As she descended the hill, she walked with an energy

4

and enthusiasm she hadn't felt for a long time. She was tired of being dormant and knew what she had to do.

She decided to un-retire.

Chapter 2

Their home was in a gated neighborhood named Ocotillo Ridge, designed for people aged fifty and older. Molly was seventy and enjoyed living with predictably nice weather, having lived most her life in northern climates. The rugged Santa Catalina mountains provided an ever-changing backdrop to their home and neighborhood and, depending upon the time of day, produced a kaleidoscope of desert colors that surprised them every day. Whether it was temperate or blazing hot, she practiced her daily yoga under a shaded ramada. In the evenings, when it was cooler, she and John relaxed in their hot tub or stared into the dancing flames of their outdoor fireplace. Dining al fresco under a cloudless blue sky or blanket of stars was one of her favorite things about living in Arizona. A small grove of citrus trees hung heavy with unripe fruit. Tomato and pepper plants, scraggly and brown from autumn's shorter days, continued to flower, despite fatigue from a long growing season. The back yard was surrounded by an adobe wall, not so much for privacy, but to keep out the coyote and bobcats. Somehow, three non-venomous snakes found their way into the garden and created unseen property lines dividing their territories. Bees and hummingbirds buzzed around the abundant flowers that perfumed the desert air with their fragrance.

Snow already capped Mount Lemmon, the

towering peak that crowned the Santa Catalina mountains, and created abundant fresh water during the spring melt, quenching the thirst of the desert plants and animals while partially refilling the human-drained aquifers that pooled beneath the foothills. Before moving to Arizona, Molly envisioned the desert as a barren landscape with sparse plant and animal life. But the desert thrived with life that had adapted over centuries and flourished by conserving and storing water. During the current droughts, water was scarce for humans and their pets. Aquifers emptied, arroyos went dry, and trees grew brittle under the unrelenting sun. Wildfires became more common. Some days, their home had little or no water flowing through the pipes, and their garden appeared parched. A brief rain shower could make everything instantly green and alive.

Molly stayed in touch with friends she had worked with during her Argonne days, and three of them were so impressed with her photos on Facebook, they decided to move to Ocotillo Ridge, as well. She was thrilled to be reacquainted with them, and their friendship picked up where they left off over forty years earlier.

The friends remained competitive with each other and battled for who would be the fastest, especially up and down hills. Breaking a sweat, they laughed about their days at Argonne together and told stories of their teaching careers after they left the labs. They shared many of the same activities they enjoyed as young women. Molly was the best rifle shot and always had been. Whether it was target shooting or skeet, she still knew how to handle a rifle and always hit her mark. Betty was the mountain climber and joked she was part goat, which was evident by the speed with which she scampered up a hill. Linda was the traveler, and Donna loved to walk, often recounting stories of surpassing the male Army recruits in both speed and endurance.

Molly Halloran, Linda Eastman, Donna Rivero, and Betty Bao had a standing lunch date every Wednesday at the Ocotillo Room—the main restaurant inside the clubhouse that served Ocotillo Ridge. Molly arrived early one Wednesday several months ago and stared at the reservation list. For the noon time slot, someone had written the word HERB. A jolt of shock ran through Molly's body as she stared at the page. *How can this be possible?* She casually asked the hostess why HERB was written under their reservation.

"Let me check. I'll ask the manager," the hostess responded. A few minutes later, she returned with an answer. "Halloran, Eastman, Rivero, Bao—first letter of your last names," the hostess revealed. "He sees you every Wednesday and has a standing reservation for you, so he abbreviated it HERB since your meals go on your account. Guess it makes it easier for him. Dunno." The hostess returned to welcoming guests and barking out orders to the kitchen staff.

When the others arrived for lunch, she told them what she had seen. Betty added, "Jesus, I would have been shocked, too. Glad you clarified it."

Donna chimed in, "That was over forty years ago. I'm sure it's just a coincidence."

Betty added, "Nothing is a coincidence. I hope nobody here has found out anything."

Linda laughed. "If they did, we can tell them *Herb Society* was about weed, like we were stoners in college, or something."

"I tried weed once and threw up, so never again," Betty offered.

"Guess I'm the group pothead." Linda laughed. "I loved it."

"We'll need to keep an eye on the restaurant manager, just in case he's in the know," Betty conspired.

"We can always say it was a club we started when we were young, in case anyone asks." Molly offered. "It's basically true."

"Yeah, true-ish," Linda replied. "The truth would curl their toes."

They had called themselves *The Herb Society* since they were in their twenties. It was an inside joke that nobody understood, and they kept it between the four of them. While the name sounded prestigious, in reality, it was a lunch club of four retired, very sarcastic ex-scientists, former teachers, and current best friends.

****

John Halloran traveled quite a bit as CEO of Phoenix Equities. Molly sat on the board and continued to advise them when consulted, which wasn't often. Molly never revealed the depth of her knowledge of the company, nor the fact that she owned fifty percent of John's majority shares, making her the company's second-largest shareholder. It was easier to play the part of the CEO's wife than an active board member. She feigned that she didn't know or care what was happening in the company, but John knew differently, and they played that game to their benefit.

The Herb Society were already seated at a table, as Molly slalomed through the tables, most of which sat couples or singles. It was lunch, and the ambient noise of loud conversations, older adults often shouting and repeating their words, sounded like a boisterous high school cafeteria. Most of the time, Molly accepted the inevitable aging process with grace, while other days she fought it, reminding herself that she had plenty of miles left in her.

"How has the single life been since John's been gone?' Betty inquired as Molly situated herself in her seat. "Have you been staying up late watching dirty movies?"

Molly laughed. "Of course!" she responded. "I've become a completely unbridled porn addict in the eight hours since John left for Dubai."

"When is John back?" Linda asked.

"About a week from today," Molly answered.

The Herb Society always seemed to have multiple conversations going at any given time, punctuated by outbursts of laugher that often drew the ire of neighboring diners.

"God, that's a long flight," Donna continued. "What do you do for twelve hours? I'd go nuts just sitting there with nothing to do. I guess I'm kind of claustrophobic."

"You used to love flying with us for work," Molly added.

"That was different. I had work to do, and we could always keep each other company. Totally different animal."

"I'm sure John gets to fly first class," Linda added. "They have these marvelous little cabin things with a seat that turns into a bed. That, plus unlimited movies and cocktails, makes it nice. I'll bet he gets some delicious privacy with no one interrupting him. Except the stewardess with more cocktails."

"They're called flight attendants now, Linda," Molly corrected her.

"Roy and I always flew first class. We even took the Concorde once. JFK to Paris in less than four hours. Did I ever tell you that?" Collective eye rolls indicated she had, more than anyone cared to count.

"Will he call you when he gets in?" Linda asked.

"Probably," Molly answered. "We don't need to talk every day. He's busy, and so am I. He'll text me a sweet emoji so I know he's thinking about me."

"Thank God we didn't have cell phones when we worked for Argonne, or Richard would have gone nuts. Not out of concern for me, mind you, but because he liked control," Betty reflected. "He was afraid I would cheat on him. Guilty conscience probably."

A waitress delivered separate checks billed to their accounts so that they would hit their food and beverage minimum for the club each month. The four women went their separate ways.

Later that night, John called Molly. "I'm on the other side of the world. Just wanted to let you know I got here safely." John sounded understandably groggy.

"Did you sleep?" Molly asked him, although she already knew the answer.

"I did a lot of prep for the meeting tomorrow. I expect it to be contentious until we actually sign."

"Are the purchase funds set to go?"

"All set, but not yet transferred," John replied. "Patrick is picking me up. I'm waiting for him now."

Patrick Aziz was the managing director of Phoenix Equities Arabia. He managed a small staff of finance analysts based throughout the Middle East. He was a

British national whose father came from Lebanon and married his mother, who was born in Northumberland. At thirty years old, Patrick was a high-potential wunderkind. He did his undergraduate studies at Cambridge and received a Master's of Business from the London School of Economics.

John had dreamed of having his son Lukas take over the business one day, but Lukas had other plans and politely declined. So Patrick became the heir apparent. Fluent in Arabic and English, Patrick was indispensable during the negotiations for Project Poseidon, so John relocated him to Dubai. Patrick enjoyed his life as an expat in a major city but shared very little about his personal life.

Molly had never met him but spoke to him on the phone, and John virtually introduced Patrick and Molly on one of his video conferences. There was something in his voice that she couldn't articulate that irritated her. Maybe it was that she felt dismissed by him or held an unconscious grudge that Patrick, and not her son, would one day lead Phoenix Equities. He certainly treated her as the wife of a very important man and didn't mask his ambitions of moving up the company ladder.

****

A week passed, and John had only texted a few times since his arrival in Dubai. She scrolled through her phone and noticed his last text, a smiley face blowing a kiss emoji, had been sent three days ago. As she walked to the Herb Society weekly lunch, she called John's mobile phone. It rang for too long, and John's voicemail was full, so she couldn't leave a message. She tried three more times, hoping he would at least text her, but there was silence. She then called the mobile phone for Patrick Aziz. The call connected and went into voicemail. "Hi, Patrick. This is Mrs. Halloran. I hope the negotiations are going well. Can you please let John know I've been trying to call him? Nothing urgent, but please have him send me a message or call to let me know how things are going."

She checked her watch. It would have been past ten p.m. Dubai time. Molly sat with her friends but felt unsettled. John always shared his location in his phone settings, so while the ladies were talking, she ran a quick scan to find his location. The cursor searched and searched before displaying *no location found* on the screen. *Is he out of range? Or did he turn off his location on purpose?*

Her pulse beat rapidly, so she began taking deep breaths to calm her rising anxiety.

"Molly, are you okay?" Betty asked her.

"I just have the hiccups," Molly lied. "I get rid of them by deep breathing for a minute or so."

When their meals came, Molly dug into her meal, distracting herself from mentally going down rabbit holes of worst-case scenarios. *He's fine, and probably out celebrating the signed deal,* she thought. When lunch was over, she decided to walk a different way home.

Linda had also picked up on Molly's preoccupation. "Hope you are feeling okay. I didn't get a chance to talk to you much, but you seemed quiet." Linda huffed as she tried to keep up with Molly.

"Sorry about that. I haven't heard from John in a couple of days, so my Irish Catholic DNA goes into disaster mode." Molly laughed.

"I'm sure everything is fine," Linda reassured her.

"Dubai is halfway around the world, so maybe there's something messed up with the satellites."

She and Linda parted, and she walked solo. It was another beautiful day, like just about every day. The sun filtered through the clouds, bathing the landscape in light that made the desert surroundings crisp with color and clarity. Molly took in a deep breath through her nostrils, both to calm her nerves and take in the scent of autumn in the high desert. Chicago autumn air smelled of crinkled, fallen leaves and had a faint hint of smoke coming from fireplaces put back into action. She missed the color palette of autumn leaves but didn't miss raking them. She craved a crisp fall apple and chatting with random strangers about how the days had become so much shorter and the nights even darker. Every year it was a ritual—a seasonal passage on the path toward winter. People reacted like it was the first time Chicago had ever experienced autumn.

Molly walked at a brisk pace and focused her mind on things that could distract her from her rumbling anxiety. She silently recited words of gratitude for her health, family, and friends as her mind drifted in and out of positive thoughts, purposely distracting herself from worrying about John. When she rounded the corner to her street, she noticed several cars parked near her driveway. She wasn't expecting anyone, so quickly dismissed it, thinking the cars must be in her neighbor's driveway. Maybe she needed a new contact lens prescription. As she got closer, she saw that the cars *were* indeed in her driveway. Her heart thumped quickly, and her mouth went dry. *Why were they here?* She saw that one of the sedans had an Arizona State Police emblem on the side of the car door. She masked her racing mind behind a polite smile as she approached the cluster of vehicles. *Did we forget to pay our property taxes? Do we have unpaid parking tickets?* she wondered.

An officer stepped out of one of the cars as she approached. He could have been forty or sixty, blotchy, red-faced, and quite overweight. Molly noticed he was sweating. "Mrs. Mary Halloran?" the man asked without introducing himself.

"Hello, yes, that's my name. Why are you here? Did we do something wrong? Is there a problem with the house?"

The man shuffled uncomfortably. "No, ma'am. Nothing is wrong with the house."

A second man, wearing a navy suit jacket in need of a pressing accented by dark brown mismatched trousers, stepped from his car. His grim, pale face made Molly's blood run cold. "Mrs. Halloran, I'm Sergeant Duncan. I'm afraid I have some news. It's about your husband."

Chapter 3

John Halloran was missing. When he failed to show up at a dinner celebrating the successful negotiation of an investment plan to support Project Poseidon, his colleagues became concerned. John had brokered the four-billion-dollar deal and had arranged the celebration himself, which made it even more odd that he wouldn't show up to his own party.

Patrick Aziz called the San Rafael hotel the following morning and learned that John had checked out the previous day, two days ahead of schedule. This sudden change was atypical for John, according to Patrick and other colleagues. He was very regimented about his schedule for both family and security reasons. It was completely out of character that John would not show up at a company event. Was he ill in a hospital somewhere?

After several hours, Patrick called the Dubai police department for suggestions on what to do. The police receptionist answered that there was not much they could do at this point, as John was not technically missing—he had only changed his schedule without notifying anyone. But the receptionist put in a search request for John's passport and business credit card numbers he received from the office manager, and in less than an hour, he had a hit.

Since John was considered a foreign executive

VIP, the police indicated they would assist to help find his whereabouts. Later that day, they discovered that John's passport was registered at the prestigious Excelsior Hotel in Palm Jumeirah, a "city" about thirty minutes from downtown Dubai. Palm Jumeirah was one of the first of several man-made archipelagos constructed with reclaimed land beneath the Persian Gulf. Shaped like a stylized palm tree surrounded by a crescent, the Palm Jumeirah was known for its lavish resorts, luxury shopping, and trendy restaurants. The Excelsior Palm was the epitome of opulence and luxury. The resort sprawled across the western crescent surrounding the Jumeirah archipelago and was significantly larger than neighboring hotels. According to the front desk, John checked into a single deluxe room overlooking the water.

Detective Abadi from the Dubai police was put in charge of the investigation. He was new to the department but aspired to become a lead investigator. Finding an American, who wasn't technically considered missing yet, was not his idea of exciting police work. More than likely, Mr. Halloran wanted to be away from the city and his colleagues. Perhaps he wanted time alone or had a special someone with whom he could discreetly spend a couple of days. It wouldn't have been the first time something like that happened. Abadi's first stop would be the Excelsior Hotel at Palm Jumeirah.

When he arrived, Abadi asked to speak with the hotel manager, who was professional but mildly cooperative, tasked with protecting John Halloran's, and every other guest's privacy. The manager confirmed that Mr. Halloran was a hotel guest, made one restaurant charge and one beach rental the previous day. He asked to see John's hotel room. "Absolutely not, I'm afraid," the hotel manager snapped back.

Abadi marched toward the beach area to see what he could learn there. He introduced himself to the beach supervisor in Arabic but quickly jumped into English, remembering the vast majority of hospitality workers were foreign, with English becoming the default language. The supervisor pointed to a young, white-uniformed beach attendant who remembered that John had rented a kayak with a friend the day before. The attendant also confirmed that Mr. Halloran had taken the requisite safety courses on how to paddle, how to flip a capsized kayak, and a general map of the Palm islands. As required, he signed a waiver. The attendant confirmed he watched Mr. Halloran enter the water on the kayak with a mandatory life vest and that he had expressed a desire to paddle around the lagoons to view the other hotels and villas from the water. The weather conditions were calm, with a gentle offshore breeze. "When did he make the kayak rental?" Abadi asked the beach attendant.

"Yesterday afternoon," he replied. "He rented it for a half day but told me he would only be a couple of hours."

Abadi scribbled some notes. "Where is the kayak he rented?"

The attendant flipped through his logbook. "It appears he has not returned the equipment yet. That's not unusual. We usually just add the extra time onto their hotel bill."

"How do you know if he is fine?" Abadi asked, mildly frustrated that he had to speak in English to a worker in his own country.

"Sometimes our guests will get confused and come ashore at another resort. Many of the Palm fronds look similar, so it's easy to get lost. Our boats are light blue and have *Excelsior Palm* stenciled under the hull. Other hotels will call us if they get one of ours. We always call neighboring hotels if we get one of their pieces of equipment by mistake."

Abadi glared at the attendant, annoyed by his lack of assistance. "Have you checked with any other hotels to see if one of your boats came ashore there?"

"I have not," the attendant answered defensively. "Normally they will call us. We let the guests have the freedom to use all of our facilities, and if they end up at a neighbor's hotel, we don't make a big deal about it. Wealthy people don't bother with confining rules."

Abadi shook his head. "Please call to see if one of your boats came ashore at a neighboring resort. We have concerns that Mr. Halloran may be missing."

An overweight hotel guest struggled to fit into her life vest and impatiently demanded assistance. "I've got to help a guest. I'll call the other hotels today." The attendant loped toward the frustrated woman.

Abadi made one more stop to visit the hotel manager. "Can you tell me the last time your guest, Mr. Halloran, used his hotel room key?"

The hotel manager glared at Abadi but complied. Fingers tapped the keyboard in search of answers, then suddenly stopped. "That's odd," the manager said as his eyes squinted at the screen.

"What's odd?" Abadi asked.

"Mr. Halloran last used his room key almost eighteen hours ago."

Abadi dropped his head in frustration. "Mr. Halloran seems to be missing. He rented one of your kayaks and apparently hasn't returned it, and he hasn't used his hotel room for a day and a half. I suggest you start a search for him." Abadi flipped him his card. "Call me as soon as you or your staff see him so I know he's safe. He's a high-profile visitor to Dubai."

The hotel manager scoffed. "Well, most of our guests are."

Abadi shot him a look that he was serious. "Call me when you find him. The next call will be coming from the United States Ambassador."

Twelve hours later, the search continued. Border control agents at Dubai International Airport were notified to check departing passengers and flagged John's passport in their system. The airline was notified, more as a formality than anything. It would be highly unlikely that he would pass through border control undetected. Hotel staff was unable to locate John or the kayak either at the Excelsior or at seven neighboring resorts. The hotel manager called Abadi to give him the update at around seven p.m.

"Thank you for letting me know," Abadi responded. "I'm ordering a water search for tomorrow morning. I've asked the officers to be discreet and to not alarm the guests. They will commence at around nine a.m."

The hotel manager obliged, reluctantly. A missing guest was the last thing he needed right now.

****

The next morning, at around seven a.m., a sleek yacht skimmed across syrupy, placid seas as the sun peeked above the horizon. The *Zafir,* a luxury fishing yacht chartered by a group of South Korean businessmen, turned toward a new fishing spot. The passengers, there for a team-building event of sportfishing, looked tired and hungover. Several napped on luxurious sofas and chairs on the main deck. They had departed at four a.m. for an early morning fishing trip, hoping to catch some marlin, wahoo, or tuna that lived in the Persian Gulf. They drank coffee and tea to stay awake. Nobody had caught anything yet.

As the *Zafir* radar searched for large fish, the captain got a hit and turned the boat in that direction. After about twenty minutes, they found the "large fish," which was actually a single person kayak floating about five miles offshore, due north of Palm Jumeirah's crescent-shaped barrier that protects the delicate islands from the Persian Gulf waves.

The captain circled the kayak in search of the kayak's occupant. They saw nobody in the water, nor were there any scuba buoys that would indicate any divers. There was just an untethered blue kayak gently bobbing in the waves. The *Zafir* captain decided to backtrack and look for a stranded swimmer, or worse yet, a body. The waters off Dubai were calm today, thanks to a light breeze. The shallow Gulf would quickly become choppy if the wind speed increased. More concerning were the recent sightings of both hammerhead and mako sharks in the area.

The captain had a bad feeling about the situation. Unmanned kayaks didn't just drift through the maze of Palm Jumeirah's islands and end up five miles off the coast near the shipping lanes. Of course, it was possibly from another region of Dubai, but someone or something had to get it there.

He decided to contact the United Arab Emirates Coast Guard. He was immediately ordered to anchor in place until an official vessel could meet them in their current location. His suspicions were correct as the Coast Guard asked few questions, which likely meant they were already searching for someone. The captain complied with the Coast Guard's request and dropped anchor. He addressed the passengers about the situation and the delay, but nobody complained. They were quite happy to have a free extension of their team-building time on the yacht.

When the Coast Guard reached *Zafir*, they quickly thanked and dismissed the crew before taking possession of the kayak. The captain knew better than to inquire what was going on but was convinced this was not about a beach boat that accidentally blew into the water.

As he piloted *Zafir* toward the Dubai Fishing Harbor, he noticed a military helicopter chopping through the air toward the Coast Guard vessel, perhaps joining the search from the air. A few minutes later, two more small helicopters and an additional patrol boat rushed toward the spot where the kayak had been found.

Someone important is missing, the captain thought. He made a mental note to check the news in the coming days to learn more, but if this was indeed an important person, it would likely remain quiet. Dubai preferred to project itself as a safe playground for the world's rich and famous, and not distract the public with unfortunate news of missing visitors.

Two hours later, Abadi was back at the Excelsior Palm resort. John had been missing nearly forty-eight hours by this point. The hotel and lagoon search found nothing; John's colleagues heard nothing. Border patrol confirmed his passport had not been scanned at the airport, and the airline confirmed, not surprisingly, that John's business class seat was empty.

During a final search of John's hotel room, the room safe, opened by the hotel security manager, revealed John's passport tucked inside, along with his wallet and mobile phone. And later that day, he learned the disturbing news about the blue kayak, that when raised on board the Coast Guard cutter, displayed the name *Excelsior Palm* on its hull.

It was time to notify the United States Embassy.

Chapter 4

Molly entered the house, stunned by the news she just received. She dragged herself toward the living room and fell into the first chair she could find. *Missing? Missing from where?* Molly's brain struggled to make sense of the news delivered by the State Police, who told her to expect a call from the US Embassy in Abu Dhabi, the capital of the United Arab Emirates. She had just spoken to John two days ago and assumed he was on a flight back to the USA to meet with his colleagues in Chicago before heading to Tucson. They usually spoke once or twice during one of his trips, just to check in. John would text if there had been an itinerary update, a flight change or delay, as John promised Molly he would never leave her in the dark on his whereabouts.

Her mobile phone rang with a number she didn't recognize. "Molly Halloran speaking."

There was a momentary delay—which made her think this may be a robocall or sales pitch.

"Am I speaking with Mrs. Mary Halloran?" a brusque male voice asked.

"It is," were the only words Molly could choke out.

"This is Officer Humphries from the US Embassy in Abu Dhabi. I understand you have been notified in person, so I am calling to confirm that your husband, John Halloran, was listed as missing by the Dubai police department this morning."

"Yes." Molly focused while she calculated the eleven-hour time difference, late last night Arizona time. "Do you have details?"

"Mr. Halloran was reported missing by some of his work colleagues when he did not turn up for a business dinner. That was over forty-eight hours ago."

Two days? Molly thought. *I'm just hearing about this now? Why didn't Patrick call?*

"We have reports from the Dubai police department that he went missing while kayaking off the coast of Palm Jumeirah," Officer Humphries declared. "This is the palm tree-shaped archipelago you may have seen in photos."

Kayaking? Molly thought. Kayaking was not one of John's interests. He hated the water, or so she believed. "How do you know he was kayaking?" she asked.

"He rented one at his hotel, the Excelsior Palm." Officer Humphries stalled. "Um, I'm sorry to tell you this, but his kayak was recently found floating several miles offshore. With no occupant."

Molly felt like she might faint and struggled to compose herself. Now wasn't the time to fall apart. *No way John would go to open water. Miles offshore? What the fuck?* Thoughts raced through her head.

"Mrs. Halloran, I don't know the latest details, but there is an active land and water search underway for your husband."

"Okay." Molly desperately tried to get her head together, but she couldn't speak more than one or two words at a time. Disjointed thoughts and tragic outcomes collided inside her mind. *Maybe I'm having a stroke.* She took several deep breaths.

"Mrs. Halloran, I know this is difficult news for you, and I promise to keep you updated," Officer Humphries assured her. "There are many possible scenarios the police are investigating now. Dubai is a big city. People go missing more than you may realize. Normally, we quickly find them within a week."

A week? Molly stiffened in her chair. "How often will I be updated?" she asked.

Officer Humphries paused. "We can update you daily if that works for you. Of course, we will notify you the minute we find him. Try and stay positive, Mrs. Halloran."

Molly held onto the phone, her other hand covering her quivering lip. Her blue eyes pooled with tears. It was like a bad dream. "Okay. I'll try. Thank you, officer." She blanked on his last name.

The phone call ended. Molly stared across her living room, still processing the ton of bricks dumped on her in the last thirty minutes. She instinctively wanted to scream or burst into a tantrum, but why? He was only missing, after all. *Stop thinking about the worst-case scenarios. Don't go there,* she assured herself. Still, her heart raced as she wrapped her head around the news from Abu Dhabi.

She decided to take a walk. That always helped her get her thoughts together. As she walked solo around the neighborhood, her mind swirled with questions and outcomes, but her panic started to diminish, only to be replaced by an array of possible negative outcomes. *What if he's dead?* she thought. *Maybe he ran off with another woman. What if he's hurt and can't communicate with anyone? Could he have been kidnapped?*

Possible scenarios bubbled like a cauldron, and none of them were positive. She decided to call her son.

****

Dr. Lukas Halloran calmly reassured his mom he would be out to Tucson later that evening, and they would work together to determine what to do next. He lived in Arlington, Virginia, but as president of his own IT consulting firm, Lukas had the flexibility to work from just about anywhere. He learned to calm himself to avoid becoming emotionally consumed by a complex challenge, and instead found ways to break the problem into manageable pieces and creatively search for potential solutions. Even with the news about his missing father, Lukas was already in action mode, his worry and emotion tucked away into a box.

This trait made him extremely successful in business and technical circles, but not so much in his personal life. He worked crazy hours, read hundreds of books a year, and was fascinated by technology and how it continued to propel the human species forward. Lukas was obsessed with Michelangelo and other artists and inventors who were boldly ahead of their time. He wondered if, like himself, these notable people were so consumed by their work and ideas that they sacrificed a chance for a personal life, or love. Lukas was an avid runner and stayed in good physical condition. He wore eyeglasses and dressed conservatively. Once, a friend told him the guys at the gym called him the Hot Nerd, which he found funny, though he felt that he was neither hot nor a nerd, despite several men who expressed interest in him. His allure was a combination of intelligence, confidence, and the gym-toned body he hid beneath his professional attire.

Molly didn't know the details of his profession, but he was good at it, judging by his lifestyle. His clients included several large banks, Fortune 500 corporations, and the United States government. She knew Lukas held high-level government security clearance but never asked him details she knew he couldn't tell her.

After she called Lukas, Molly called both of her daughters. Her eldest daughter, Catherine Halloran, was working on postgraduate studies in microbiology and parasitology at the National University of San Marcos in Lima, Peru. Catherine was passionate about health and ridding the tropics of parasites and deadly viruses that incubated in the jungles of the Amazon basin. She had applied to San Marcos, the oldest university in the Americas, never thinking she would be accepted. But to her surprise, she was admitted and had called Lima her home for the last several years. She lived with her boyfriend, Enrique, whom she called *Kiko.*

When Catherine hung up with her mother, she was speechless. "My dad is missing," she told Kiko, who immediately took a place on the sofa next to her. "He somehow disappeared in Dubai. He was kayaking." She shook her head. "He hates the water!"

"Do you need to go to your mother?" Kiko asked her.

"My brother is on his way now. I have clinicals this week and next." She put her face in her hands while Kiko tried to comfort her. "At least Lukas can help Mom in the short term."

Molly's call to her second daughter, Amanda Fowler, went quickly, as the mother of three was in the middle of feeding her twin boys, Alex and Max.

"Missing? Dad? Where? Is he okay?" Amanda asked as Alex let out a scream that could wake the dead and drowned out her mother's attempted response. Molly and Amanda normally texted each other for this very reason. Amanda was usually just getting by managing her three boys. "Mom, can I call you back?"

"Don't worry. I don't know anything more than I've told you. Your dad is missing. Your brother is coming to Tucson. I'll text you when I hear something."

"Sorry, Mom. I'll call you when the twins are napping. Stay positive, Mom, and take care of yourself. Let me know when Lukas arrives."

Now that her kids knew about the situation, Molly made a call to Linda so that she could tell the rest of the Herb Society. Linda was shocked at the news. "You need to be around people. And food," Linda stated in her normal direct manner.

"I don't feel like either," Molly responded.

"When will Lukas arrive tonight?"

"Around nine thirty, I think," Molly responded. "He's getting picked up and will be here shortly after that." Molly didn't disclose that Lukas was flying in a chartered jet for some reason she couldn't articulate. She felt it wasn't her place to share that information, and she didn't want to come across as bragging to her best friends. Lukas was extremely guarded and private. He had been since he was a boy, always downplaying his intelligence and achievements.

"We'll keep you company until he arrives," Linda insisted. "I've already texted our Herb Society chat group. See you shortly."

Before Molly could protest, Linda hung up. She

heard her text alert and saw the message that Linda sent the group. *Maybe a night with my friends is what I need now.*

Within thirty minutes, the other three women had arrived at Molly's house. They brought whatever food they could find, as well as wine, beer, and vodka. Linda and Betty arranged a table of food, and Donna popped open a bottle of Sauvignon Blanc.

Molly didn't have an appetite, and her silence added to the pallor of the room. "This is weird," Betty announced out of nowhere. "I'm not sure how to react to any of this."

Molly wasn't surprised by Betty's directness, but at least she said what was on everyone's mind.

"Yeah. I know," said Molly. "I'm in limbo. Worried, for sure. Kind of sick to my stomach. My mind is racing."

"Don't let your mind go to a bad place. We attract what we think about, good or bad," Linda replied. "Think about positive things, like John is alive and just unreachable."

"I try to think like that, Linda. I normally think positively, but this…the boat they found just…it gives me a terrible feeling."

The other ladies were silent. Molly had already told them about the news from Abu Dhabi. *John's kayak, empty and adrift, miles from shore in the Persian Gulf.* It didn't sound good.

"One second, I think I'm overreacting and too negative, and the next minute, I feel I could collapse into a heap," Molly explained, burying her face in her hands.

"Sometimes I try to prepare myself for the worst,

but hold out hope for the best," Donna offered. "Don't give up, but do something that makes you feel in control of a bad situation."

Molly continued to pace. She tried to call Patrick and the call went to voicemail again. She was frustrated, looked at her watch, and noticed it was four a.m. in Dubai. *Damn you, Mr. Aziz.*

"I don't know who to call now," Molly shared.

"Can you call Phoenix Equities to see if they heard anything?" Linda asked.

"I don't want to panic anyone without real facts. Since the pandemic, Phoenix has operated as a virtual company—everyone works remotely," Molly replied. "Plus, if there's even a hint of doubt about John, a few board members would be hungry to become interim CEO."

The minute she said the words, she realized she forgot to take a very important step. *Their attorney needs to know, to create a timestamp for the company, for insurance, for succession. A lot has to happen if John is dead.* "Excuse me, ladies. I need to make a call," she said as she walked toward her bedroom.

Chapter 5

Lukas Halloran was the oldest of Molly and John's three children. He was also the only boy, and both taunted and protectively oversaw his two sisters growing up. As a young boy, he scored a genius level IQ. Although they were a lot alike, Lukas and his father had a complicated relationship. There was an awkward formality about them, especially evident when they greeted one another—each man oppositely going for a handshake or a hug, and eventually landing on the hug. There was no animosity whatsoever, no alpha male competition, and each man respected the other, despite viewing the world differently. They just didn't have much in common.

John scoffed when Lukas announced he was taking three months off after graduating with his Master of Science from Stanford. John thought he should be working for Phoenix Equities or looking for a job, not gallivanting through French Polynesia with his friend Drew. Lukas and Drew shared their adventures in an email distribution newsletter they sent to family and friends. John was not a fan of reading about his son's playful adventures when he felt Lukas should be focusing on his career options. He only saw updates Molly would show him. They were two handsome men, sailing the islands and having lots of experiences. In most of the photos, they were shirtless and in bathing suits. John had never seen Lukas so relaxed and happy. Their newsletters showed swimming with sharks and manta rays in Bora Bora, climbing jagged volcanic peaks in Moorea, and scuba diving in the crystal-clear turquoise waters of surrounding islands throughout the archipelago.

Molly gave John updates every few days on their adventures and their upcoming itinerary. John long suspected that Lukas may be gay, and the photos of their adventures in paradise left him with little doubt, not because of anything overt, but it was how the men looked at each other. They looked like they were in love and wanted to share that with the world.

John felt excluded, even though he was the one who deleted the email updates. Molly read each note to John, anyway. John was both disappointed and hurt to be left out of important things happening with his son. "Why doesn't he include me in his life?" John would complain to Molly. "I don't know who this Drew guy is. Is he a friend or something more? He only tells me the formalities of things but doesn't share the personal stories with me."

"He probably thinks you don't want to know," Molly answered. "Besides, he knows you're a Republican, and the party stance on LGBT civil rights isn't exactly rooted in the twenty-first century."

"I'm not a registered Republican. I vote for the best candidates and my finances," John protested.

"Candidates who always seem to be Republican, John. What do you expect him to think? It would be helpful if you showed a little sensitivity to him. The party you support is often hostile toward people like him."

"Yeah, wait until he's working and paying taxes. Then he'll know where I'm coming from."

Molly sighed. "Come on, John. When your basic rights are threatened, it's hard to prioritize tax rates as your biggest concern. I'm not telling you how to vote, but you need to explain to him that you support him as a priority, first and foremost. Most of the people in this country support rights for gay people, regardless of party. You need to tell him that you do, too."

"He knows I support him. I don't know if he's gay. He never told me." Before the words were out, John realized what Molly was trying to explain.

"Lukas once told me something," Molly explained. "He lives his life openly and lets people figure it out that he's gay. Straight people don't have to come out, so why should he explain his life to anyone?"

"He's got a point there," John responded.

"Lukas is strong, but he's sensitive. He never assumes how a person will react or say when they find out he's gay. Lukas looks for what people don't say, what they conceal, and how they behave. He's not stupid, John. I'm sure he's experienced a lot of rejection in his life, so he prepares himself by being stoic, formal, and cautious. You need to make the first move. Don't assume he knows how you feel."

John gave her a kiss. "Thank you for telling me that. I've really blown it, huh?"

"He loves you, John, but he's terrified you won't accept him," Molly finished. "And no, you haven't blown it. Just reach out and tell him you're happy for him and his life.

Several weeks passed. Molly informed John that Lukas and Drew had finished their journey and were now flying back to the United States from Tahiti. When Lukas landed in San Francisco, he texted his mom. Molly let John know.

After they cleared immigration and customs, the men went to wait for their flight to Denver. Drew's parents had a home in Breckenridge that was a couple of hours by car once they landed. After months of warmth and humidity in the tropics, they both looked forward to the crisp mountain air.

When Lukas' phone rang, he saw it was his father calling him. "Oh shit," he muttered. His dad called rarely, and it was usually about something bad. Lukas tensed when he answered.

"Hi, Dad, is everything okay?" Lukas attempted to not sound anxious.

"Hi, Lukas, it's good to hear your voice, and I can't wait to hear about your trip." *Did he and Mom get a divorce or something?* Lukas thought, still believing something bad had happened to spark John's call.

"I was wondering…I mean, your mom and I were wondering if you and Drew would like to spend Thanksgiving with us next month. Here in Arizona. The weather will be nice. You don't have to answer now but think about it."

Lukas was stunned. *He's inviting both of us?* He whispered to Drew while he was on mute, "My dad wants you and me to come to Thanksgiving in Arizona." Drew smiled and gave him a thumbs-up. "Seriously?" Lukas whispered. Drew nodded.

"Thanks, Dad. We'd love to come. What can we bring?"

"I'll let your mother answer that one, but we'll fix up the downstairs bedroom for you guys. The one with the best view of the mountains."

Lukas was taken aback. His father was talking about the bedroom with the king-sized bed. *One* king-sized bed. "Okay, Dad, sounds good. Tell Mom we said hi."

"Will do. Enjoy Colorado," John replied.

Lukas glanced at Drew. "I was not expecting that."

Drew simply smiled and put his arm around Lukas. "I look forward to finally meeting them."

****

From that point onward, Lukas and John's relationship grew closer. Having Drew join the family Thanksgiving was a big step for Lukas, and he did his best to maneuver through uncomfortable silence, lots of questions for Drew, and the general awkwardness that comes with bringing a boyfriend home to meet the family. Lukas' family was very different from Drew's in terms of energy and engagement. His sisters befriended Drew and immediately treated him like a new family member, with an inclusiveness Drew had not experienced with his own family. As the night wore on, Drew secluded himself on a sofa, engaged by his phone, while the rest of Lukas' family laughed while playing games.

Thanksgiving night, as they lay naked in bed together, Lukas felt relief that Drew had been accepted and engaged by the family. It was the first time Lukas had ever been one-half of a couple in the eyes of his family, and he loved that feeling. The happiness he felt, plus the lingering effects of the wine they had all enjoyed all night, made Lukas feel a bit horny. Already aroused, he slid over to Drew, kissed his chest and stomach before making his way down to take him in his mouth. Lukas had never done anything sexual in his parents' house, which added to the excitement.

Drew stared at the ceiling, his mind somewhere else and his penis not showing any interest in fooling around. "Are you feeling okay?" Lukas asked him.

"I'm fine, just not in the mood. Maybe I drank too much."

"My sisters loved you. My parents, too."

Drew gave a flat smile. "Nice people."

Lukas kissed him on the cheek. "Thanks for being so great with my family. I was nervous about how it would go, but we did great." Drew glanced at him uncomfortably. "I love you, Drew." It was the first time Lukas had said those words to anyone. Drew was asleep, or at least pretended to be, as Lukas rolled over and dozed off himself.

The next morning, they made their way to the airport to fly home. In the car, they hardly spoke. It was the same at the airport despite Lukas trying to engage Drew in conversation. Lukas sensed that something in Drew had shifted, but Drew said he was just tired. When they boarded the plane, Lukas was surprised when he saw Drew take a seat in first class. "I upgraded," Drew explained. "I need to sleep." As the plane took off, Lukas had a sinking feeling he shouldn't have used the *L* word with Drew. Now Drew was alone in first class, and he was stuck in a middle economy seat for the next four hours. Lukas worried, but he tried to rationalize Drew's behavior as simply needing some alone time after three days of being surrounded by his boisterous family. When they landed, Lukas caught up with Drew at baggage claim. "Did you forget I was in steerage? Hope you got some sleep?" Drew nodded once silently. They collected their bags and walked toward the exit.

"I'm gonna take a taxi home," Drew told him matter-of-factly. Lukas and Drew each had their own apartments, but usually stayed overnight together.

"Thanks for going with me." Lukas reached to kiss Drew, but he maneuvered into a hug.

"See you whenever," Drew said coldly as he marched away.

Lukas took a taxi home alone. *What's going on?* Lukas thought, as his mind raced on what had happened in Tucson. He arranged for them to get together and talk. Drew didn't want to come to his apartment, but instead suggested a restaurant for dinner. Two nights later, at one of their favorite Italian restaurants, the inevitable questions came up. Lukas was right— something had shifted in Drew. He wanted to break up.

"What did I do?" Lukas pleaded with him. "Everything was fine before Tucson, and now you want out? Was it my family?"

Drew shifted uncomfortably. "Your family is very nice. Your sisters are great, and they made me feel welcome. Your parents, too. They're great people, Lukas."

"Then why? Was it something I did?" Lukas asked.

Drew thought for a minute and took a deep breath. "No, it's something I did."

Lukas sat back and tried to process this. "What did you do?" Lukas had to ask, but he knew he wouldn't like the answer.

Drew was silent for a minute. "I've been messing around with other guys, Lukas. I know we said we were exclusive, but I can't do it. And now I've met someone."

A cannonball hit Lukas in the stomach. He wanted to throw up, cry, scream. "Why did you go to Arizona with me then?" was all Lukas could say.

Drew thought for a moment. "You are the kind of guy every man dreams of marrying, Lukas. I hoped that being with your family would somehow snap me out of this whore phase I've been going through. But I don't want that coupled life yet. I'm into hooking up, having fun, partying, hooking up again with ten guys at once. I'm only twenty-four, and I'm not ready to settle down."

"What about this person you met?" Lukas remained calm, but the wheels in his brain were on hyperdrive.

"He wants the same things. We're moving to Europe together. Do the party circuit for a couple of years, I don't know."

A second cannonball hit Lukas in the chest. He was in shock. "When do you plan to move?"

"Next week," Drew responded.

The following week, Lukas volunteered to drive Drew to the airport for his flight to Europe. The men hugged each other. Drew kissed Lukas on the cheek and walked off to the terminal.

Lukas was gutted, heartbroken, and confused. Tears streamed down his cheeks as he focused on the road. He felt like he couldn't go on living another minute, but Lukas drove home alone and vowed to never let himself be hurt like that again.

****

A spotless black Denali rumbled outside as the driver awaited his passenger. Lukas descended the private elevator from his penthouse condominium down to the lobby, dragging three rolling suitcases, loaded and heavy. "Good afternoon, Dr. Halloran," the driver greeted him and helped with his bags. It was a cloudless day, the golden and orange autumn leaves complementing the cerulean sky. Lukas gazed up at his penthouse and wondered when he would be back home. He would miss his views of the Potomac River and Georgetown, and, beyond that, the headquarters of his largest client, The United States government.

As the driver pulled away, Lukas still reminisced about that final goodbye to Drew and the unbearable pain it left behind in his heart. *That was almost fifteen years ago,* Lukas thought. But here he was, being chauffeured to a jet he chartered. Never did he imagine he would have such a luxury to take him across the country for a family emergency. But Lukas was organized and resourceful and jumped into professional mode whenever confronted with a challenge.

Lukas didn't know when he would be returning to the office, so he packed up enough clothes, and more importantly, his office equipment so he could work from his parents' house until they found his father. At least that's what he hoped.

As the Denali pulled into the private jet area of Reagan National Airport, he saw a sea of private aircraft sitting on the tarmac awaiting passengers. The SUV dropped him off in front of a gleaming white jet, much larger than what he had expected. The captain greeted him from the cockpit door as Lukas climbed into the plane. "Looks like I got upgraded," he said to the captain as he surveyed the luxurious, spacious cabin. "All this for me?"

The captain smiled. "Yes, Dr. Halloran. The CEO sends his compliments and appreciation for your continued business. We hope you enjoy the ride."

As Lukas got himself settled, he felt awkward that all of this was for him. The captain re-emerged from the cockpit. "Is everything to your liking, Dr. Halloran?"

Lukas smiled, "Please call me Lukas, and if I knew you were sending a Spectrum 6, I would have invited about fifteen friends."

The captain laughed as Lukas smiled, knowing he didn't have fifteen friends, not even close. He buckled himself into the soft, plush leather seats. "Are you ready to go, Dr. Halloran?" Lukas gave him a thumbs up.

As the jet taxied to the runway, Lukas reflected on the surprising turn today's events had taken. His mother's surprise call interrupted his meeting at the Pentagon, and now he was headed to Tucson to stay with her until they found his dad. He reclined slightly and closed his eyes as the jet's engines accelerated for takeoff, and the plane quietly lifted off into the air. A quick glance at his watch confirmed that he was on time. Within forty-five minutes of leaving his home, he was now in a sleek private jet climbing above the clouds.

The sound of the cockpit door opening woke him from his light nap. A tall, well-built man emerged, wearing what could have been either a pilot or flight attendant uniform. He approached Lukas with a big smile and the greenest eyes he had ever seen. *Is he the flight attendant?* Lukas thought, trying not to stare at the man's tight pants and the assets they concealed.

"We should be landing in Tucson in less than five

hours. Even faster if we can get above the jet stream. There's a pretty strong headwind today," the man explained, having taken the seat across from him. Lukas wasn't paying much attention, as he was captivated by the man's face and felt himself blush. "I'm Taylor, the co-pilot, by the way." He extended his hand in introduction.

Lukas shook Taylor's strong hand. "Hey, I'm Lukas," he replied, noticing Taylor's green eyes were focused on him a bit too long. "How is the weather on the way out west?"

"We may hit some bumps over the Rockies, but otherwise, it should be a smooth ride." Taylor smiled. "Are you heading out for business or pleasure?"

Lukas thought. "Neither, actually. I'm visiting with my family." Lukas chuckled. "I guess that's pleasure, right?"

"Depends upon the family," Taylor joked as he stretched to stand, giving Lukas a view of his muscular biceps and overall well-toned body.

"What do you guys do out in Tucson? Will you hang out for a while?" Lukas hoped he didn't sound too inquisitive.

"I'll be out there for a couple of days. Jerry, the captain, is heading to Phoenix to see his mom. She's turning ninety-five. It all worked out. Since you're doing a one-way trip, we'll have to wait for our next customer heading east, or we'll come back empty on our own dime. I love the mountains around Tucson. I'll take a few days off and keep myself busy."

"You like to hike? I've got some great trail recommendations," Lukas said as his cheeks reddened. *Am I actually flirting with my pilot?* Lukas thought he saw Taylor blush.

"That would be really nice. By the way, thank you for your business with Nimbus Aviation."

Lukas suddenly wondered if he had met Taylor on one of his other trips.

"Can I get you something from the bar before I head back to the cockpit?" Taylor asked him.

"I'm okay. I can make a drink if I want, but I don't like to drink alone, and you're flying the plane, so I guess that rules you out." Lukas kept tripping up and silently admonished himself for babbling. *Just stop talking, Lukas*, he told himself.

Taylor paused and stifled a smile. "Well maybe we can get one after we hike one of the trails you recommend."

"Deal," Lukas answered. "If you want, leave me your number…"

"I'll definitely do that," Taylor responded a bit too quickly. "I've got to get back to work. Nice talking to you."

Why did I just ask him for his number? Lukas chided himself, slightly embarrassed.

He moved himself over to a long leather sofa that ran parallel with the fuselage, propped up some pillows, kicked off his shoes, and rested his eyeglasses on the console before laying himself on the sofa. Thoughts of meeting Taylor, his kind face, his sexy body, those eyes, bubbled through his mind. *Probably a party boy*, he thought. *I'm definitely not his type. No thanks.*

He was intrigued by Taylor, but tried not to think about him. It only made him think about him more, even though he estimated there was zero chance he would see Taylor after this flight. He soon drifted off to sleep, and the aircraft continued southwest, silhouetted by the fiery red sky of the setting sun.

Four hours later, the jet made its approach toward the Tucson area, a few minutes ahead of schedule. Marana Regional Airport was closer to his parents' home, so he opted to land there. Once they landed, the jet pulled close to the terminal as another large black SUV approached.

"Looks like your ride is here," Taylor remarked as he opened the cabin door.

"Thanks for getting me here so quickly," Lukas responded. "I fell asleep, so it felt like only a few minutes."

The limo driver and Taylor helped Lukas unload his bags from the jet's luggage compartment. There were three large bags in total. "Looks like you're gonna stay for a while. What you got in here? Lead?" Taylor asked him as he lifted the largest bags.

Lukas tried to think of a witty response, but now that he was in Arizona, his father's disappearance took on a sobering reality. "I'm staying with my mom for a while. My dad went missing a couple of days ago. We're gonna figure out what to do next."

Taylor looked shocked. "Oh shit, I'm sorry. I shouldn't have—"

Lukas interrupted. "Hopefully we'll find him soon."

"Where was he? I mean, is he?" Taylor immediately backtracked. "Sorry, that was way too personal a question."

Lukas responded, "I appreciate you asking. He was…is…in Dubai. I'm going to talk to my mom about what we do next. I don't have a lot of confidence in the current search. Maybe we need to go there and find out what we can."

"By going to Dubai?" Taylor asked.

"Not sure yet. If we decide, you can fly us…" Lukas joked, but immediately realized he sounded like an idiot.

With the bags packed into the large vehicle, Lukas shook the hands of both the captain and Taylor and thanked them for getting him to Arizona. The SUV driver held open the door as Lukas ducked inside.

"Don't forget to give me your number. I'd like to take you up on a hike if you've got time. I know you've got a lot on your plate, but…" Taylor handed him his own card. "Good luck with everything. Let me know if you need help getting to Dubai."

Taylor's smile was wide and bright. Lukas could have sworn he winked at him again. Lukas paused before answering. "I don't think I have a bank account big enough for that, but thanks anyway."

Taylor smiled. "No problem, and thanks for being a great customer. Hope to see you in the mountains."

The two pilots walked toward the parking lot. The SUV driver closed the back door, and they headed for the exit.

Taylor turned his head to look back at Lukas, smiled, and waved. Lukas thought he felt butterflies in his chest as he watched Taylor disappear into a dark parking lot.

He leaned back and stared up through the large moon roof extending the length of the SUV. The night sky was aglow as he surveyed the desert sky and the mass of stars, planets, and galaxies swirling above.

He looked at the business card in his hand. *Taylor J*

Pastore — CEO and Pilot — Nimbus Aviation. Interesting, Lukas thought as he tucked the business card into his briefcase, with no plans to ever call Taylor Pastore.

Chapter 6

When Lukas opened the door to his parents' house, he was happily surprised to see his mom with her friends. He immediately gave his mom a big hug, at which point she started to cry.

"I'm so happy to see you, honey. Thanks for coming."

Lukas was also emotional but kept himself stoic as he didn't want to make his mom more upset. He hadn't expected that seeing her would suddenly make all of this seem very scary and real, and it was surely the same reaction for Molly.

"Honey, you remember my friends."

Lukas walked over to them. "Ms. Bao, Miss Rivero, and Mrs. Eastman, thank you for being here with my mom. She's a very lucky lady to have such great friends." He hugged each woman and returned to his mother's side. Nobody seemed to know what to say.

Finally, Linda Eastman broke the ice. "Lukas, dear. You must call me Linda. This Mrs. Eastman shit is what my students called me. I had a minute of PTSD just now."

Lukas smiled. "Of course, Linda. I can make you a mean martini to take the edge off that PTSD. How's that sound?"

Linda looked at Molly. "Handsome, polite, and he can make cocktails? Where've you been all my life, darling?" Lukas blushed. "I still can't believe some man hasn't snapped you up!"

"Thanks, Linda. Maybe you can coach me in that department."

Molly loved to watch her children navigate life as adults. Make good choices and mend the bad ones. Lukas was here for her, as she knew he'd be.

Betty joined in. "You better call me Betty, too. I'm not an old lady like the other ones in the room. You look like you need some food. We have a kitchen full of goodies."

"Thank you, Betty. I ate a bit on the plane, but it's past midnight on my body clock. Not sure if I'm hungry or just need to go to bed."

"Oh, I'd stay up at least until eleven," Donna chimed in. "Get a good rest, and we can start fresh tomorrow."

Lukas was touched to hear the *"we"* part of this. Surely his mom's friends had no intention of leaving Molly just because her son arrived. "Sounds good. I'll fight to stay awake for another hour but forgive me if I pass out on the sofa and start snoring," Lukas replied. "Thanks again. I'm glad you're here for us."

The ladies left an hour later, and Lukas sat on the sofa with his mom. "It's all so surreal, Lukas. I'm worried, anxious, sad...paralyzed. I have scary thoughts that he's not alive, and then five minutes later, I expect a call from the embassy saying they found him alive and well."

"Yeah, Mom, I know. It's normal to—"

"I hate not being in control," Molly interrupted. "I hate sitting and waiting by the phone. I feel useless."

"There's nothing worse than waiting, Mom. I'm

here, and I'll be waiting with you. At least you'll have some company." Lukas held his mom's hand.

"I feel like getting on a plane tonight and flying to Dubai," Molly interjected. "I'm not sure what I'd do, but at least I would feel like I was close to him."

"That's always an option, Mom. Let's table that thought for a day and see if we hear from the embassy. It's Thursday here, so it's Jumu'ah in the UAE."

Molly looked at him, confused.

"Friday at noon is the Jumu'ah, the day of prayer. Most people still work on Friday, but some offices are closed. I would imagine the United States embassy will be open as normal, so they will keep us informed if there's any news." Lukas searched for the embassy hours online. "We can check in with them Sunday night our time, which will be Monday morning there. Then we can decide what to do."

It was almost midnight, and Lukas could barely keep his eyes open. "What can I make you for breakfast tomorrow?" his mom asked.

"I'll definitely need coffee. I'd like to go for a run in Catalina, first thing. Can I borrow your park entry pass?"

"Sure, honey. Use your dad's car." She took a deep breath. "I'll be here when you get back, but I'll make sure the espresso maker is warm when you get up."

Lukas tried to protest, but Molly stopped him. "It has a timer that I set for six a.m. Is that early enough?"

"Perfect, Ma. We can have breakfast when I get back. Probably around nine, okay?"

"Go get some sleep, Lukas. You've had a long day. And thanks for coming to be with me."

"Wouldn't want to be anywhere else, Ma."

****

The next morning, Lukas awoke and had the momentary disorientation one gets when waking up in a new place. He still wasn't used to his parents' new home. When he realized where he was, he felt a pit of sadness in his chest and stomach. *His father was missing. It wasn't a bad dream.*

Even with only six hours of sleep and a three-hour time difference, Lukas was up and ready to go for a desert run, something he made time for whenever he was visiting. He slipped on his T-shirt and running shorts, grabbed a double shot of espresso, and checked himself in the mirror before heading to the garage. As the lights flickered on, two vehicles appeared under the fluorescent lights: his mom's spotless Mercedes SUV and his dad's mud-splattered Jeep Wrangler. John Halloran always wanted a Jeep with a removable soft top, but the Chicago winters made this type of vehicle mostly a summer extravagance his practical business mind couldn't justify. When they built the new home in Ocotillo Ridge, he purchased a used Jeep and left the top off most of the time. Tucson was the land of sun, so the expense was justified in his mind.

As Lukas drove, the warm morning air rushed through the Jeep while he sipped his double espresso. He admired his legs, still strong and reasonably tan for this time of year. *Not bad for thirty-eight,* he thought. Catalina State Park lay in the foothills of the Santa Catalina Mountains. The park is home to abundant wildlife and desert vegetation—most notably roadrunners, quail, bighorn sheep, coyote, and the ubiquitous saguaro cacti that stippled the hills and canyons. Runners and hikers had already embarked on their treks, and he found a shaded parking space. Lukas liked to run the Romero Canyon Trail—a fourteen-mile trail that slowly ascends the mountains to an elevation just shy of six thousand feet. He didn't have time, nor the energy, to do the whole trail, so he planned to run up to the Romero pools and then head back. Starting out early, he could make it up and down in a little over ninety minutes, finishing before the intense Arizona sun hit its peak.

The trail started out flat, first crossing an arroyo that was currently dry as a bone, and then heading into the foothills. He paced himself as he climbed the sandy part of the trek, which led to the more challenging part of the trail leading up to the Romero pools. The sun and fresh, dry air revitalized him as he studied the saguaros and other plants that dotted the landscape. It was common to see wildlife, especially in the cooler mornings. Birds and lizards were abundant, and every so often he would see snakes either sunning themselves on the rocks or coiled up in the shade of a rock ledge. Rattlesnakes ranked as the most dangerous animals, although Lukas had not seen any up close. A few years back, a hiker encountered a mountain lion. Lynx and bobcats also roamed the area and together, the carnivores kept the rodent and rabbit population under control. He encountered the familiar sign forbidding dogs from entering the protected wildlife area. This was when Lukas had to kick into high gear, as the trail became a steep climb through the rocky canyon.

When he made it to the Romero pools, he noticed that the water levels were lower than he had seen in the past. He dipped his baseball hat into the water to act as a makeshift air conditioner for his head on his trip back down the canyon. This was a trick his father taught him years ago, and it worked. His hat would be bone dry by the time he reached the parking lot.

When he made it down the most technical part of the decline, he decided to take a detour down another trail since he had made good time and could still make it in time for breakfast with his mom. He veered off to the Canyon Loop trail—which was mostly flat and populated with saguaro, barrel cactus, mesquite, and ocotillo. It was perfect for a cooldown jog and walk.

Lukas looked ahead and saw a figure about one hundred yards in the distance and couldn't tell which direction the person was running. Soon, he confirmed that the person was jogging toward him, and looked to be a *preener*—Lukas' term for a tan, muscular dude running without a shirt, obviously displaying his physique for the world to see. Seeing a preener ignited something in Lukas that was both irritating and alluring. When he was young, Lukas was skinny and hadn't developed much in terms of musculature. He felt self-conscious around other boys who were more developed and confident in their appearance. As his teenage sexuality was still developing, he felt jealousy and shame for his own body, combined with a yearning attraction to their bodies. Despite years of working out, Lukas accepted that he'd never have the bulky muscles that preeners possessed. His own body was muscular and athletic, but not bulky. He dealt with these feelings of envy by diminishing the preeners as shallow, attention-seeking showoffs, and kind of pathetic.

There was something familiar about the approaching runner. He smiled and raised his hand—a typical acknowledgment from one runner to another—

then his mind froze as the runner passed and smiled back, masked behind mirrored sunglasses and a hat. Lukas hoped the other guy didn't notice him.

"Hey, Lukas!" Taylor Pastore called out.

Lukas stopped and feigned surprise when he turned around. "Hey, captain!" He couldn't remember his name. "Funny meeting you here. Sorry, I was in my own world there," he fibbed.

"Me too. I'm Taylor, by the way, in case you forgot." Taylor quickly put his shirt back on, but not without Lukas getting a quick glimpse of Taylor's impressive physique. "You were right—this place is amazing. Thanks for the tip."

"I didn't recognize you without your pilot uniform on." Lukas realized how that comment must have sounded. *Shut up Lukas*, he thought. Lukas smiled and removed his sunglasses—a lesson in etiquette his mom taught him. "Don't let other people guess where your eyes are directed," she would say.

"How is everything with your mom? Any news on your dad?"

Lukas shook his head. "My mom is a tough lady, but it's hard on her. The uncertainty and all."

"You're a good son to be here," Taylor reinforced.

"It's nice to come out here…clear my head, you know?" Lukas looked at his watch. "Speaking of which, I should head back. She likes to make me breakfast."

"I don't blame her." Taylor chuckled, then looked embarrassed. "That didn't come out right."

Lukas smiled at Taylor's awkward attempt to make small talk. There was something endearing about watching Taylor try not to be nervous. "Nice to know that even a handsome pilot gets tongue-tied. Thought it was only me. I'm walking toward the parking lot if you're going that way."

Taylor nodded and followed. *Did Lukas just call me handsome?*

"Any idea when you're heading out?" Lukas asked him.

Taylor shook his head. "No idea. There's a nationwide pilot strike looming, commercial and private. Nobody's booking flights for fear of being stranded. The union is being cagey about the status of negotiations, and the pilots are getting pissed. They may go wildcat, so everyone is holding their breath."

"Shit, that sucks. I hadn't heard about it. Can you fly yourself out?"

They continued to walk together. Their conversation was casual, and it felt like Lukas had known Taylor for much longer than twenty hours.

"Technically, yes," Taylor answered, "but I would have to fly a plane certified for only one pilot. Not many of those out there. I couldn't take the G back home for sure."

They soon arrived at the parking lot and walked toward the Jeep. Taylor's eyes grew wide. "I love Wranglers...especially the sport edition. Nice ride, Lukas."

"Actually, it's my dad's. I'm just borrowing it, you know, while I'm...here."

Taylor shook his head. "Of course. Hey, listen...looks like I'm going to be here for a few more days than I expected. Is there anything I can do for your mom or you? I know you're going through a lot, and I feel kind of useless. I could cook you all dinner or cut your grass."

Lukas laughed. "You mean cut the gravel? I appreciate the offer. How is your family doing back home knowing you may be stranded?" Lukas asked, trying not to sound like he was prying, which he was.

"Just me. My company keeps me on the move," Taylor responded. "I've been a nomad for most of my adult life...first the Air Force and now Nimbus."

Lukas noted a twinge of loneliness in his voice.

"Long story I'll spare you from." Taylor fumbled with his hair nervously. "Look, I know this is a shitty time for you and your mom. I'd be happy to help, you know, with whatever. Totally cool if you don't need me to. I don't often get to meet customers. You seem to be a nice guy."

"I like to keep my hobby as a serial killer on the down low," Lukas joked. He usually made jokes when someone complimented him. Especially a handsome guy.

"I'll try and look past that," Taylor answered.

"I'll let you know. We will hopefully get some clarity this weekend. I've got your number, but I'm a regular at Catalina. Maybe I'll see you around here."

Chapter 7

The next morning, Lukas decided to try a new trail in Oro Valley, the sprawling area abutting Tucson and the Santa Catalina mountains. Oro had grown significantly over the years, which was why his parents decided to build their home in the familiarity of Ocotillo Ridge. The sprawling Oro Valley's population grew with an onslaught of retirees, snowbirds—people who liked to temporarily escape the cold—and residents who worked in several of the businesses in the area. It was situated between Tucson and Phoenix and was predicted to grow in population due to its high desert climate and over two hundred eighty days of sunshine in a given year.

Unlike Phoenix, the Tucson area had more distinct seasons. One year, while Lukas was visiting his parents for Christmas, they received over six inches of snow in one storm. It melted within a day, but the temperature remained in the forties for a week. Spring was when the desert bloomed, summer weather was *Hell's Front Porch,* as Lukas liked to call it, and winters were generally mild.

Since Ocotillo Ridge sat at an elevation over 3,500 feet, the air was dry and the nights were cool. Towering nine thousand feet above Oro Valley was Mount Lemmon, the highest point in the Santa Catalina mountains. Sunsets were spectacular, as the sun turned the mountain range into a dazzling palette of oranges, pinks, reds, and purples.

Lukas asked his mom to join him this morning. She was an avid walker and hiker but had mostly stayed at home since the news of his father's disappearance.

Molly protested at first, saying she was tired, stressed, and needed to be by the phone.

"Mom, they have your cell phone number. You need to get out of the house and move a bit so that you're not tired and stressed. You usually exercise every day, and I'm not taking no for an answer."

"Ugh, fine." Molly sighed. "I know better than to argue with you."

Lukas smiled. "I had a good teacher."

After a twenty-minute drive, they arrived at Honeybee Canyon. Lukas had researched this walk so that it wouldn't be too challenging. His mom was understandably preoccupied, so he wanted something more moderate, yet picturesque.

Molly took off onto the trail as Lukas tried to keep up. She was a formidable power walker who seemed to get faster every year. She liked to be active and exercised every day as long as Lukas could remember. At thirty-eight, Lukas was in great physical shape, also worked out daily, ate well, and got plenty of sleep, thanks to Molly's influence growing up. As a mom, she was strict with sugar and had her kids snack on fruits and vegetables, while other kids filled themselves with potato chips and cookies.

It's probably why most people would never think Molly was seventy years old, and most of Lukas' friends thought he was only in his late twenties or early thirties at most.

In less than two years, Lukas would turn forty. Most days, he thought about what the next phase of his life would bring. While marking a new decade of life can mean many things, turning forty nagged at him for reasons he couldn't articulate. Career-wise, he was successful, he was healthy, generally happy and financially secure, but with his father now missing, his future seemed murky. He hadn't thought much about life without his parents or death in general for several years. Approaching forty brought these thoughts to the forefront and now he dealt with that potential loss in real time.

I have to stay focused for Mom, he thought. Now was not the time for spiraling into worst case scenarios. He had not shared this with anybody, but his intuition told him that his father was still alive.

Lukas had zero facts to back this up, but he remembered back several years ago when his grandpa died. He was in Croatia on business and was in a deep sleep when, suddenly, he was jolted awake. He awoke, shivering and extremely cold, and felt certain that his grandfather had just died. It was like his spirit passed right through Lukas as he slept. It was three a.m. in Dubrovnik. Lukas and his grandpa were close, and he knew his grandfather wanted to let him know by passing through him on the way to wherever.

Three hours later, his phone rang, and he saw it was his mom.

"I know. Grandpa died," Lukas stated, not asking a question.

His mom stumbled. "Yes, how did you…?"

"What time, Ma?"

"It was just after eight in the evening. We had a

nice dinner, and Grandpa said he felt full, so he went to lie down on the sofa. I went to wake him up for one of his shows, and he was gone," Molly replied. "How did you know? You're the first one I've told."

"Grandpa told me, Mom." Lukas quickly calculated that when he was jolted awake in Croatia, it was eight p.m. in Chicago.

Since then, Lukas was no longer afraid of death. Einstein's law of conservation, *energy can neither be created nor destroyed—only converted to another form,* proved this phenomenon and explained why, with absolute certainty, Lukas knew his grandfather's energy had transitioned to a new form after passing through his grandson. He felt death was not the end, but simply a change. This was a big statement for an agnostic like Lukas to make.

****

Lukas debated telling his mom that he didn't think John was dead, even though he trusted his intuition. He didn't want Molly to get excited or disappointed if his guess this time was not correct. And why did his grandpa choose him to pass through and not anyone else in the family? What if his father was dead, but Lukas didn't get a sign? All scenarios were possible, which was why he was keeping his thoughts private. Still, he didn't believe his father was gone.

They walked for an hour. Molly was quiet and reserved throughout the hike. Lukas would point out a certain desert plant, or a colorful hummingbird, and Molly's distracted response was vague and distant. He knew his mom was stoic when dealt with a challenge or bad news, and he knew her well enough to know she was preparing for the worst yet hoping for the best.

She called it her "Irish Curse." She could not allow her guard down, believe everything was okay, and then be clobbered with a negative surprise. Her approach was pragmatic, but not negative. Lukas told her she was superstitious, but she did not catastrophize or plunge into a dark vortex of worry. She simply learned to accept worst-case scenarios and pray they never happened.

He inherited those traits, as well, which helped him both personally and professionally. Boyfriends had been both bothered by and turned on by Lukas' cool, confident style. He didn't succumb to mind games or get caught up in drama, but he was constantly processing and analyzing information, reactions, and emotions. He was not without feelings or emotional responses; far from it. When faced with a challenge, his mind would be chaotic or frenzied while working through his thoughts. Sometimes he would panic, think the worst, or feel like shutting down. But on the outside, people would remark how calm he would be in a crisis. Yet Lukas knew that the story inside his brain was far from that. His mom once told him that he was like a swan—graceful and elegant on the surface of the water but paddling like hell beneath it.

As they drove back home, Lukas asked her to share her thoughts with him.

"Well, honey, I'm thinking about going to Dubai. I'm not happy with the radio silence, so I want to go there and…"

"And what, Mom?" Lukas asked.

"Help? Look for him? I don't know. I'm not good just staying here wringing my hands. He's a missing person case to them, but he's my husband and your dad, and we've waited almost a week and have heard nothing. I know you think I'm crazy, but I'm going to go."

Lukas smiled and touched his mother's hand. "I don't think you're crazy, Ma. You have been incredibly strong these last few days. I think you should go, too."

Molly looked at him with surprise. "I thought you would be against it. I've talked about it with the ladies, and they think I should go. They volunteered to go with me, if you can believe that. Even Donna, the claustrophobic flyer."

"Count me in too," Lukas emphasized. "We can start looking at flights tonight."

"Really, you'd want to do that?" Molly asked.

"Of course, Ma, but let's try and get an update from the embassy when we get home."

"Good idea. Are you sure it's okay with work and everything?"

"I think the boss will approve." Lukas pointed his thumb at himself. "He's an awesome guy who lets me work from anywhere in the world."

****

Molly called Linda to tell them they were going to go, and that Lukas was going, too.

"So does that mean you don't need us?" Linda asked. "Because I, for one, am packed and ready to go."

Molly replied, "It's up to you all. It will be expensive to book tickets at the last minute. Can you call Betty and Donna? I can make woodfired pizzas tonight. Talk to you later."

Molly appeared a bit more buoyant. Her posture returned, and her eyes reflected the clarity of regaining control. She had decided, and she would stick to her decision, even though she had no idea how they would get there or what they would do.

"I hope we can find flights this late," she said.

In the back of his mind, Lukas remembered what Taylor told him about the potential pilot strike. Being unable to fly out of the United States was one thing, but not being able to fly back home was what concerned him the most. That gave him an idea.

"Mom," he asked Molly. "Would you mind if I had someone over for dinner with you and the ladies? I know it's kind of an odd question, considering what's going on."

"Do I know this person? Of course, you can, Lukas. We all need our friends around us at such a difficult time."

Lukas rubbed the back of his neck. "I wouldn't say he's quite a friend. More like a nice guy I met on the flight out here who is kind of stuck here for the next couple of days. I ran into him out at Catalina yesterday morning. He likes running there, too."

"Honey, you've uprooted your life to be out here with me. I can imagine it would be fun to hang out with someone other than a bunch of old ladies."

"I love hanging out with all of you. It's more like, I kind of feel sorry for him, Mom. His name is Taylor. It's kind of my fault he's stuck in Tucson."

Molly looked perplexed. "Your fault? May I ask why?"

He didn't share a lot with her, especially about his business life, and on the rare occasion he had one, his love life.

"He flew me here."

Chapter 8

Molly, her friends, plus Taylor and Lukas dug into the woodfired pizzas they made together. Taylor blended in quickly, charming everyone with his flying stories and overall wit. Lukas had obviously never seen him in a social setting, and considering this was a tense time for everyone, he knew how to be appropriately engaging. "Mrs. Halloran, your pizza tastes like it was flown in from Naples," Taylor complimented.

"Please call me Molly, and thank you, Taylor."

Linda chimed in, "How long have you and Taylor known each other, Lukas?" She winked at him, signaling her approval—for what he could only imagine.

"We just met a few days ago. Taylor lives near DC, but we met on the flight out here."

"Here on business?" she asked.

"I'm a pilot, ma'am," Taylor explained.

"Interesting. How long have you been flying?" Donna inquired.

"More than twenty years. I was in the Air Force, Special Operations Command, mostly deployed throughout the Middle East. Spent time in Iraq, Afghanistan, and Pakistan." Lukas was learning things about Taylor he didn't know.

"Thank you for your service," Donna interjected. "I was in the Army."

"Thank you for yours."

Donna smiled at the acknowledgment. "People are nice to military folks, but I wish they would say thank you to teachers, doctors, nurses, and social workers, as well. My mom was a teacher. I know it's a thankless job," Taylor noted.

Taylor instantly won over the crowd with four very grateful teachers. "Okay, I love him, Lukas," Betty interjected, not aware that he and Taylor were not an item he was showing off to his mom and her friends.

Lukas just shrugged and raised his eyebrows. Taylor acknowledged the awkwardness by smiling back at him.

Hoping to change the subject to get Lukas off the hot seat, Molly asked, "So, ladies, who is going to Dubai with me? No pressure, but I've just got to get this damned trip booked already."

Linda and Betty immediately raised their hands. Donna slowly did the same, a bit hesitant and perhaps submitting to peer pressure.

"I'm going to call the embassy tomorrow morning early," Molly informed them. "It's been two days since they called last, and they didn't have any news about John anyway. I get more worried each day."

"If I may offer a perspective," Taylor interjected, "the fact that they have not found his body could be a positive sign." Lukas, Molly, and their friends were taken aback. "I do not mean to sound gruesome, but if your husband had…you know. They would have probably found his body in the water by now. It's a very busy area. Lukas told me only a little of the story. I'm sorry if that was an insensitive thing to say."

Molly was stunned. "No, no please. You've told

me more in two minutes than the embassy has told me in almost a week."

"You can take the boy out of Special Ops, but you can't...well, you know the saying. One of my duties in the Air Force was search, rescue, and recovery." Taylor stumbled. He looked nervously at Lukas, who nodded, signaling it was all good.

Linda spoke up. "So you think John is alive?"

Taylor suddenly wished he'd never opened his mouth. "Linda, I have no idea. It's just experience, and odds are if a body hasn't been found in the water, on the beach, a hospital, a morgue, or somewhere else, there's a pretty good chance he's alive out there."

"But it's the open ocean," Betty mentioned. "I mean there's fish, sharks..."

"The detective in Dubai confirmed with the hotel that John was wearing a life vest," Molly reminded them. "Even if, God forbid, he did drown, wouldn't that still float?"

"Theoretically yes, Ma," Lukas answered. "So would his paddle, and they never found that either."

"How long has the search been going on?" Taylor inquired.

"About five days, assuming it's still on," Molly responded.

"Lukas, do you have a laptop I could borrow?" Taylor asked him, and he walked past and returned with his laptop. Taylor fired it up. "Password?"

Lukas entered the password and several biometric checks—fingerprints, facial recognition, and speaking voice. "I've got government data on here, so it's protected like Fort Knox."

"In that case, I'm not touching it." Taylor searched

on his cell phone for some information.

He handed his phone to Lukas, who entered the identical URL to be able to pull up the map on his larger screen. It was a map of currents in the Persian Gulf. Taylor studied the map and asked everyone to move closer so they could see the screen. "Okay, so this is the northeastern part of the Arabian Peninsula. There's Qatar, Abu Dhabi, and up here toward the point is Dubai," Taylor explained.

"That's the Strait of Hormuz, right?" Donna asked.

"Yep, and right next door is Oman. Dubai is closer to Oman than it is to Abu Dhabi, the capital of the UAE," Lukas pointed out.

"So what does this have to do with John?" Linda asked. "Other than showing us where Dubai is located, what are you suggesting?"

"Not suggesting anything right now, but wanted to show you something," Taylor replied. "Lukas, can you click the animation on this map?"

Suddenly, the arrows within the map started to move as Taylor studied it. "See how the currents churn counterclockwise? That's pretty consistent from what I remember. The current is affected by salinity and water temperature, so as it churns, it creates a system of lower pressure in the middle...more or less a gyre."

Lukas pointed his finger to follow the current. "So if Dad's boat was found off the coast of Palm Jumeirah, his paddle and life vest would have likely circled this gyre and ended up right back where they started." Taylor nodded.

Molly jumped in. "The search supposedly focused on where they found the kayak, but Taylor, you're saying the boat had probably traveled a bit. John would have only been missing hours by this point, not days. How could his kayak still be relatively close to Dubai?"

"I'm going to take a stab here," Taylor jumped in. "If currents were relatively predictable and there were no storms, which I don't imagine there were since John probably wouldn't have ventured out. But let's assume it was normal, in thirty-six hours, John's boat would have been closer to the coast of Iran than to Dubai."

"The search was focused on the waters off Dubai. That's what the embassy told me," Molly responded.

"Mom, add that question to your list when you call the embassy. Ask them where the search has been conducted and where it will go next."

Molly jotted that down. A question had been on her mind. "Isn't the Persian Gulf pretty crowded with ships? I read there are traffic jams going through the Strait of Hormuz."

Taylor nodded. "You have hundreds of oil tankers from the UAE, Bahrain, Qatar, Kuwait, Iraq, Iran, and Saudi Arabia going in and out of the gulf every day. It's a prime target for terrorists and also disputes between Oman, United Arab Emirates, and Iran. Iran has threatened to shut off the Strait due to sanctions imposed by the Americans."

"So it's a pretty busy place," Molly confirmed.

"And a disaster waiting to happen," Donna commented.

"Which is why it's so heavily patrolled," Lukas added. "I read that about twenty-five percent of the world's oil passes through the Strait and Persian Gulf every day."

"Molly," Taylor asked, "Lukas said the kayak was

found by a pleasure boat out on a fishing trip, correct?"

Molly nodded. "That's what the embassy told me."

"Fishing areas usually begin about forty miles offshore. I wonder why the boat that found the kayak was closer to shore...five miles, wasn't it?" Taylor asked.

"Maybe it was more like a booze cruise," Linda commented.

"Mom, I think that could be another question for your call tomorrow," Lukas added.

It was already ten p.m., and Molly and her guests were fading. "I've got my alarm set for three a.m. tomorrow so I can speak with the embassy during their business day. We spent so much time talking we didn't have time to check flights."

"We can do that tomorrow," Linda answered. "I'm way past my bedtime."

After cleaning up, Linda and Betty boarded Donna's golf cart. "No way I'm walking home tonight," Betty said. "Too many coyotes out. We'll see you tomorrow, Molly. I hope the embassy has some good news."

Lukas walked Taylor to the door. Molly gave him a big hug. "Thank you for talking to us tonight. You sure know a lot about the world. I feel more informed, but there is something that doesn't add up. You touched on it, Taylor, and it's been nagging at me."

"And what part was that?" Taylor asked.

"The paddle and the life vest. Why wouldn't everything be in roughly the same place; the kayak, paddle, and the life vest, regardless of whether John's body was in it?" Molly pointed out. "I can't understand why search and rescue has not turned up anything else.

"I don't know, Molly. I thought about that, too. The search and rescue part of me is wired into my DNA."

"Well, good night, and I hope to see you again, Taylor." Molly returned back into the house, leaving Lukas and Taylor alone on the front porch.

"Well, you are a bountiful supply of information," Lukas thanked him. "Thanks for engaging my mom and her friends. That was sweet of you. I think you gave my mom a bit of hope."

"Look, Lukas, I didn't want to say this in front of your mom, but I think it's strange that the embassy hasn't been calling you around the clock with updates. Your dad is a big executive, and he's missing. A lot of what I'm hearing sounds...odd. I wonder how much they really know or are actively looking for your dad."

"I hope we can learn more tomorrow. I really appreciate you giving her information. She's a scientist and a detective at heart. I can already see her wheels turning."

"I only told her what I can see from the information provided," Taylor responded.

Lukas reached his hands to massage his neck. "Let's hope we get some clarity soon."

Taylor nodded. "So, meet up tomorrow morning at Catalina? Seven a.m. I'll bring the espresso."

"Seriously?" Lukas laughed. "I'm fucked up on sleep, have a stiff neck and jet lag."

"Best way to cure that is to keep moving," Taylor answered.

"Are you my personal trainer now?"

Taylor shrugged. "Maybe. Thanks for inviting me over tonight. It was nice to hang out with some fun people...even in this shitty situation." Before Lukas could respond, Taylor embraced him in a bear hug that left him surprised. "See you tomorrow morning. Sleep well." Lukas felt engulfed by Taylor's muscles and had never been this close to him.

Lukas smiled back and nodded. He couldn't even remember the last time a man hugged him.

Chapter 9

Lukas and Molly were up at three a.m., as planned. It was dark outside, and the sun had another two hours before it would begin to turn the sky orange. They sat at the kitchen table with Molly's phone on speaker as they tried to connect to Abu Dhabi. Finally, someone picked up and transferred to their case manager, Officer Humphries. "Good morning, Mrs. Halloran," Humphries answered with little to no inflection in his voice. "What can I answer for you today? I have no updates, unfortunately."

Molly flipped him off and silently told him to fuck off while she composed herself. "My husband has been missing for over a week. Have you confirmed that there has been a search of area hospitals, morgues, or other cities in the UAE? Also, can you confirm whether the sea search is still going on and approximately where?"

Officer Humphries cleared his throat. "Mrs. Halloran, I will confirm those things for you and call you sometime next week."

"I'd like a call back today, Officer," Molly said pointedly. "If I do not hear back from you by this afternoon, Arizona time, I'm calling my congressman, senators, and the FBI. I need to know what is going on with my husband, and I'm not waiting until next week. My patience is at its end."

There was silence on the other end of the phone

while Lukas high-fived his mom. "Mrs. Halloran, I will get whatever answers to your questions within the next four hours. If I don't have answers, I'll tell you that, too. I apologize, as I know this must be very difficult for you."

"I appreciate that, Officer Humphries. I will speak with you later, and I have this phone with me at all times."

"I got flashbacks to my childhood just now," Lukas replied. "You still terrify me, Ma."

"Let's hope I terrified Officer Humphries. Thanks for your help preparing me. Thank your friend Taylor, too."

"I'm meeting up with him at Catalina in a couple of hours."

"Well he's a nice man, Lukas. Smart and handsome, too."

"Mom...I don't even know if he's gay, or married, or a...witch doctor...we literally just met a couple of days ago."

"I'm pretty sure he's into you, Lukas. What straight man would come spend an evening with a bunch of old ladies?" Molly pointed out.

Lukas smiled. "Mom, the guys that are into me are usually sociopathic party boys, unavailable, or have googled my net worth because they're gold diggers."

"Honey, I have a sense about people. I think he's a good guy."

Lukas rubbed his temples. "Honestly, I do, too, Ma. That's what worries me. I never seem to attract the good guys, so I'm not getting my hopes up. I'm gonna grab a quick shower, some breakfast, and then head out."

"You're taking a shower before your run?" Molly smirked. "Whatever you say, dear."

Lukas hugged his mom. "You're impossible."

He pulled the Wrangler into the parking space a few away from Taylor, who was doing calf stretches against the wheel of his Hyundai Tucson rental car, while talking on the phone. Lukas threw on his sunglasses quickly so that Taylor didn't see him staring at his muscular legs and butt, nicely accented by the running shorts. *Holy shit,* Lukas thought. Taylor hung up and waved to Lukas, who had been sitting in his Jeep until Taylor was off the phone. Taylor walked over and hugged Lukas again. *He must be a hugger,* Lukas thought, enjoying the embrace.

****

"My daughter called, and I had to help her through a financial and personal crisis." Taylor laughed.

Another piece of the Taylor puzzle revealed. *He has a daughter?* "No problem. I didn't want to disturb you," Lukas replied.

"You wouldn't have. We talk a couple of times a day. She's a pilot, like her dad." Now Lukas was perplexed. *Taylor's daughter is a pilot?* He assumed his daughter was about ten, not old enough to be a pilot. *What other surprises did he have?* Lukas' heart sank a bit, the air let out of the balloon. He chided himself for this stupid crush he had.

"I can see you doing mental math," Taylor joked.

"Hmm? Sorry, what do you mean?" Lukas asked, playing it cool.

"Hey, do you mind if we don't run today?" Taylor asked. "We can walk and talk if that's okay. I got to spend so much time with you and your family last night at a really difficult time in your lives. I thought about it last night that you don't know much about me, other than I fly airplanes."

Lukas was not feeling like a run, so he didn't protest the suggestion. "Okay, this is what I know about you. I got to personally witness the pilot part. You were in the Air Force Special Ops, Iraq, and Afghanistan…and some other country I can't remember. You own Nimbus Aviation, live in the DC area, apparently like Hyundai rental cars, and you have a daughter who is a pilot. Oh, and you like woodfired pizza. Other than that, you're a mystery to me, Taylor Pastore."

"Very good, Dr. Halloran."

Lukas flipped the question back at Taylor. "Tell me what you know about me, although I'm not nearly as complex as you?" Lukas asked.

"I know you've been a customer of Nimbus for the last couple of years. Your mom is a lovely lady with lovely friends. You like hiking and running. You live in Arlington and do something with computers." Taylor laughed. "And I can tell you have a good soul."

"Ha! Got you on that one," Lukas responded. "I'm not convinced I have a soul."

"That's the first thing I noticed, your kindness. I see how you treat people and make them feel important. Your mom, her friends, me. People see the kind of person you are just by looking at your eyes. The first time I met you, I knew I could trust you," Taylor explained. "That never happens to me. Even in your sadness about your dad, you still think of others. It's remarkable really."

Lukas didn't know what to say. "Thanks, Taylor.

That's really nice. Now I feel bad about saying pizza as one of the things I knew about you. Tell me about your daughter and the rest of your family," Lukas asked as they walked along a dusty desert path.

"My Tory is something else. Her mom and I had her when we were both really young. I wasn't even nineteen yet. She didn't want the baby, so I convinced her to go through the pregnancy and that I would raise it. My dad was a wealthy man and paid for her prenatal care until the baby was born. He probably gave her money, but not completely sure. I named her Victory—after the *Winged Victory of Samothrace* sculpture. I once took her to the Louvre to have her see her namesake. And yes, my daughter has a head, unlike the statue," Taylor clarified. "I was a dumb kid thinking I could raise her on my own, especially when I was in the Air Force, but we did it."

"Who helped you with raising her?" Lukas asked.

"Ahhh. That's a story in itself. Short version is that she lived with my parents and had a couple of nannies to help out. I would come home from wherever I was in the world as much as I could. My mom and dad loved her and treated her like a princess. I think my mom always wanted a girl, so she was all-in with Tory. It made it easier when I had to go back on duty."

Lukas tried to imagine Taylor as a young father.

"When I was away, Tory would look up to the sky to see if I was flying. She was probably around three then. My mom would point at a bird, and Tory would say *Daahd*. I was more like a big brother to Tory at that point, but she knew I was her dad. One time I told her that my airplane looked like a goose, which she remembered. Every time a goose would fly overhead, she would point and say *Daaddy*."

Lukas' heart warmed at the story. "That is so adorable."

"It helped that my dad had money and was able to provide for her. He was also a kind man, like you. He would give you the shirt off his back."

"What happened to Tory's mom?" Lukas asked.

"It was a one-night stand kind of thing. She was relieved I took care of the baby, so she basically took off. It was the first and last time I'd slept with a woman, but I got Tory for it."

"And how did you get to what you're doing now?" Lukas asked.

"I left the Air Force during Bush 2's second term. I was tired of the whole *Don't Ask, Don't Tell* thing. If I wasn't good enough to fight as a gay pilot, I decided I was not going to pretend I wasn't. My dad set me up in a business that eventually became Nimbus Aviation. And here I am, an old gay dad with a badass daughter who flies planes for Nimbus."

Puzzle pieces 2, 3, and 4, Lukas thought.

"So that's me," Taylor stated. "Pretty boring, no social life. I work a lot, never got into the gay scene, raised my daughter, built my business, and here I am, stranded in the desert with you."

Lukas paused for a moment, thinking how he could respond. "Thanks for sharing all of that with me. You've had a pretty spectacular life."

The two men walked silently together, the words not coming together like water in a raincloud. *Fuck it, I'm just gonna say it,* Lukas thought. He took a deep breath. "I'm happy to hear that you are gay. I wasn't sure," Lukas fumbled.

Taylor smiled. "I wasn't sure you were until fifteen seconds ago."

Lukas laughed. "My mom and her friends are probably planning our wedding as we speak, in between calls to the embassy, of course."

"I wasn't sure, you know? I never assume."

"Nor do I," Lukas responded. "I have this bad habit of falling for guys who end up being straight, psychotic, or wanting a daddy with money. I never get my hopes up."

"When I saw you asleep in the Spectrum's cabin, I almost gasped," Taylor continued. "I came back again when you were awake, and let's just say you're quite a stunning man, Lukas. You have incredible energy."

Lukas blushed. "I bet you say that to all your clients."

"Just the hot ones," Taylor retorted, "which brings that total to...one."

"Good answer. I don't think I've been called hot for a long time." Lukas confirmed, "And I hope I wasn't drooling when I was asleep."

"Buckets full. That's why I came back when you were awake," Taylor joked.

"I'm glad you did," Lukas continued. "I'm a sucker for a man in a pilot uniform."

They made small talk on their way back to their cars. Both men had similar lives, owned companies, worked non-stop.

"Sometimes I wonder what life would have been like if I had just focused on having fun, meeting people, playing around, you know?" Lukas added. "Part of me wanted to sow my oats, or whatever. It was scary for me not to have everything planned out, so I chose the path I thought I should take."

"I kind of understand. I went from being a horny gay teenager to a dad to a pilot. Not much time for anything else," Taylor explained.

"You also raised a daughter as a single parent. That's pretty impressive," Lukas pointed out.

"I've had a good life, Lukas," Taylor said. "I often wonder what my life would have been like if my folks hadn't adopted me. One more detail I forgot to mention."

"That's cool, Taylor. Do you know anything about your birth family?"

"Nothing more than they are probably from the village near the place I was born outside St. Petersburg." Taylor paused. "Russia, not Florida."

"Russia is way more exotic," Lukas added.

"I had some tough times growing up. My father and mother were very religious but good-hearted. I told them I was gay when I was around seventeen. They handled that news by arranging for me to meet a girl, have sex with her, and get that out of my system. Tory is my souvenir from that experiment, and I'm very much still gay."

"How did they react when you didn't change your evil ways?"

Taylor laughed. "They were infatuated with Tory, so they focused on her. I never talked about my remarkably boring sex life with them, and they didn't ask. My family was the original Don't Ask, Don't Tell culture I would later find in the Air Force. My folks were good people, Lukas. I think they felt that me being gay was caused by something they did. They were worried I'd be alone my whole life. They're both gone now."

"I'm sorry about that, Taylor," Lukas said. "I'm sure they would be very proud of you today. I'm fortunate to have both my parents, well, as far as I know I have both."

Lukas mentioned his own feelings about turning forty and fears that his best years may already be behind him. He realized the older he got, the more likely he'd grow old alone, a concept he more or less accepted. "Did you have any...you know, boyfriends your parents got to meet?"

"They met a friend of mine from the Air Force. He was kind of a boyfriend but mostly just a guy to fool around with. But they did meet him."

"Did they know he was, um, a fuck buddy?"

Taylor laughed. "Ha, no way! They just assumed we were friends from the Air Force, which is basically what we were. With benefits, of course."

Lukas felt a weird twinge of both jealousy and arousal when he imagined Taylor naked with some other airman in a barracks somewhere. Then there was his Russian lineage, which explained his exotic, sexy appearance. His mind drifted to all sorts of places when he heard Taylor speak.

"The strike is supposed to start either tonight or tomorrow."

Lukas refocused. *Oh, the strike,* he thought.

"Tory is coming in this afternoon from Colorado so she can fly the Spectrum back to D.C. with me. Gotta have two pilots," Taylor explained. "If we don't get out soon, I'm afraid the strike will spread to other unions like airport workers, fuel operators, baggage crew, flight attendants, folks like that. I think this is the air travel industry fighting back on all the shit they've had to deal with during the pandemic and after. Can't say I blame them with all these nuts flying these days. But we're all screwed if that happens as the airports will be forced to shut down until the strike is resolved."

Lukas immediately thought about the potential flights to Dubai. "I'm sorry I won't be able to meet your daughter Victory—*with a head.*"

"Who says you can't? She'll be here by two this afternoon. I can drive her by your mom's house," Taylor offered.

Lukas looked at his watch. "Shit, I'm supposed to be back home by now in case the embassy calls back. Text me and let me know about Tory. I'm around all afternoon." Lukas hopped into the Jeep, but not before Taylor stroked his arm.

"I've really enjoyed hanging with you. Thanks for everything you shared."

Lukas responded by giving Taylor a kiss, nothing passionate, but hopefully enough to convey that he liked Taylor and hoped to see him again. "There, I raise your hug to a kiss." Taylor's smile was genuine and bright. Lukas already was falling for his dimples.

As he fumbled for the keys to the Jeep, Lukas' phone buzzed. It was his mom.

He looked up at Taylor. "Uh oh, it's my mom." Lukas was stone-faced. "Hey, Mom. I'm on my way home. Any news?" He heard faint sounds and thought he had a bad signal, "Mom?" he asked again. There was a pause, and then he heard his mom utter a single word he could barely understand amidst her stammering, "…Dad."

Chapter 10

Lukas raced back to his mom's house with Taylor in close pursuit. He had called Betty en route to let her know his mom got some bad news, from what he could tell. By the time he pulled into the driveway, Donna, Betty, and Linda were standing outside waiting for Lukas. Taylor pulled in behind him.

"How is she?" Lukas asked them.

"We haven't been inside yet. We were waiting for you," Linda explained. "You see how she is, and if she doesn't want visitors, we'll come back later."

Lukas looked over at Taylor's car. "Thanks for following me home...hopefully I didn't break any laws or speed records."

"Let's just say you didn't get caught. I wanted to make sure you got home okay. I'll head out but keep me posted if you can. I know you have a lot on your mind right now." Taylor put the car in reverse to back out. "Let me know if I can do anything."

Lukas walked to his mom's front door and entered the code on the keypad. He stepped inside the dark foyer and saw his mother sitting alone on the living room sofa, and she was listening to something on the phone's audio speaker. Molly continued to replay what sounded like a voicemail, over and over. She listened calmly. No tears and a slight smile on her face. She was so focused on the voicemail she hadn't noticed Lukas walk in. As he walked closer, he could hear a recorded voice speaking through the phone. Whoever it was had a British accent.

"Mom?" Lukas spoke softly so as not to startle her.

"Hi, honey, when did you get here?"

Lukas thought she was faking her calmness, or maybe she was in shock. "Just now. I rushed over after you called me. What happened to Dad?"

Molly's lips shook, and she fought to compose herself. "I don't know. Please listen to this."

She handed Lukas the phone, and he pressed the voicemail playback.

Hello, Mrs. Halloran. This is Patrick Aziz calling from Dubai. I work for Mr. Halloran. I'm sorry to leave this message for you, but it's imperative you know what has been unfolding quickly. I have been informed that Mr. Halloran is being held against his will. He is unharmed, from what I understand. I've been given instructions to call you and no one else. Lukas felt sick to his stomach. His mom continued her blank stare. *Mrs. Halloran, I'm afraid I do not know much more than that. They instructed me not to contact the Dubai police or the US embassy, or Mr. Halloran would be killed. I have not contacted anyone but you. Today, I received a phone call at the office informing me of this unfortunate situation. Whoever these men are, they know all about you, where you live, and your phone number. I am to let you know that they will be calling your mobile with further instructions at twelve p.m. your time. Mrs. Halloran, I am at your disposal at any time. I believe you have my mobile number.* Patrick recited it to her anyway.

Please let me know how I can assist you. I have

told no one in the office about this. Call me at any time. Thank you.

Lukas tried to sound positive. "At least we know he's alive." Molly didn't reply.

He ran to get her friends standing outside. "Please look after her for a few minutes. I have to make a call." Lukas quickly dialed Taylor's number to get his viewpoint on this situation.

"How is everyone?" Taylor asked.

"My dad's been fucking kidnapped! His colleague in Dubai left a message on my mom's voicemail. He's heard from the kidnappers, and they are going to call us in less than an hour. He said not to call the police or the embassy, or they would kill him. Fuck! My mom's in shock. She really hasn't said anything."

"Jesus, I knew this was a potential scenario. What else did they say?" Taylor asked.

Lukas tried to remember. "He said the kidnappers are calling us at noon. That's less than fifteen minutes from now. I don't even know what to say to this guy…assuming it's a guy," Lukas mumbled.

"I'm turning around. Don't call anyone. I'll be at your place in less than ten." Taylor hung up.

Lukas explained to Linda, Betty, and Donna what was going on with his dad and the mystery surrounding what was next.

"My God," Donna said in disbelief.

"I've never seen your mom like this. I can't tell if she's just calm or in shock," Linda said.

"I think it's a little of both," Betty chimed in. "I don't think any of us expected this."

"I don't have a clue of what one does in a situation like this," Donna added.

"Taylor is on his way here," Lukas explained. "He did search and recovery in the Air Force. Maybe he knows more about a hostage situation, or whatever this is, than we do."

It was eleven fifty-five when Taylor walked in the door. "Sorry for just walking in, but I know the call is coming soon."

"What call?" Linda asked.

"The kidnappers are calling to explain more about what we do next," Lukas explained.

Taylor addressed the group. "Okay, this is what we need to do. The kidnappers don't know that we are all here with Molly, at least I don't think they do. Molly needs to be the only person talking. They probably know Lukas is here with her."

"How would they know that?" Betty asked.

"If these guys are what I'm afraid they are, they know that and a whole lot more," Taylor responded grimly.

It was eleven fifty-seven.

"Molly," Taylor asked, "are you okay to take this call? We should all take notes and then compare afterward to make sure we got the whole message. Lukas, can you please record the call?" Lukas nodded. "Information we need from them: 1. How long they've had John and any clues as to where he is being held. 2. What do they want? This could be ransom money, and let's hope that's all. And 3. Who they are, who they work for, and what is their agenda?" Taylor explained.

"What else could they want other than ransom?" Molly interjected from the sofa.

"Some will hold hostages for social or religious causes. Sometimes it's a prisoner swap, but I doubt it's that."

Eleven fifty-nine. "Final thing to ascertain is timing," Taylor explained. "If they want a ransom, they will want it to be transferred somewhere they can get it. They may give us a deadline of, say, forty-eight hours."

"And then what?" Donna asked.

Taylor knew there were many grim outcomes if a deadline was missed. "Let's cross that bridge when we come to it."

It was twelve noon. They all stared at Molly's phone for what seemed like an eternity.

12:02 p.m.

"Why aren't they calling?" Molly's voice raised in agitation.

"They are trying to establish control by being fashionably late and making us wait for them. They could make us wait for an hour," Taylor mocked. "They will call, just remember to be calm and…"

Molly's phone rang. "Unknown caller," Molly reported. Taylor nodded at her to answer.

"Hello, Molly Halloran speaking." She hit the speakerphone.

"*Hi, honey. It's John. I'm okay, but I know you must be worried about me, so I wanted to call and tell you that I'm okay.*" Lukas froze in horror. It was his dad's voice, but he was not speaking like his dad. *He is reading from a script,* Lukas thought. "*I'm being held by a group of men who kidnapped me. They are treating me well. So far. They will ask you for money in order to secure my release…*" A shuffling sound came through as if someone grabbed the phone from John.

A digitally disguised voice began speaking. "Mrs. Halloran, we are calling about your husband."

"Yes, can you hear me?" Molly answered.

"Yes, I can hear you," replied the odd robotic voice. "The instructions are as follows. You, Mrs. Halloran, will meet our representative at the Dubai Al Maktoum International Airport at the FBO Terminal." Lukas scrawled notes as fast as he could. "You will meet us within forty-eight hours at the stated location. Once confirmed, we will send you a text with a number for you to call once you clear customs. That number will give you further instructions," the mechanical voice continued. "Finally, we kindly request a fee of five million US dollars for Mr. Halloran's safe release. This will be paid in several installments, the first one starting tonight as a guarantee that we know you understand this situation. Please prepare two hundred and fifty thousand US dollars drawn on cryptocurrency and deposited to an account I will specify later. The balance, you can pay in cash or cryptocurrency when I give further instructions."

Lukas couldn't believe what he was hearing. First, there was the money, and how could he get five million dollars together in forty-eight hours? Second, the entire country's airline fleets would likely grind to a halt in less than twelve hours when the strike commenced.

"And, Mrs. Halloran," the emotionless robotic voice continued, "do you, by chance, have your son by your side now?"

Molly looked panicked about how to respond. Taylor nodded to her to answer truthfully.

"Yes, I do," Molly answered. "Would you like to speak to him?"

"Not now," the voice answered, "but I've been told he can be quite creative. That is good for you to have him close by. Maybe he can accompany you to Dubai. It's a dreadfully long trip to make alone. Your airlines will strike soon, so you best get moving." No more sound emanated from Molly's mobile as the robot hung up.

Lukas grabbed his head and rubbed his temples. "Fuuuuck," was all he said.

Taylor had also been taking notes. He put down his pen and exhaled. "Excellent job on the call, Molly. You played it very cool and sounded professional."

"I felt like I was going to throw up," Molly responded.

"What do you think, Taylor?" Lukas asked.

"These are professionals who know what they're doing. I need to make a phone call," Taylor said as he left the room with his phone.

"Taylor," Molly said. "Can I speak to you after your call?" Taylor affirmed with a nod.

Lukas looked toward his mom. "How are you doing?"

"Well," Molly replied. "I'm pissed as hell. They aren't going to make this easy. What was he saying about an airline strike?"

"Nothing we need to worry about right now, Ma."

Taylor walked back into the room and motioned Molly to come talk to him. They exchanged a few brief words, and Taylor nodded before continuing on to meet Lukas at the dining room table. "I called Tory. She's delayed but will be landing in Tucson. The strike is definitely going on at midnight eastern. She said the airports are crazy with people trying to get home."

Lukas knew what he had to do next. "Shit, I'm gonna check to see if I can get to Mexico or Canada in the next couple of hours so I can get to Dubai before the deadline," he said, exasperated. "At least you should be getting some calls from folks who want a charter."

"Yeah, the phone's been ringing off the hook," Taylor responded. "She's bringing her boyfriend. Some guy I've never met. She's a smart one. She thinks of everything."

Lukas was confused. "That's good. I'm glad you can get out of here."

"Not that I want to," Taylor said. "But I got a client."

Taylor acted preoccupied with something, Lukas thought. *Why is he talking about his daughter's boyfriend now?*

Taylor got a phone call and started to fire off questions to the person on the line. He wrote notes in his notebook and was now on hold. "Great. Do you think that'll be a problem?" he asked the person. "Yeah, me neither. Okay, I'll check back in ten."

"Who were you talking to?" Lukas asked.

"The aircraft mechanic. Just checking the plane before we head on out."

"Okay, hey, I'm going to look for flights to Mexico now. I don't think my mom needs to go."

Taylor either didn't hear Lukas or was, again, preoccupied. His phone rang again, and he quickly answered. "Awesome. How soon can you have her ready?"

Chapter 11

Lukas called his banker to get the $250,000 cashed and transferred to Bitcoin. The banker assured Lukas that he would have access to the funds by midnight at the latest. It was a hefty chunk out of his portfolio, but quicker to access his money than trying to get to his parents' funds. They would pay him back anyway. "Mom," Lukas said as he walked into the room. "The pilot strike starts at midnight eastern time, so nine p.m. here, so less than six hours from now."

Molly nodded but said nothing. "Mom, I'm gonna go. I'll get to Mexico tonight and find a flight to Dubai tomorrow. I think you should stay here. I'll be back in a couple of days, hopefully with Dad."

Molly said firmly, "I need to be there. Didn't you hear the kidnapper? I must deliver the ransom. They want me. Therefore, I'm going."

Linda chimed in, "Molly, I'll go with you guys too, for moral support."

"Count me in," Betty shouted.

Lukas understood the need for his mom to go with him, but with Linda, Betty, and maybe Donna, things would get complicated. "Okay, let me secure the tickets to Mexico City first. That's a little under two hours, and then I can look for the Dubai tickets. Those are going to be expensive, Ma, last minute and everything."

Molly nodded her understanding.

Linda chimed in that she wanted business class. "It's a long flight, I'm worth it."

"I'm not sure it's worth it," Betty added. "I'll just do economy. I'm little."

"Mom, you are going in the front of the plane whether you like it or not," Lukas informed her. "I'll take whatever ticket I can get."

Betty started giving Lukas her seating preferences. "I like a window seat, so I can sleep."

Lukas buried his face in one hand, massaging his temples. This was going to be a shit show.

Just then, Taylor came into the room and witnessed the chatter about seat preferences, special meals, and frequent flier points that could be redeemed. Lukas was on his phone checking out flights to Mexico City. "Lukas, can I speak to you for a minute?"

"Sure." Lukas followed Taylor into the kitchen.

"I don't want you to be mad at me, but I have something to tell you," Taylor told him.

"Mad at you about what?"

"What I'm about to tell you."

What's he talking about? Lukas thought.

"The stuff with my daughter, her boyfriend, it was all arranged, well not the boyfriend part, that was her idea, but she's right. We'll need three of us to do the job."

Lukas nodded, still clueless as to what Taylor was talking about. *What job?*

"Sorry, I'm thinking out loud. It's about my client. We needed three pilots, and Tory figured it out."

"Taylor, I'm not really following you on all this, but I've got to get back to booking flights.

"No, you don't." Taylor smiled. "*You're* my client,

and I'm taking you to Dubai."

Lukas reared back, stunned. "What? I can't afford a private jet to Dubai!"

Taylor chuckled. "It's not as bad as you think. Plus, Tory and I are your complimentary pilots—free of charge. Her boyfriend will be, too, at least if he wants to remain her boyfriend."

Lukas paused, unsure he heard correctly. Taylor's grin confirmed that he had. "Jesus, Taylor, I don't know what to say."

"Say you'll have dinner with me in DC after we get your dad home. Have you ever been to Delaware Room?"

"For the record, I would have gone with you to Delaware Room or Joe's Pizza Shop regardless of you flying me halfway around the world. You don't need to—"

Taylor checked his watch. "Good answer, and I appreciate that, but the clock is ticking. Gotta get going," he interrupted. "I already filed the flight plan, and the *Goose* is being fueled as we speak. We can depart in an hour."

"You named your plane the *Goose*?" Lukas asked. Taylor smiled. "Ah, that story about Tory as a little girl," Lukas remembered. "Of course. That adorable story." Lukas shook his head. "Let's go tell everyone else."

Once Molly, Linda, Betty, and Donna were informed of the change in plans, they sat together quietly. "So you have a plane that can fly halfway around the world without stopping?" Linda asked.

"Yes. It's a Spectrum 6 XR for extended range. It will be tight, but we should be able to make it non-stop

91

if we have a strong tailwind. If not, we stop and refuel. Not a big deal."

"I've never been in a private jet," Betty remarked.

"Lukas, can you and your mom call the guy at your dad's company in Dubai? His name escapes me," Taylor said.

"Patrick Aziz. What do I tell him?"

Taylor pulled out his notes. "I'm planning on wheels up at 19:30 hours Pacific time." Molly scribbled her own notes. "Landing at DWC approximately 20:00 hours local time. We will need a pickup at the DWC Jetport and probably need some hotel rooms."

"DWC?" Molly asked.

"Dubai World Central," Lukas replied, his eyes reading the smartphone search results. "It's a newer airport, less crowded, and looks like they have a nice reception area for business travelers."

"It's also where the kidnappers want to meet us, so we'll have the *Goose* there, if needed," Taylor added.

Molly looked at Lukas for clarification. "He calls his plane *Goose*?"

"I'll explain later, Ma."

"Okay, folks," Taylor announced, "we have less than two hours to go. If you're going with us, pack lightly, bring your passports, and be back here in thirty minutes."

"Will they have food on the plane, or should I buy some?" Donna asked. "I'll need a gallon of whiskey to calm my nerves anyway."

"I've ordered full catering and bar service for ten people. If you want to bring some snacks or a special drink, that's fine. Just remember, this is an aircraft and not an RV. And don't forget your medications. Bring them in the original containers if possible."

Taylor looked over at Lukas and whispered, "Lukas, I'm gonna get over to the airport about forty-five minutes before we take off. You should come with me. Do you think your mom is going to need help with getting anything?"

"I'll get her documents together. I don't know what this kidnapper meeting is about or what I need to do, but I'll need wireless internet on the flight. Is that possible?"

"That will cost you extra," Taylor joked. "Yeah, we have satellite Wi-Fi the whole way."

"Good, I need to find $5 million in the next twenty-four hours." Taylor and Lukas left for Marana airport to get the plane ready.

Molly was in her bedroom, calmly packing her clothes. She walked over to a large safe in their closet, punched in the entry code, and pulled open the heavy door. Inside sat her unloaded rifles, some jewelry, cash, and family documents. A high-end laptop sat on the safe's bottom shelf. She picked it up and placed the laptop and its power cords in a black computer bag hanging in the closet. She re-armed the safe and shut the door, waiting for the lock to engage.

She exited the closet and grabbed her phone, sat on the edge of her bed, and prepared to make a call.

When the phone connected, Molly began to speak. "It's me. I'm getting ready to leave. Please inform the board at nine a.m. tomorrow that I initiated SP4A.2 at eighteen thirty hours Pacific Standard Time. Please send me an email or text when this has been completed."

"Yes, ma'am," said a voice on the other end of the

line. "Understood."

Molly calmly walked with her luggage to stand with her friends as they waited for their driver. Each woman had a small bag, as instructed, their electronics, travel documents, and snacks. Donna actually did bring a half gallon bottle of scotch with her.

"Why didn't you just bring a barrel?" Betty jibed.

"Look, I'm a nervous passenger, and this is all I had at home."

Linda went on, "Donna, honey, nobody is judging you. Just save some for me."

"I'm judging you, by the way," Betty jumped in. "But I may have a sip, too."

About a minute later, the car showed up, and a uniformed driver popped out of the black Suburban. He quickly grabbed their bags and other supplies and placed them in the trunk. "Everyone confirm you have your passports, cellphone, wallet?" the driver asked. The ladies gave him a thumbs up.

Within twenty minutes, they pulled into the Marana Regional Airport and unloaded their luggage. They sat in a lounge awaiting further instructions. "I've always wondered what it was like in here. I drive by all the time," Linda commented. A few minutes later, a porter rolling a luggage cart met them in the lounge area and asked them to place their bags on it and follow him. The Spectrum sat gleaming on the tarmac. It was spotless, and the setting sun accentuated the designed curves and proportions of the aircraft. Sunset was on its way. "Wow, what a beautiful plane. Is that for us?" Linda cooed.

"Where do we go through security? I think we missed security," Donna said with a touch of panic in her voice, imagining TSA agents tackling them to the ground.

They waved at Taylor in the cockpit and noticed Lukas walking toward the back of the fuselage, where the luggage door was open. "Mom, I'm back here." The porter wheeled the cart toward the back where Lukas helped to place the bags in the hold. "Good job packing light, everyone. Make sure you have everything you need out of your suitcase. Taylor told me it's like a maze to get to the baggage hold from inside the plane."

As Lukas finished placing bags inside, the front door of the aircraft started to open downward, revealing a set of stairs built into the door. Taylor stuck his head out and welcomed them on board. Molly complimented him on his crisply ironed pilot's uniform. The group stared silently at the spacious interior with warm colors, wood-tone paneling, and cognac-colored leather seats. Taylor pointed out the circadian lighting that changed throughout the flight to reduce the effects of jet lag.

"Welcome aboard, ladies. Please choose a seat you'd like for the next fifteen hours. Each of the chairs transforms into a lay-flat bed." They stared in awe.

"It's really a beautiful jet, Taylor," Molly said, as she clutched an orange leather designer bag.

Taylor smiled. "There are a few sofas that can be used as a bed, and you can turn your seat pods to face each other if you want to play cards or eat together. There's an enclosed stateroom, which I'm reserving for the pilots, but feel free to use it if it's vacant. There is an aft lavatory with a vanity and small shower, and there's a second small lavatory up front."

Linda excitedly asked, "This plane has a shower? My gosh."

Lukas climbed on board. "Pretty nice, huh?"

"I could get used to flying like this," Betty stated.

"We're just about ready to go," Taylor announced, "but we're still waiting on two pilots that should be here within the next ten minutes.

"This jet is capable of carrying eighteen people, including crew. We will have eight of us, so hopefully you'll find it spacious and comfortable." Taylor walked toward the galley. "You have a full beverage selection in here, and one of the pilots will serve your meals when we get in the air. We have plenty of meals and snacks, so help yourself whenever you are hungry."

As Taylor walked toward the cockpit, Lukas appreciated his posterior view. "Lukas, can you join me for a second?"

"Has anyone told you that you have an amazing ass?" Lukas told him brazenly. Taylor just smiled, and Lukas thought he detected a slight blush on him. Lukas moved to the co-pilot seat. "Sorry, I should not say the first thing that comes into my head," Lukas said, a bit chagrined.

"I'm not complaining." Taylor smiled while he pointed at a small dot in the sky. "That's Tory. She'll be here in a few, and we're ready to go."

Lukas grabbed Taylor's hand. "Thank you so much for doing this. I can't even imagine…"

"It's strange, Lukas," Taylor commented. "It feels like I've known you for months. Like I'm doing this for a friend." *Friend?* Lukas thought, but he smiled anyway. "I clarify, a very hot friend who I can't stop looking at," Taylor pushed to get a reaction.

Lukas smiled. "Back at you, but I know what you mean. I never predicted my week would end like this. It kind of feels like a big, weird dream."

"Fate, I guess." Taylor smiled. "And we're just getting started with the interesting part. Are you ready for this?"

Lukas nodded. "I've got a question, though. This plane is impressive and all, but I can't grasp how it can fly over eight thousand miles on one tank of gas."

"That's a great question, Lukas. These planes are pretty advanced. Musk has one. So does Bezos. Oh, and one of the Kardashians, plus hundreds of businesspeople and celebrities who need to get around the world quickly," Taylor explained with pride. "It's the longest-range business jet around, holds seven and a half thousand gallons of jet fuel, and can fly at over fifty thousand feet in altitude where we can almost hit the speed of sound."

Lukas told him, "I'm at least paying for the gas."

"We'll negotiate that later." Taylor smiled. "Let's go get your dad."

Out of the corner of his eye, Lukas noticed a smaller jet pulling up close to the *Goose*. When the door opened, a tall woman with shoulder-length, straight blonde hair stepped onto the aircraft stairs. Next followed an attractive man in his late twenties or early thirties. All Lukas could see was that he was tall, had jet-black hair, muscular arms, and he deduced he was Tory's mystery boyfriend. "Well, he looks…nice," Lukas commented.

"Stop it, bad boy. That could be my future son-in-law." Taylor rolled his eyes. "I haven't met Taylor's boyfriend in person, so this is the first time. I've only seen him on video chats. He's taller than I expected."

The duo climbed up the stairs to the *Goose,* and

Tory immediately ran to hug her dad.

"There's my girl. I'm so happy to see you!"

"Wouldn't miss it, Dad." She looked at Lukas, and she went to hug him. "I'm assuming you're Lukas, or I'm just hugging a random man. You didn't tell me he was so cute, Dad."

Taylor nodded. "Well, what would you expect?"

Lukas approached Tory. "Your dad has told me about you, and I can't thank you enough for being here."

"I love flying the *Goose* with Dad. And I'm here to get your dad, too. This is my boyfriend, Diego."

Diego reached out his hand to Lukas first. "Hello, Mr. Lukas. Mr. Pastore, it's nice to see you live and in person." Diego Paul was six feet tall, had an athletic build, dark wavy hair, and bright blue eyes.

"Are you living in Mexico?" Lukas asked.

"Yes sir. Mexico City." Lukas thought his accent sounded slightly different from other Spanish speakers he knew. Maybe Diego just lived in Mexico but came from somewhere else or even a different part of Mexico. Lukas was good at understanding some accents, but others were a mystery to him. They would have plenty of time to get to know each other, so he made a note to ask him then. Diego had a genuine, warm smile, and Lukas immediately felt comfortable with him.

Taylor whispered to Diego, "Thanks for coming along. I owe you one."

"No problem. It's nice to finally meet you, sir."

Taylor closed the aircraft door while Lukas took Tory and Diego to meet his mom and her friends. There was a double ping that indicated they were ready for departure. "Tory and Mr. Pastore will fly the first leg," Diego explained to the passengers. "I'll try and get some rest, and then I'll take over for one of them. We will rotate every three to five hours. Mr. Pastore is the captain, and we will follow his direction."

Donna fidgeted with her seat controls while Diego spoke to them. She was visibly nervous about flying so far, so she focused on the view out the window. "I hate being a passenger," she grunted softly.

Taylor's voice filled the cabin. "Ladies and gents, we're about to take off, so I need you to make sure your seatbelts are fastened. Our route will take us in a northeasterly direction where we will cross the Canada border, then we will head north close to the pole. We will then dip down over central Russia and follow that to cross over Georgia, the country not the state, Armenia, Turkey, and then Iraq. We are restricted from flying over Iran due to our aircraft being registered in the United States. After that, it's a straight shot to Dubai. We will be flying high today, about 50,000 feet, and at a speed of Mach .93, which is just below the speed of sound. The strong tailwind will help us save fuel."

It still boggled Lukas' mind that Taylor's jet could fly so far so fast. He wondered how much this was going to cost him, but he quickly put that thought out of his mind. Finding his father and getting him home was the priority now. The whir of the engines intensified as Taylor piloted the plane down the taxiway onto the runway. "Folks, we have a pretty short runway here at Marana and some tall mountains we have to cross, so I'll be taking a pretty steep climb out. Please keep your belts fastened and try not to move around until we give you the go-ahead."

Lukas was sitting across from his mom, who had her eyes closed. What was she thinking about? "Ma, you good?"

"I'm fine, honey. I still can't believe all this has happened in such a short amount of time."

"It's surreal." The plane pivoted 180 degrees and lined up with the runway. "Looks like this is it. Ready, Ma?"

Molly smiled and nodded.

The Spectrum's engines roared, providing thrust to power the plane to takeoff speed as it lurched ahead down the runway. The plane's power was evident as the acceleration force held them in their seats. This plane was designed to go fast, and the cabin was surprisingly quiet. As they hit takeoff speed, Taylor pulled back, and the nose lifted off the ground, followed shortly by the rest of the plane. The landing gear retracted immediately into the fuselage.

The passengers quietly stared out the large porthole windows as the *Goose* climbed out of Tucson. It was almost dusk, and Lukas spotted thousands of saguaro cacti dotting the sides of mountains that cast distorted shadows that looked like goblins. The exhilarating views captivated everyone. That is, for everyone except Donna, who sat rigid in her seat, hands clenched and her eyes squeezed shut. Lukas shot her a thumbs up in thanks to Donna—already not a fan of flying, but all in for a fifteen-hour flight halfway around the world just to support her friend. The plane's angle leveled off, and soon Taylor emerged from the cockpit, curious how well the passengers had settled into their home for the next fifteen hours. Linda and Betty had their eyes shut, as Donna distracted herself with her laptop.

Taylor walked back to the crew stateroom for a few minutes. He and Diego had a brief conversation before Diego walked up to the cockpit. Lukas moved toward the back of the plane to set up his inflight internet connection and workspace.

Linda and Betty awoke, startled and disoriented after their brief power nap, while Donna adjusted their seats to face each other, a small table between them. Betty remarked that it reminded her of a train.

"How're you doing?" Taylor asked Lukas.

"Just trying to get set up here. I've got a lot of work to do on the way to Dubai. I need to connect with my team in Croatia to get some data and ideas on how I can get this ransom together. It's still early morning there, so I'll wait a few hours."

"Why don't you get some sleep until then?" Taylor suggested. I'm gonna try to myself. You mind?" Taylor pointed to the empty seat next to Lukas.

"Of course not." Lukas stood to let him in. Taylor sat and reclined his seat. "I changed my mind. I'll let the kids do the first leg, then I'll replace one of them, and we rotate like that."

Lukas saw that his mom and her friends were already starting to doze off, no doubt tired from the frenetic day. "Why don't you sleep with me?" Taylor said, and then caught himself. "I mean not with me but next to me—you know what I mean. You make me all tongue-tied, Dr. Halloran."

"Sure, I could use a nap. I'm relieved we're finally on our way." Lukas reclined his seat to the same angle as Taylor's. The cabin was mostly dark, except for the LED accent lights that glowed a cool blue.

Taylor reached out and touched Lukas' hand. "Is this okay?" He then intertwined his fingers with Lukas'.

"This is better than okay. Sleep tight." Lukas raised their joined hands and kissed the back of Taylor's. Pretty soon, their hands were on each other's thighs. Heat rose from Taylor's athletic legs.

Despite the sadness, stress, and emotion of this week, Lukas appreciated the kind soul sleeping next to him. As he was resting, Lukas suddenly felt a rush of panic. *What am I doing?* Random memories of Drew raced through his head as he tried to calm himself. He tried to rationalize his thoughts. *Yes, I just met this guy. Yes, I promised myself I'd never get hurt again. But he's such a nice man. What if he's psycho?* He pulled his hand away from Taylor and eventually calmed his mind and drifted off to sleep. When Lukas woke up, he noticed his mother sitting with her eyes open, staring at nothing, either deep in thought or terrified of something. Lukas walked over to her. "Ma, are you doing okay?"

"I think I'm okay. I just have a lot on my mind."

"I know. This has got to be tough for you…"

"Honey, I'm not talking about your father. Of course, I'm concerned about him, but it's only a matter of time until we can see him, hopefully."

"Then what is on your mind? I'm not a little boy; you can tell me anything."

"I know I can, sweetheart." Molly looked out of the plane window. "I wonder where we are?"

Taylor, awake now, stared out the window. "We are making good time. Just passing over Hudson Bay."

Molly nodded. Lukas saw the look of worry in her eyes. She rustled Linda, Donna, and Betty awake. Linda instinctively knew what was going on. "You gonna tell him?" Linda asked.

"Can we get some space for the six of us?" Molly asked. "Taylor, you can inform your daughter and her friend, okay? Actually, it won't mean much to them. Scratch that thought."

Taylor nodded.

Lukas thought, *tell him what?* as he pondered Linda's question.

They found a spot where all six of them could sit. Molly sat down, brushed the wrinkles out of her slacks, and sat back tall in the chair.

"Ma?"

Molly cleared her throat. "As of six thirty p.m. Pacific Time yesterday, I invoked article SP4A.2 in the Phoenix Equities corporate charter. The board will be informed tomorrow morning at nine a.m. that I am now CEO and Chairman of the Board."

Lukas sat in stunned silence. "Does this mean you don't think Dad's coming back?"

"On the contrary," Molly responded. "I want to ensure that we can make fast decisions without a lot of squabbling and interference from the board. Article SP4A.2 not only names a temporary successor, but it also nullifies their power to screw with decisions I need to make."

"Do they know you can do this?" Lukas asked.

"If they don't, they didn't read their contract. Once the crisis is over, they will be reinstated and compensated for their time." Molly looked at Lukas. "I've been able to amass the ransom and pay you back, Lukas, for the Bitcoin transaction you made today. That was very sweet of you."

How did she know about that? Lukas thought.

"And finally," she concluded, "I was able to charter this beautiful jet to go rescue my husband, thanks to Taylor and his daughter...and don't even think I'm not paying you for your time." Taylor looked over at Lukas and lifted his eyebrows, indicating that he was sworn to secrecy.

"I have one more thing you need to know. It's about Poseidon." Molly took a deep breath. "I believe that's why your father was taken."

"Why would he be kidnapped for investing in a company? What does this company make?"

"Poseidon is a technology, an amazing technology. The company was built around it, and Phoenix bought it. Your father is so idealistic, which is what I love about him."

"So what does this technology do that someone would want to hold dad hostage?"

Molly took another deep breath and calmly said, "The technology itself is sound, but there have been people who have tried to manipulate it."

"To do what?" Taylor asked.

Molly lowered her head for a moment. "Something I never thought was possible."

Chapter 12

He had no idea where he was, what day it was, or whether it was day or night. John Halloran assumed he was in an underground bunker as there appeared to be no windows. He chided himself for being gullible enough to be led into a trap on Palm Jumeirah. He hated kayaking, but he went anyway at the request of an original Poseidon investor, Malik Bawadi, who expressed interest in running the new acquisition and taking a position on Phoenix's board.

At forty-eight, Malik was a self-made businessman. John knew he considered himself Syrian, but he had been born somewhere else. His family was extremely poor, and he found himself orphaned at an early age. Malik spoke several languages and now lived in between his homes in Paris, Damascus, and Dubai. John found him to be ambitious and intelligent, but there was something that bothered him. Malik did not have, or at least show, a trait that John considered to be non-negotiable for a business partner or board member—trustworthiness.

As the two men paddled among the fronds of the man-made archipelago, John had to admit that the engineering used to design and then build up what was once Persian Gulf was quite impressive. By using a combination of dredging, landfill, and enough architectural savvy, the Emirati were able to create new beachfront property to allow for the massive hotels and shopping malls that entertained billionaires and tourists alike.

That was where John's memory started to fade. He remembered a motorboat approaching them, some yelling and confusion, and then nothing. Next, he recalled being very groggy and slightly seasick as the motorboat navigated through choppy waters. Someone threw his kayak overboard. *Why would they do that?*

The next memory he had was reciting a written statement to his wife while being recorded. He made a mistake, and he felt a blow to his head. When he woke up, he had a headache but repeated the script and didn't make a mistake this time. He heard the creak of a door open. A large, cloaked figure entered with a tray of food and placed it on a bench near John's bed. Two more figures entered the room. They were careful to make sure their faces were covered. When they spoke, John could not make out a word. Having traveled extensively around the world, he knew basic words in the major world languages. Really basic; *yes, no, thank you, hello, beer, toilet* made up the extent of his vocabulary, and whatever these guys were speaking didn't sound like anything he'd heard.

One of the captors walked over to him. John could see that he was wearing a clown mask and wondered if the man meant to make him laugh or terrify the shit out of him. *Lovely*, he thought, and decided it was the latter. Clown Face spoke something into his phone. Someone on the other end answered him, and John could have sworn it was in English.

I hope she invoked article SP4A.2, he thought. *Some folks on the board could use my absence to forward their own agendas.*

He reached for the food tray and politely bowed to the man who brought it in. At least they had fed him and given him water. The cuisine tasted a bit like Indian, but different. He'd never eaten anything similar to it in the past. The two men and Clown Face turned and left the room, leaving John alone. He was bored, had nothing to read or even scenery to look at. He sensed he was in a precarious situation but didn't know why or how. After he ate, he lay back on his cot and attempted to meditate, during which he promised himself to take everything as it came and hope for the best. When meditation didn't work, he tried pushups and sit-ups. Those tired him out and at least made him want to take a nap. The last thing he remembered before he fell into a nap was the distorted mask of a clown face.

Chapter 13

Lukas processed the information his mother shared with him, but he sensed there was something more to the story. Taylor approached him and put his hand on Lukas' shoulder. "I'm sorry I didn't tell you your mom chartered this flight. I wanted her to tell you."

"Actually," Lukas responded, "I'm kind of relieved. Now I don't have to go on that date with you in DC."

Taylor felt a brief lightning bolt zap through his heart but maintained his composure. "Lukas, I'm…"

"Oh, just stop it. I'm teasing you. But you're paying for dinner." Lukas answered.

"Well, actually, you should pay. Your mom just saved you a boatload of money."

Lukas smiled. "Fine, then you have to take me somewhere really cool."

"Maybe I'll fly us to Paris. Would you like that?" Taylor smiled.

Lukas had no response. The mere idea of being able to jet over to Paris with this man was incredible.

Taylor sat down next to him. "We should be able to see the Aurora Borealis tonight after we cross the pole. I'm glad we got out when we did. There is a ground stop on all US flights. Now the United States air traffic control is on strike."

"I thought Reagan made that illegal?" Lukas asked.

"So did I, which was why I didn't see that coming," Taylor answered. "Let's hope Europe doesn't follow suit." Lukas nodded in agreement.

"I wonder if we should have called the FBI, or the embassy, or somebody. I feel like we have no idea what we've gotten ourselves into," Lukas speculated.

"I don't know, but in my experience, the worst thing you can do is get local or Federal law enforcement involved in something like this. They play by the rules too much," Taylor replied.

"Isn't that good?" Lukas asked.

"Sometimes, and theoretically, yes, it's good they follow the rules, or else you'd have chaos with guys making decisions not knowing the broader story."

Lukas nodded. "Hey, look. I see them."

Lukas and Taylor saw the Northern Lights on the horizon, glowing with vibrant colors and appearing almost unreal.

"That's a view I never get tired of," Taylor commented.

Lukas agreed. "I've probably seen them twice now, both times in the air. It's pretty fascinating."

"You know," Taylor interjected, "it's always so peaceful up here, it's easy to forget all the conflict, suffering, and strife that goes on down there." Taylor leaned back on the jet's sofa, adjusted his arm, and placed it over Lukas, whose back rested on Taylor's chest. Despite his thoughts earlier, Lukas felt good with Taylor. More importantly, his gut feeling was to trust him. *Trust and verify*, he told himself, which was one of his mantras he used with his employees regarding data accuracy and the conclusions they drew from it.

Molly quietly walked toward them, smiling at how

content Lukas looked with Taylor. "It's nice to see you both so comfortable. You make a handsome couple," Molly observed. "Taylor, Lukas will probably yell at me for saying that, but I say what I think. Which reminds me, can I make a phone call from up here?"

He looked at his watch. "In about an hour. We get better reception when we're over land. That work?"

Molly nodded. "I need to call Mr. Patrick Aziz and tell him I'm his new boss. I'd love to be a fly on the wall when he learns that."

"Why do you say that, Ma?"

"Your father thought Patrick could possibly be his successor one day, and I'm sure Patrick knew that, too. He followed your dad around like a puppy, but he had no time for me. I was just the dutiful wife."

Lukas chuckled. "If only Patrick knew who held the real power in the Halloran household."

"I've been involved with Phoenix since Dad started it," Molly commented. "I know a lot about the company, its holdings, strategy, and stuff like that. Your dad would bounce ideas off me, and I'd tell him my honest opinion."

"Did you ever disagree?"

"Most of the time we disagreed." Molly chuckled. "Your dad was the visionary. He could see things that most people couldn't see."

"Sounds like a good team," Taylor stated.

"Yep. My husband was the dreamer, I got shit done, and that still works for us."

"Mom, what did you mean when you talked about Poseidon? You make it sound like it was something bad. That doesn't seem like something Dad would want to get involved with."

"I'll explain it to you since you should know what's possibly at stake. Taylor," Molly asked him, "can you get Tory and bring her back here? I'd like to explain this one time so I don't have to repeat it."

"Molly, I'm afraid I can't do that unless I take her spot in the cockpit. We need two pilots up there, even when we're on autopilot, unless it's just a quick pee break."

Molly turned around and spotted Donna, who was engrossed in watching a movie on her tablet, along with her sound-canceling headphones. "Donna. Donna!" Molly waved her arms to get Donna's attention.

"Yeah?" Donna yelled, not knowing how loud her voice was due to the headphones.

"They need another pilot while I explain Poseidon to them. Can you…"

"Roger. Finally get to have some fun." Donna rose from her seat and headed toward the cockpit. "I didn't drink the booze, in case you were wondering."

"Mom, what is she doing? She's terrified of flying!"

"Didn't you know? Donna was a pilot in the US Army back in the day. She's kept her license and has flown bigger planes than this. I think she gets nervous when other people fly. She's not afraid of flying. She's afraid of being a passenger. Don't take it personally, Taylor."

"Mom, you never told me that."

"Didn't I? I must have forgotten."

Donna opened the cockpit door and pulled out a badge. In a few seconds, Tory walked back to where the passengers were meeting. "What'd I miss?"

"Is she okay up there, Tory?" Taylor asked

nervously.

"Diego's up there, and Donna showed me her pilot's license, so they should be okay. She's trained to fly Spectrums, which is a coincidence."

"But, Ma" Lukas stammered. "Shouldn't she hear this conversation about Project Poseidon?"

Molly had a slight smile as she glanced over at Linda and Betty. "She already knows."

Chapter 14

They were over Greenland and dipped south. Outside the aircraft, the sky was a cerulean blue that indicated dawn was breaking in whatever time zone they were in. Lukas saw the slight curvature of the Earth crested with the golden light of day due east. They were six hours into their flight. Taylor reported that their fuel consumption was well below what he expected due to the strong tailwinds pushing them along. "Diego, what's our ETA at this speed?" Taylor asked.

"So far it looks like we will get in about forty minutes early, sir. Want me to slow down?"

"Affirmative. Let's ride the wave and save some fuel. I don't think any of us have any social engagements tonight in Dubai, do we?"

"Taylor, dear," Molly called out. "Do you think I can make that call now?"

Taylor nodded. "Voice over Wi-Fi should be good to go. You don't need a password. Give it a shot."

Molly dialed, and after about thirty seconds she heard the ringtone on the other end of the line. "Patrick Aziz speaking."

"Hello Patrick, this is Molly Halloran, John's wife. I believe we met virtually in London and have spoken on the phone a few times."

"Good day, Mrs. Halloran. To what do I owe this

surprise? Are you calling from the plane?"

Molly rolled her eyes. "Have you been informed about the recent organizational change?"

"Yes, ma'am, I have. One of the board members called to let me know."

Interesting, she thought. "Do you have any questions?"

"No, ma'am. You are now the temporary CEO, so I report to you now."

Molly gritted her teeth. *Pompous shit.* "Patrick, I hope it's temporary and that we find my husband. There is no *temporary* in my title, which includes CEO and Chairman of the Board, just to be clear."

Patrick swallowed audibly. "Excuse me, ma'am, I didn't mean to sound…"

"Think nothing of it. I look forward to seeing you in person. We should be arriving on time. Oh, and Patrick, would you be able to arrange hotel rooms? I think we will need—" Molly counted the number of heads. "—looks like six rooms."

"Oh, I didn't know you had guests, ma'am."

"We need six rooms. Thank you, Patrick, goodbye." Molly disconnected the call. "I don't know why that guy rubs me the wrong way."

Taylor laughed. "I bet he's well aware of that now."

"Lukas," Molly said. "I got one room for you and Taylor. I hope that's okay. If not, you boys can figure something else out."

Lukas looked awkwardly at Taylor. Taylor's expression indicated that he was fine with that arrangement. "Thanks, Ma."

Molly stood to stretch her legs. "Okay, now that we

have that settled and eight more hours of flying, right, Taylor?"

Taylor nodded at Molly. "Just about seven and a half."

Molly opened her laptop and typed in her password. "I need to tell you a bit more about Poseidon." Taylor, Lukas, and Tory inched closer to the screen. "Poseidon, if you might guess, is about water. What is the one thing that makes this planet unique and also something every single life on this planet depends upon?"

"Water, I guess. But isn't there water on other planets?" Lukas asked.

"Yes, there is water on other planets, or was. But so far, we have not found life on other planets, and we've only examined a few, so I'd take that with a grain of salt. The theory out there is that water was brought to Earth via meteors and asteroids billions of years ago. More and more asteroids hit the Earth and brought water, or components of it like hydrogen and oxygen, with them. I'm talking asteroids the size of cities that pummeled Earth for eons. You with me so far?"

"Are these asteroids like the one that killed the dinosaurs?" Tory asked.

"Great question, and I'll put this in perspective. The Chicxulub asteroid was about ten kilometers wide. Six miles! Imagine the force! When it hit Earth near the current day Yucatan peninsula, it was traveling at almost forty-five thousand miles per hour. The impact kicked up trillions of tons of matter that was ejected into the atmosphere, and the shock wave created tsunamis three hundred feet high. That was 66 million years ago and led to a massive extinction of seventy-five percent of all animal and plant life, including the dinosaurs."

Lukas sat back and watched his mom bring science to life. No wonder she was such a great teacher.

Molly pointed to her screen and showed the location of the impact crater as a small red circle. "That asteroid was huge by our standards, but compared to the Earth, it was like a small stone you skim across a pond. Still, it was devastating, life-altering, and nothing like it has repeated in nearly seventy million years."

"Mom, I've been to Yucatan and saw some of the cenotes that were formed in the aftermath. How does this relate to Poseidon?"

"Good question," she continued. "I told you that story for perspective. Now imagine the Earth is only a couple of million years old. A baby planet, if you will. No life or atmosphere, as we know it, exists. This baby planet gets hit by several asteroids almost 400 miles wide! That's the size of Colorado. These asteroids brought water in the form of ice, hydrogen, oxygen, and other elements. The force of these impacts was so strong and so hot atoms were sheared and re-bonded to create many of the compounds we have today."

"Like water?" Tory asked.

"Yes, Tory. Like water," Molly continued, "So over four billion years, the amount of water increased, precipitation and evaporation cycles occurred, but the bottom line is that Earth has roughly the same amount of water now that it had hundreds of millions of years ago."

Molly drank a glass of water. "So fast forward to today. Over six billion people on Earth and growing rapidly, climate change continues to accelerate the planet's warming, and we have parts of the world that are in drought and other parts that are flooding or being submerged. It's feast or famine. The glaciers, our largest source of freshwater, melt into the oceans and become unusable for anything on land, but that disrupts the ocean currents and can create more wild weather. Aquifers are drying up due to over farming. Less than three percent of the water on earth is considered freshwater, and we aren't making more of it. Our population grows, yet the amount of Earth's water stays roughly the same."

Taylor raised his hand. "I never really thought about that. I always hear about dwindling resources, but it's actually the increase in the number of people that makes that happen." Taylor laughed. "Did I just raise my hand?"

Linda laughed. "Teacher's pet!"

Molly continued with her story, "And so now we have Project Poseidon, a new technology that actually creates water."

"From what?" Lukas asked.

"Oxygen and hydrogen, just like all water," Molly explained. "But it sounds simpler than it is in reality. Remember that water is two hydrogen molecules bonded with one oxygen molecule."

"This is the fun part," Linda interjected. "So the oxygen we breathe is actually two oxygen molecules bonded together, right?" Heads nodded. "So we have to shear those oxygen molecules apart, which isn't easy, and then bond two hydrogen molecules together, which also isn't easy."

Betty jumped in. "And this is where Poseidon

comes in. It's a technology that creates synthetic water, almost from thin air."

How do they know all this? Lukas thought, feeling a bit left out.

"But it's not like dumping ingredients into a bowl and mixing them up. We're talking about splitting molecules apart and joining others together," Betty continued. "This takes a massive amount of energy and can result in a massive release of energy."

"Like an explosion?" Tory asked.

"Yes, an explosion, and potentially a big one," Molly jumped back in. "Hydrogen is extremely flammable, so this is not something that is easily done, but Poseidon has been able to create water in just this way without burning down the laboratory."

"How flammable is hydrogen?" Tory asked.

"Google a video of the *Hindenburg*," Molly answered grimly.

Lukas, Tory, and Taylor let all of that new information settle in their heads. Molly continued to work on her laptop, while Linda and Betty reclined in their seats.

"Mom, I get how this technology would be useful, but I don't get why Dad would be abducted for it," Lukas finally said.

"Your dad sees this technology in a humanitarian way. Think of all the droughts in the world where crops wither in the sun, and people starve to death. That's who your dad has been thinking about in acquiring this technology. Saving people, babies, animals that don't have water where they live because it's on the other side of the world. And weather patterns change, so it's difficult to predict long term where rain will fall and where it won't."

"So is Poseidon commercialized?" Lukas asked.

"The technology works in a laboratory setting and was successfully piloted in a small reactor. Theoretically, we can scale it up, but the company needed the funds to figure it out. Your dad bought this technology to help people. He wants it to be his legacy. He's not planning to make money on it," Molly explained.

"I agree with Lukas. This is an amazing technology, but I'm still missing why someone would want to kidnap him," Taylor asked.

"Well," Molly started, "I see two ways this technology could be misused. One, imagine a future where water is a scarce and precious commodity because it's the very essence of life. I would imagine someone, not now but in the future, would want to make money off of that scarce commodity, don't you?"

"Like oil today?" Lukas asked.

"Oil is such a part of the global economy, and we have proven time and again that we, as humans, do or pay almost anything for it. Governments stockpile it. Nations like the one we're soon to be visiting have unbelievable wealth because of oil's value. The irony is that dependence on oil is driving a scarcity of water due to climate change."

"So someone with this technology in the future could leverage the shortage and get rich off of supplying water, or at least the technology to make it synthetically," Lukas stated.

Molly nodded. "When you get to be my age, you see that people don't really change. Someone wants this technology so that they can start a new industry and bring life to barren deserts."

"So there's the economic angle," Taylor stated. "But why not just buy it from your husband? I mean ideally someone like Mr. Halloran would do this for the betterment of mankind, but if someone finds a way to make a profit off of it, they will get extremely rich."

"John has been challenged by entrepreneurs, governments, and large utility producers to buy the Poseidon technology, but the inventor of it wanted John to have it because they shared John's vision and passion for helping humanity. The inventor was less concerned about the money."

"It truly could help the world," Tory said.

"Yeah, and potentially rebalance economic power in the next century," Lukas responded. "I get why Dad was so protective of this. No telling what people would do to get it."

"Maybe we're finding that out now," Taylor said as he walked toward the cockpit. "I'm just gonna see if they need anything. Be right back."

As Taylor walked back to the group, he asked a question that had been nagging him. "So, this is a crazy question, but could this Poseidon be used for something negative, other than economically? Like a weapon? I'm picturing a hydrogen bomb and the *Hindenburg*. Could that be at play?"

"I don't think like a psychopath, so I can't say for sure, but the short answer would be, probably." Molly rubbed her forehead. "You guys know I was a physics teacher, so I've got a scary scenario in my head that I don't even know is possible, one that could have a significant impact on all life. I believe the physics are theoretically possible. And if it were to happen…well, it terrifies me."

"What are you suggesting, Ma?" Lukas' eyes opened wide the second after he said it. "Wait, hold on, is that even possible?"

Taylor and Tory appeared confused. "Is what even possible?" asked Taylor.

Molly took a deep breath. "Poseidon running in reverse. Destroying water and returning it to oxygen and hydrogen molecules."

"Speeding up the shortage of water to drive up the value?" Lukas asked.

"Yes, but there's also a worse scenario," Molly said somberly. "Every living thing on Earth consists of water, and a large percentage of it. Most mammals are seventy percent water."

"Oh shit." Lukas' eyes went wide, as did Taylor's. "The ultimate catastrophic weapon. No explosion. No radiation. People wouldn't even know what hit them. Poseidon could also be used to vaporize and destroy life."

Chapter 15

He was jostled awake by someone dragging him out of the cot. A man threw a bowl of water onto John's face and motioned for him to wash up. John now had more than a week's growth on his beard. He knew he looked awful, having been deprived of daylight and basic human interaction.

The bodyguard he called Big Man had grabbed John by his arm and led him down a corridor lit only by fluorescent bulbs that flickered and buzzed. John really had no concept of how long he had been detained. The windowless room could have been underground or in someone's home, for all he knew. Nighttime or morning? He had no idea. He ate the food he was given, when they gave it to him, or they would take it away, and John would go hungry until the next meal, John learned the hard way. He slept when he was tired or bored due to the lack of stimulation or routine. While he thought he'd been detained for about a week, he had nothing but his beard growth to gauge how much time had actually passed.

Big Man and John arrived at a door. There was no window in the door to give him a glimpse of what was waiting on the other side. John suppressed the anxious reality that came with being a prisoner. Torture or death could come at any moment without warning.

The image of an American journalist, who had

been kidnapped by extremists, came to him in nightmares, and John experienced the terror of watching the journalist be beheaded time after time whenever he fell asleep. *Maybe that's what is on the other side of this door?* John thought but pushed the idea from his mind. He didn't need to panic now.

The door opened, and he saw another windowless room furnished with five empty wooden chairs. Next to the chairs was a long plank, some cloth, and a bucket. *I'm going to be tortured,* John thought as his pulse quickened. Images of waterboarding flooded his mind.

I wish they would just kill me or let me go, he thought. Big Man pushed down on John's shoulders, indicating that he should sit. He did as commanded. The big man held up his hand. *Stop? Stay? Be right back?* He had no idea.

John once learned from a security consultant that if kidnapped, one should cooperate with the abductors, but to not be submissive or overly emotional. *"That's one way to get a bullet in your head real fast." Cooperative but not weak,* was what he remembered. John waited for his hands and feet to be bound to the chair, but to his surprise, Big Man turned and walked out the door without restraining him. *Are they just gonna shoot me?*

A few minutes later, the door creaked open, and Clown Face walked into the room. John acknowledged him with a brief nod while Clown Face searched for something in his robe before pulling out a smartphone. Clown Face spoke into the phone, and John could not understand a word or discern what the language was. It sounded like Arabic, but with an accent he couldn't place. Maybe it was a local dialect. Sounded Middle

Eastern, maybe African. It could have been either an official language of wherever they were or some village dialect. Google dealt with major languages, hundreds of them, but not regional dialects.

Google Translate replayed, and Clown Face turned up the volume. The digital female voice spoke back. *Your wife will be in Dubai today.* John stifled a laugh that the voice of scary Clown Face was female. *We will go and see her at the appropriate time. For her sake, I hope she has what we expect from her.*

Clown Face spoke into the phone again, the digital voice asked, *Do you need anything?*

John shook his head. *Are you comfortable?* John nodded his head.

Do you want to see your wife? John froze. In a split second he had to answer. Of course he wanted to see Molly, but he didn't want the kidnappers to think that seeing her was important to him. He shook his head no.

Chapter 16

The *Goose* was somewhere over Northern Europe when Lukas woke up from another short nap. Something about the cabin air and the occasional bump here and there always made him tired. He was still processing what his mom told him about Poseidon technology and how it could be a miracle if used as intended or a devastating weapon if used for destruction, as many despots in the world would happily attempt. Questions swirled in his mind also about how his perception of people had changed in the last couple of hours.

Donna was flying Taylor's Spectrum jet like it was the most normal thing in the world.

How did Linda and Betty know about the Poseidon technology? How did his mom suddenly become CEO and Chairman of a multimillion-dollar private equity firm less than a year after retiring from teaching? How did she know intricate details of the Poseidon technology? What was the recital on asteroid history all about? He knew his mom was smart, but again, he was surprised at the level of details she knew. Lukas couldn't make sense of it.

He looked for Taylor in the cabin and, after not finding him, walked to the cockpit and knocked on the door. Diego opened the door, and Lukas saw that the two of them were piloting together. Lukas felt sorry for

Diego, trapped in a confined space with his girlfriend's father, who was undoubtedly peppering him with questions. "Do you guys need anything?"

Diego visibly relaxed when he saw Lukas. "I'm fine, thank you."

Taylor winked at Lukas and promised he was not torturing Diego too badly.

"Good to hear. I know pilots can't drink, obviously. I'll buy you a cerveza in Dubai." Lukas smiled.

"We've got meals ready if any of you are hungry," Taylor offered. "I can show you how to heat it up."

"Contrary to popular opinion, IT people can actually operate kitchen appliances."

"Impressive," Taylor shot back. "This I've got to see."

Taylor unbuckled his seat belt and entered the galley where Lukas was getting the meals ready. He put his arm around Lukas' waist.

"How's the father of the potential bride?" Lukas joked.

Taylor didn't respond, but whispered in Lukas' ear, "You're the damned sexiest flight attendant I've ever met," and then kissed him on the neck.

Lukas tensed, not sure if he was comfortable with Taylor's sudden advance or not. He couldn't remember the last time a man had shown physical interest in him.

After an uncomfortable pause, Taylor asked, "Did I just cross a line?"

Lukas hugged him back. "Yes. But it's okay. I want to get used to it. Keep crossing them until I tell you to stop." Lukas smiled. "My head is kind of spinning right now. It's nothing about you."

Molly and her friends were asleep, but Lukas didn't want them to hear. "I feel like I have all these puzzle pieces thrown at me, but don't know how they fit together. Did you ever have that feeling like everyone in the room knows something you don't? That's how I feel."

"Did you ask her? Your mom?"

"What would I ask her? She's always just been my mom, and now I see this new badass side to her that I can't wrap my head around. It kind of knocked me off center."

Taylor ran his fingers through Lukas' hair and massaged his temples. "I think we grow up believing our parents live just for us, and when we become adults and leave, they just stay the same, pining away for their kids to come visit them." Taylor laughed. "At least that's what I thought about my folks. And then suddenly, you're an adult, and you realize they are just people, you know? They have their interests, talents, faults, secrets, and you see they are more complex than you imagined when you were a kid. They have lives, and maybe some baggage. That's why you should talk to her."

"I'm pretty sure my mom and dad have a docile life where they are now. They travel, work, volunteer, and stay active," Lukas explained.

"I don't mean their lives now, Lukas," Taylor continued. "I'm talking about their lives before you were even born."

Taylor returned to the cockpit. Molly awoke from her nap and was hungry. She went to the galley to check out the food options. Lukas sat in the back of the plane working on his computer and saw an opportunity to talk to his mom, with Betty right beside him working on her computer. "How are you feeling, Ma?"

"I'm so glad we could take our own jet, but still, I feel gross. It'll be nice to get to the hotel and take a shower. I feel awkward using the one on the plane. That probably sounds like an awful thing to bitch about."

"There's just nothing like airplane sweaty body, Ma. I promise I won't tell anyone you complained about your private jet." Lukas joked.

"You know, Lukas, I know it's your romantic life, and you don't need your mother meddling in your affairs, but Taylor is quite a catch if you ask me. You two look so natural together, like you've known each other forever."

"I hope you mean that in a good way, Ma." Lukas blushed a bit. His mother could see right through him. "I'm waiting 'til he reveals he's a psychotic serial killer. That's usually how my relationships go, well, not the serial killer part, but definitely the psychotic part."

"I think you should go for it, for what it's worth. And why are you so negative about relationships?"

"Mom, I've known him for a week and during one of the most awful, chaotic weeks in my life. I'd like to see how we get along in a normal setting, like normal, boring life. Watching Netflix, making popcorn, folding clothes, you know? Simple life stuff. That's when you know whether you're with the right person or not."

"You haven't changed much, Lukas," his mom pointed out. "You look at everything with logic, precision, follow the rules, and with as little variation as possible. You've been that way since you were little, and I love that about you, but you have to let yourself feel emotions. Allow yourself to be vulnerable and take a leap of faith. You're not a Klingon, for God's sake."

Lukas held back a laugh. "I think you mean a Vulcan, Mom."

"Let me ask you something, Lukas. How do you feel when you're around Taylor?"

Lukas pondered. "That's easy, Ma. I feel like I'm right where I want to be. I feel joy, fear, happiness, then scared and vulnerable. Panicked and terrified he's going to walk away."

"Like Drew, you mean?"

Lukas paused. "Yeah, Ma, like Drew."

"You live once, honey. You're almost forty, and before you know it you will be my age. It's best to share a life with someone, not run probability formulas to predict success or failure. Sometimes, you just have to jump and know, that no matter what happens, you'll be okay."

"What did you and Dad do before I was born?" Lukas quickly changed the subject.

Molly was taken aback. "Um, well, we had a lot of adventures, that's for sure. Not much money, so we both worked a lot, but we had fun."

"Mom, how did you meet your friends, you know, Linda, Betty, and Donna?"

"We worked together."

"Teaching? Lukas asked.

"Not teaching. We worked together at Argonne National Laboratory before teaching."

"What did you guys do there?"

Molly thought about a response. "Lots of stuff."

"Mom, can you tell me more than that?"

Molly let out a sigh. "Not every story is my story alone to tell. I have to get the ladies to explain some things. It's a long story, so let's go get them so we can tell it."

Molly summoned Taylor again, so Tory took over for him in the cockpit. Diego was already up there. Molly gathered her three friends, along with Lukas and Taylor. "This plane is turning out to be like a confessional at forty-five thousand feet," Molly joked. "Lukas asked me how the four of us met, so I'll tell my side of it and, ladies, feel free to jump in any time," Molly started out. "We became friends about five years before you were born, Lukas. Your dad and I had recently married and had the time to try some new things. We didn't have money, but we had love and energy."

Lukas wondered what "new things" meant. *Please don't tell me you're swingers*, he thought, not that he had anything against swingers; he just didn't want to know if his parents did that stuff.

"The four of us"—Molly pointed to her friends— "were in different areas working at Argonne, and we became friends working on a project together."

Linda took over. "Argonne is part of the Department of Energy, and, mind you, this was fifty years ago. We had already started to develop clean energy solutions like solar, wind, and hydrogen power. Develop, not invent. The basic technology was already there."

"All of us were young and scientifically astute," Betty continued. "One day, and I think this was before we met, wasn't it?"

"I think I had met you already," Donna chimed in.

"No, I'm pretty sure it was before, Donna. You're thinking about the orientation meeting," Betty stated.

"Anyway...whether we had met before or not isn't relevant. We were brought into a meeting room, just the four of us, with a bunch of guys in suits. They asked us our names and where we went to school, although they already knew, I'm sure," Molly said.

"They had to have known," Betty commented. "How would they know who to call to the meeting?"

Molly steered them back on course. "The men asked us if we wanted to travel overseas, so we said, sure! We were young and adventurous, so why not?"

"We should have smelled a rat when they told us where we would go," Betty explained. "We're thinking the travel was to places like Paris, London...places like that."

Lukas jumped in, "So where did you end up going?"

"More like where we *didn't* go. All over the place, mostly in the Middle East. They told us we would be doing *energy research*." Linda used air quotes. "Cities like Tehran, Amman, Cairo. We did get to Paris a couple of times, though, which was nice."

Taylor asked, "So what did you do besides energy research?"

Molly interjected, "We actually didn't do any research. Not after the first trip, I mean. The US, Japan, and Europe were already way ahead in developing alternative energy. But most of the world still relied upon fossil fuels like oil, gas, and coal."

"Back then," Betty commented, "climate change was not the driving force behind alternative energy. It was about money, dependence on oil-rich countries, and finite resources. Everybody knew fossil fuels would eventually run out, whether it was in fifty or five hundred years."

"And where do you ladies come in?" Lukas asked.

Donna spoke up. "Oil brought trillions of dollars to the countries who sold it, and money makes people do awful things. Rogue forces got involved because the money didn't flow to the people on the street. It was hoarded by the governments and oil companies, and people became angry and fought back."

"Who are these rogue forces? Terrorists?" Taylor then asked.

"Yes, but not the terrorists we know today," Molly answered. "I would use the term, *organizers* to more accurately explain what they did."

"Organizers started popping up everywhere. It was like Whack-a-Mole, and many of these guys got violent, sabotaging oil fields, kidnapping and killing westerners, all the things you hear about, but still pretty vanilla compared to today," Linda continued, "The US was in a tight spot. These groups were not affiliated with the government, so there was no country we had to fight, just these terror cells as they came to be known. Nobody took ownership for reeling them in."

"Central Intelligence had a theory and got involved recruiting young people to fight these groups, to basically have them pose as undercover tourists and students and get paid some money," Betty explained. "Pretty good money, to be honest."

"Their theory was that they needed to cut off the head of the snake and let the terror cells dissipate," Linda clarified. "So they asked us if we were interested."

Molly got serious. "The CIA offered us what today would be called a side hustle. So we figured, why not?"

Taylor looked over to Lukas, unsure of where this was going. Lukas shrugged and looked at his mom in disbelief, trying to follow where this was going and fearing it wasn't good.

"Boys, you're looking at the prototype unit for Operation Rosemary."

Chapter 17

Lukas rubbed his temples as he tried to get his head around this new information. Like everyone else, he was tired and groggy, so perhaps his brain wasn't as sharp as usual. *My mom continues to surprise me,* he thought. "Mom, do you have any other stories I need to know?"

"Well, you didn't *need* to know either of those stories. I chose to tell you to help put things in perspective. Did they help?"

Lukas nodded. "You've had a way more adventurous life than I would have imagined."

Molly shook her head. "My life was adventurous, as you say, and I'm grateful for everything I've done that has led up to today."

"So," Lukas started, "I'm afraid to ask this, but what exactly did you ladies do on these trips?'

"At first, not much," Linda responded. "We were in Baghdad, I think it was, and supposed to act like college girl tourists. You know, all laughy and ditzy—something non-threatening. There were always a few CIA guys around, so we knew we were relatively safe most of the time. And being young, we trusted everything they told us to do or say."

"That was our first real trip out there in the real world, wasn't it?" Donna asked.

"Yes, we were green and probably looked pretty

nervous. Our job was to look for an address the CIA gave us, have local people lead us confused young ladies to the general vicinity, and nail the bad guy. Well, actually, the CIA sharpshooters nailed him."

"Mission accomplished," Molly said. "But we were smart and resourceful, so we started to get creative, and not only find the bad guy, but to take him out, without the CIA's help."

"But we had their blessing," Donna interjected.

Lukas buried his face in his hands. "Please tell me this isn't happening," he whispered to Taylor.

"I'm afraid it is," Taylor responded.

"We got good at finding these bad guys because nobody would think that young women would be any kind of threat. Most of the time, the terrorists were hiding in plain sight, like in someone's house in the city," Molly continued. "Kind of like bin Laden. For years, the military combed the mountains, caves, and bunkers in Afghanistan. Then they found the asshole living in an upper-class neighborhood in Abbottabad, Pakistan, right under everybody's nose. The Navy Seals took him out when he was watching TV."

"We did that for about, what, three years? Linda asked.

"Three, four max," Donna answered.

"That's when we started calling ourselves the Herb Society," Molly recalled. "Acronym using the first letters of our last names."

"We were not allowed to use Project Rosemary in conversation, so we substituted Herb Society for it," Betty concluded.

"Then I got pregnant with Lukas, so we stopped traveling, and Project Rosemary was mothballed. We thought the tie-in with Rosemary and Herb was cute, so it stuck."

Taylor asked what he knew Lukas wanted to know. "So did you all ever carry out...um...the deed?"

"Oh sure," Betty chimed in. "We probably took out ten to fifteen guys during our time. Maybe more than that. No women that I can remember."

"We did not shoot them, guys," Molly said to Lukas and Taylor. "We'd usually use poison or explosives...throw a pipe bomb into their house, that sort of thing."

"Actually, you shot two guys, Molly. Can't remember their names but you were accurate. I think it was Cairo," Linda reminded her. "Your mom is an awesome shot, Lukas."

"I stand corrected," Molly said.

"So, does Dad know any of this?"

"About Rosemary? Well, yes, but not every detail. Much of it was classified, and he respected that. I felt I owed him a little information so he wouldn't worry."

"If I knew my partner was out busting up terrorist cells, I would have been *more* worried!" Lukas said dryly. "Ma, I want to make sure I understand this. The four of you would go to some city harboring supposed terrorists, find them, and take them out?" The four ladies nodded. "Like you killed them?" More nods.

"They were bad guys, Lukas. We were young and idealistic, trying to make the world better and safer," Molly explained. "The US Government gave the orders. We just executed them."

"Bad choice of words," Linda said, attempting to lighten the mood.

"Well, this has been an enlightening flight." Lukas

took a deep breath and exhaled. "So the four of you, the Herb Society or whatever you called yourselves, were basically global assassins?" The four friends eyed each other, waiting for one to speak up.

Molly spoke, "I guess that's what you could have called us."

Chapter 18

The wing flaps extended, and the *Goose* began to slow, creating a soft rumbling sound that rolled through the darkened cabin. Linda's stomach dropped as they descended in altitude, the slowing of the plane causing her to shift her balance. In the back of the cabin, Lukas and Betty worked feverishly on her laptop, their focused faces illuminated by the screen. "That should do it, and it's a nasty one." Betty was interested and stifled a smile. "Let's hope we don't need it."

The tired passengers peered out the window. "I don't know about you, but I'm ready to get out of this tin can," Donna interjected. The metropolitan area glowed with the orange-hued sodium vapor streetlights. The Dubai skyline twinkled in the distance, adjacent to a massive void of blackness that was the Persian Gulf. The *Goose* received clearance for its final approach. The jet touched down on the runway of Dubai's Al Maktoum International at approximately eight p.m. local time. Taylor and Donna, who insisted on serving as a co-pilot to keep her claustrophobia under control, made a perfect landing and reverse throttled, the force so strong that Lukas almost lost grip of his laptop as the plane slowed to a near stop. "I guess that's why airlines make you stow your electronics during takeoff and landing," Lukas commented to Betty, The *Goose* came to a near stop before pivoting onto a taxiway and held their position. The mood in the plane reflected a combination of fatigue and relief, draped in the enormity of the tasks that lay before them. The fifteen-hour flight had gone smoothly, having had the fortune of strong tailwinds, but there was an unspoken somberness regarding why they were all there, to rescue John Halloran. The idling *Goose* was approached by a small ground support vehicle with a large, illuminated *Follow Me* sign. Taylor had not been to Al Maktoum for a few years and noticed how much it had grown since the last time he had utilized this airport. "We get an escort since our tail number hasn't registered for the last few years," Taylor commented to his daughter, sitting in a nearby jump seat.

"Maybe you flew the older plane here last time," Tory responded.

"Okay, folks," Taylor announced over the intercom, "We are being escorted to the FBO terminal reserved for private aircraft. Either the customs official will board the plane and check our passports, or we will deplane first and do that in the terminal."

When the ground crew chucked the wheels and the engines powered down, Taylor released the entry stairs, and two men came on board requesting passports. The emotionless agents were all business and stamped their passports without much scrutiny. They went to the rear of the plane and performed a perfunctory inspection of the cargo hold, and finding nothing suspicious, told the passengers they were free to deplane. "This is the way to fly," Linda smirked as they began to disembark just three minutes after arriving.

Linda, Donna, and Betty grabbed their things and made their way to the jet's exit. Donna carried her large bottle of liquor and threw it in the waste bin the cleaners brought on board.

"Didn't need it after all! It feels so much better when I get to pilot a bit. Thanks, Taylor and Tory. Nice wings ya got there."

Porters were already unloading suitcases from the luggage hold while an airport escort helped the older ladies down the stairs.

"Little do they know my little old mom could probably snap their necks like a twig," Lukas commented to Taylor.

The FBO lounge looked nothing like an airport terminal. Plush leather seats surrounded ornate coffee tables loaded with reading materials and adorned with either sculptures or floral arrangements. A full-service restaurant, complete with white tablecloths, was available to passengers, along with showers, a spa, and sleeping rooms. A tuxedo-wearing pianist played softly on a lacquered grand piano.

"Reminds me of Marana," Taylor whispered sarcastically, referring back to their very basic departure airport in Tucson.

"I'm kind of slaphappy right now. How are you doing?" Lukas asked the pilots. "You did all the work flying us here."

Taylor answered, "I pulled rank and let the kids and Donna fly most of it so I could spend time with you."

"Glad you did. You were emotional support for me after learning about my mom's sordid past." Lukas winked. He checked his watch and continued, "We gotta watch our step. Homosexuality is illegal here. We don't need to get lynched in the town square."

"I'll be discreet, I promise. Your mom can always save us if needed," Taylor replied. Lukas wasn't sure if he was kidding or not.

They walked toward an area where limo drivers awaited their passengers. Lukas texted the number the hijackers gave him. Molly was the only one who had seen what Patrick Aziz looked like, so everyone relied upon her to spot their companion, who would take them to their hotel. Suddenly, a handsome, well-groomed young man stepped out to greet them. He wore a slim-fitting tailored suit that looked expensive. "Madam Chairman, it is good to see you, and welcome to Dubai."

"Hello Patrick"—she extended her hand—"It's good to see you, and please call me Molly."

Patrick smiled politely. "I will try and remember that, ma'am," Patrick replied, knowing he would never call his boss by her first name. Lukas could tell from his mom's demeanor that she was being ultra-formal with Patrick. Maybe even chilly. She was now his boss, and her normally warm, engaging style evaporated. "This is my son, Lukas, and his friend Taylor, who is also one of our pilots." Each shook Patrick's hand. "These are my friends, Linda, Donna, and Betty."

"Nice to meet you as well and—"

"And this," Molly interrupted, "is Taylor's daughter, Tory, and her friend, Diego."

"Again, welcome to Dubai, and I'm sorry it's under distressing circumstances. I have asked the porters to take your luggage to the car."

"I hope he has a bus," Linda whispered to Donna as she eyed the small mountain of luggage next to them.

As they exited the building, a hot blast of dry air

hit them in their faces that reminded Lukas of opening a hot oven door. Having been in the temperature-controlled environments of the jet and arrivals lobby, the sudden wall of heat felt like a shock. "From one desert to another, it feels like a sauna!" Taylor heard Tory say.

Lukas' phone buzzed, notifying him of an incoming text. He stared at the number. It began with 971, the country code for the UAE. "I've got to make a quick call." Lukas diverted to a corner and dialed the phone number given to him by the kidnappers, as instructed. "The Halloran family has arrived," Lukas spoke, hoping for a response.

"Please meet in the parking lot of the FBO terminal at 17:00 hours tomorrow. I will text or call you beforehand with further instructions." The person on the other side immediately disconnected the call. The abruptness of the response gave Lukas pause. Why would they need to wait almost another day to receive instructions on what to do next?

As the van drove toward the city center, Lukas stared in amazement at the Dubai city skyline. Impossibly tall and unique buildings were colorfully illuminated, some with huge moving advertisements dancing across their façades. Other buildings pulsated with animated art and graphics like fireworks and fountains. Even from miles away, they could see the city's focal point—The Burj Khalifa—the tallest building in the world. Standing at over 2,700 feet, the Burj towered over the city and was surrounded by a series of man-made lakes.

"I can't believe that building is over a half mile tall," Donna reacted.

"Over there is the Burj Mall—the largest in the world," Patrick explained. "It's actually more like an indoor city with shops, an amusement park, Michelin-star restaurants, and a massive indoor aquarium."

"Interesting," Lukas commented. "A Michelin-star food court. Imagine something like that in Tucson."

"Take that, fast food joints of the world," Taylor zinged back.

Patrick also pointed out the Dubai Fountains, where visitors could be treated to a choreographed water show like no other in the world.

The city glowed with an aura of newness and obscene abundance of money and luxury. Expensive cars were the rule, not the exception. Taylor pointed at a Rolls-Royce adorned in taxi livery. Hidden occupants were cloaked behind tinted windows as the vehicles cruised the motorway. Excess abounded in the vehicles, the architecture, and the shops like Dubai won a contest no other city could even enter. The neo-futuristic Burj Khalifa dominated the skyline like a towering middle finger with an overt message to the world: *Fuck off and don't even try to top Dubai.*

Patrick booked them at the San Rafael Hotel, one of the best-known luxury hotels in downtown Dubai. It was also the same hotel in which John stayed just over a week ago. Its exterior was illuminated in shades of blue and purple lights that reflected in the canal that snaked beneath it. Another welcoming committee greeted them as the van pulled into the hotel entrance. Patrick handed out six hotel key cards. "I've already checked you all in."

Patrick explained the general layout of the hotel, the locations of the gym, spa, and pool, as well as restaurants. "Of course, the hotel offers twenty-four-hour room service."

"Thank you, Patrick," Molly said. "We need to meet the men who have Mr. Halloran at five p.m. tomorrow, right, Lukas?"

Lukas nodded. "They said they would call us for next steps."

"We should meet here at four tomorrow afternoon," Patrick suggested. "It's not a long drive to the airport."

"Thank you, Patrick." Molly remained icy and followed her porter toward the elevators.

Taylor and Lukas rode up in their elevator in silence, discreetly declining the porters to carry their own luggage. "There are probably two twin beds in there," Taylor said as he stared at the elevator floors whiz upward.

Lukas nodded. "Probably."

"Are you okay with the sleeping arrangements? I can get my own room if..." Taylor interjected.

"Yes," Lukas answered. "There are two beds, but you should know that I snore. I'm giving you fair warning."

Taylor laughed. "We can see who is louder."

They got to the room. Lukas paused and walked in. It was a spacious suite with floor-to-ceiling windows overlooking views of downtown Dubai. There were two king-sized beds outfitted with elaborate pillows and bedding. They checked out the room in awkward silence.

"I'm gonna take a shower unless you want to go first," Taylor nervously told Lukas.

"You go ahead. I'll go after you."

While Taylor showered, Lukas explored the room's features and was surprised by its simple elegance and size. Fresh flowers graced a large table, and the room smelled of lavender and citrus. There were multiple electrical outlets and USB ports for visitors who came from around the world. Taylor's shower was quick, and he stepped out of the bathroom cloaked in a towel and surrounded by steam. Lukas turned his gaze away from Taylor, hoping to avert staring at his magnificent room companion. Soap and the scent of Taylor's clean skin emanated from him, and it reminded Lukas of a locker room. He was instantly turned on and entered the bathroom to take his shower.

As Lukas showered, he tried not to think about what could potentially lie ahead. He didn't want to assume anything, and maybe Taylor would already be asleep in bed, exhausted from the lengthy trip. But his heart still beat rapidly in anticipation, and his body parts reacted to the vivid things that Lukas' mind imagined. He visualized them both naked, hard, and hot, anticipating the attraction the two of them felt for each other and hoping Taylor felt the same way.

When Lukas finished showering, he emerged wearing only a towel and without his eyeglasses. Taylor sat on the edge of the bed, stood up, then walked over, held Lukas' head in his hands, and started kissing him passionately. "Is this okay?" he asked. Lukas nodded and kissed him back. They were hungry for each other, and soon their towels fell to the ground. The room was dimly lit, and the two naked men stood staring at each other, slowly taking in every detail.

"My God, you are perfect," Taylor said as he ran his hand up Lukas' sculpted stomach and chest.

"You're gonna make me fucking explode." Lukas reached around and grabbed Taylor's muscular ass, pulling them closely together.

Lukas pushed Taylor onto the bed and straddled him, passionately kissing his lips, neck, and chest. Both men were lost in primal thoughts, and decades of pent-up passion boiled to the surface. Lukas jumped up to close the drapes. "Just in case the morality police are watching." He smiled and lay back down on Taylor's muscular chest, their warm, damp skin touching in so many places that Lukas felt like they were glued together. "Let's break some laws."

Taylor hungrily grabbed at his naked torso and ass, mesmerized by the heat and scent radiating off of him. He was lost in a dream and wanted to devour Lukas. "Let's break them all."

The next morning, Taylor and Lukas lazily took in their view of the Dubai skyline, including an unobstructed view of the Burj Khalifa that dwarfed everything surrounding it. Their room was a large suite with floor-to-ceiling windows that also had a view of the Dubai Canal and the boardwalk that ran parallel to it. "I never pictured Dubai to have so much water running through it," Lukas commented. "We can take a run on the boardwalk later if you want."

Taylor looked at him and smiled, which Lukas took as a sign that Taylor had other plans in mind for the two of them this morning. Wearing the plush robes provided by the San Rafael, a finished breakfast sat between them. They opted for room service in order to spend more time together, and held hands across the small table, which they could do behind closed doors, but not in public.

"You are beautiful, Lukas".

Lukas squeezed Taylor's hand. "You are more."

"Hey, listen," Taylor started. "I know we, uh, you know, didn't use…"

"I'm negative, so you know," Lukas interjected. "I got tested less than a month ago for my annual physical, and I've lived like a monk for the last five years, anyway. Maybe my reaction to you naked gave that away?" Lukas smiled.

"I'm negative, too." Taylor squeezed Lukas' hand back. "I was so into you, your body…everything. I didn't stop to…think."

"How many times did we…?"

"I lost count," Taylor answered. "Four or five times maybe? We were kind of animals."

"That's so not like me. I'm usually more…reserved." Lukas blushed at the memory as he pushed his eyeglasses up the bridge of his nose. "It's been a dry spell, well, actually a dry decade. Still, I'm not normally that irresponsible."

"Me neither. Dads don't get a lot of time to hook up, which isn't my style anyway."

"What's it like being a dad?"

"It is pretty great," Taylor reflected. "There were days, though, I envied freedom. Tory went through a pretty monstrous phase as a teenager where I kind of lost my will to live." Taylor smiled.

Lukas laughed. "She seems like such an angel."

"She is, but nothing can prepare you for the teenage years. You just get through it because what choice do you have?" Taylor fidgeted with his fork, stabbing a leftover slice of honeydew melon. "What about you? Do you want kids?" Lukas was quiet for a moment. "I mean, in general," Taylor clarified. "I didn't mean necessarily with me. Not that I would mind that if it ever…"

Lukas pulled Taylor to him and kissed him on the lips. "I want to have kids someday, while I'm still young enough. And I haven't ruled you out just yet."

"Can I ask you a question?" Taylor asked.

"I think you will anyway, so go ahead." Lukas smiled.

"Have you ever been in love? Like in a relationship?"

Lukas froze and thought about how he would answer Taylor's question. "I was." Lukas filled his glass with sparkling water. "It was a long time ago. I was very much in love with him. Drew was my first boyfriend. We sailed through French Polynesia together. I'd never been so happy in my life. I thought we'd be together the rest of our lives."

Taylor gazed at him. "What happened?"

Lukas let out his breath. "He didn't want me. He wasn't ready nor wanted a monogamous relationship. He met someone and ended up moving to Europe with him."

Taylor rubbed the top of Lukas' hand. "I'm sorry, babe. How long ago was that?"

Lukas chuckled. "Over ten years ago. I never heard from him again. He broke my heart, so I built an iron wall around what was left of it." Taylor's eyes took on a concerned look. "I promised myself that I would never feel that kind of pain again. I never let myself get too close to anyone, buried myself in work, built the company, dated sometimes, but nothing serious. Sounds kind of pathetic when I say it all out loud."

Taylor gazed into Lukas' eyes. "Thanks for telling me that, Lukas. Did you know the guy Drew ran off with?"

Lukas shook his head. "Some mystery guy who Drew was willing to completely change his life for. That's all I needed to know."

Taylor put his hand on Lukas' knee. "Sorry you got your heart broken, and I hope you'll trust me. I was never in love before, but even right now, I would feel…really sad, if you didn't want to be with me."

Lukas stood and straddled Taylor's legs, and his robe opened as he kissed him. "You are starting to melt the iron wall," Lukas told him. "And I'm both happy and terrified of it, just so you're aware."

Taylor pulled him close, their chests touching and arms wrapped around each other as they kissed some more. "Baby, I've got a confession to make," Taylor stated. Lukas looked at him with expectation. "I have had a crush on you for some time. I made sure I scheduled myself on your flight to Tucson so I could meet you. I never expected…"

Lukas kissed him gently. "I'm glad you did."

They made their way to a bed and flopped down together, passionately rolling and rubbing their bodies together. This continued for several hours. Intense sex followed by a post-sex nap, and the cycle would start again, making time seem irrelevant.

After one of these short naps, Lukas awoke and glanced at his cell phone on the nightstand. "I've got to meet my mom in the lobby at four. That's in one hour. Ready for another round?"

Chapter 19

The lobby of the San Rafael was relatively quiet, as guests milled about looking at the multiple paintings and sculptures on exhibit, while some enjoyed beverages from the daily afternoon tea service. There was a quiet murmur of guests having conversations. Donna, Linda, and Betty wore comfortable, practical clothes. After all, how does one dress to meet kidnappers? Lukas and Taylor stood rigidly, overcompensating to cloak their passion and any evidence of the deliciously bad things they had engaged in during the last eighteen hours. Lukas was dressed in jeans, tee-shirt, and a sport coat. Taylor complimented him and said he looked sexy before they left their room.

The men flanked Molly, who was typing something on her smartphone. Tory and Diego sat next to each other on a sofa, having spent the day visiting Dubai Mall and the observation deck of the Burj Khalifa.

At precisely four p.m., Patrick Aziz entered the hotel dressed immaculately in a navy-blue tailored suit that accentuated his trim frame. Perfect black hair was slicked back and lush. His cognac shoes, polished and gleaming, clicked on the marble floors. "Good afternoon, everyone. I hope your first day in Dubai has been a pleasant one."

Other than my husband being held hostage, it's

fabulous, Molly thought. "Hello, Patrick," Molly replied.

Patrick clapped his hands. "How many will be going to Al Maktoum?"

Seconds after Patrick asked the question, Lukas' phone buzzed with a text number to call.

"I've got to take this. I think it's about Dad." Lukas found one of the lobby sofas and entered the telephone number he was sent. The call connected.

"I am watching you right now," an accented male voice answered. "You have people with you. I told you no police."

"We have not contacted the police," Lukas spoke, creeped out that someone was watching him. "Besides my mother and me, there are three of her friends and the…flight crew that brought us here."

"Just you," the voice said.

"Just me, what do you mean?"

"You come alone. I have a car waiting."

Lukas fumbled for a response. This was not going to plan. "Where is the car?"

"Front of hotel now. Driver standing by a dark blue Bentley. You have one minute. If you are followed, you will be killed. As will your father."

Lukas looked at his watch. Forty-five seconds left. He quickly walked to the group to tell them the change of plans in as calm a manner as he could. "I need you to listen to me. One of the kidnappers is watching us. He has instructed that only I go to talk to them. If anyone follows, I will be killed, and so will Dad. I have my phone with me. Hope they let me keep it, but I doubt it. I'll be in a dark blue Bentley."

"I'm going with you," Molly interjected.

"Just me, Ma. They just want me. I'll be okay." Twenty seconds remained. Lukas walked toward the main door.

His mother and Taylor followed him, distress evident on their faces at this sudden turn. "Don't worry. I promise I'll be okay." He went to hug his mom. She grabbed his face and stared into his eyes, then brushed off his lapel.

"I want you to look good for Dad. Please be safe."

He acknowledged Donna and Linda, then Betty approached him and gave him a big hug, which took Lukas by surprise. Betty was not a hugger. "I dropped a little surprise in your jacket pocket," Betty whispered in his ear. "Swallow it when you get there. It will help us find you."

It was an odd interaction with Betty, but he played it as nonchalantly as he could, assuming he still had an audience watching from wherever.

Now the hard part came. Taylor's face was etched with concern and longing, having spent an incredible night and morning together. Taylor took a deep breath. He wanted to kiss and hug Lukas, drink in his scent, and tell him not to worry. Neither man could show affection in public, which only increased the pain of separating. Lukas longed to make him feel better, even though he was terrified of what was awaiting him.

He checked his watch. It was time. "I've got to go." He ran for the Bentley, and the chauffeur opened the door for him. Lukas tentatively stepped into the expensive vehicle.

Taylor felt his heart drop to his stomach as he watched the Bentley disappear into traffic.

****

The second Lukas stepped into the car, he was grabbed by a man who slid a hood over his head and zip-tied his ankles together to prevent any chance of escape. They left his hands unbound. Lukas' first reaction was panic. The black hood felt claustrophobic, and he struggled to get his breath under control. He couldn't believe he'd been stupid enough to be lured into a trap. He didn't know at the time that his father had been lured in a similar way.

The driver maintained a steady speed and made enough turns that Lukas assumed they were driving in circles to cloak their route in confusion. He thought it ironic that, being his first time in Dubai, they went to such lengths to hide their trail. In reality, Lukas would have no idea where he was had they driven him to the location in an open-air tour bus. He didn't have the greatest sense of direction and made a mental note that he should study maps more often.

He could still smell Taylor on his clothes, which gave him a sense of comfort. How could this man he had known for such a short time make him feel so wonderful and grounded? Maybe Taylor was his soulmate who took almost thirty-nine years to find. Lukas was used to keeping his emotions and passions boxed up and hidden, yet Taylor smashed that box open with a sledgehammer. Surprising to Lukas, he didn't feel vulnerable or exposed. He felt seen and loved, or at least liked.

The Bentley stopped and turned, driving down a small hill, and the echo, combined with the dank smell of concrete and car exhaust, suggested to him that he was in a parking garage. The car stopped, and one of the men got out and helped Lukas step outside. The man removed the hood and snipped the zip ties around his ankles but bound his wrists together instead. Lukas' eyes ached with the sudden exposure to the dull light of the garage.

At least he could see where he was now. One man stayed behind in the car while the zip-tie guy escorted Lukas forward. Lukas avoided looking at his face, but he could tell he was a big, strong man. Zip-tie whisked Lukas up a flight of stairs and into a hallway. He pulled the black hood over Lukas' head again. Lukas didn't struggle. He remembered his dad telling him about being cooperative but not dominated by a captor, a lesson learned from one of his security advisors. Lukas didn't have a security advisor, so he took his father's advice.

****

The buzz of what sounded like fluorescent lights added to the confusion about where he was. Lukas continued to breathe and not let anxiety or fear take hold. They stopped walking, and he heard a door creak open. Lukas felt Big Man's strong arm shove him forward, and he stumbled before crashing to the concrete floor, his bound arms partially able to cushion the blow. Dazed and bruised, Lukas righted himself to sit, blindfolded, unsure what was coming. The door closed, and Lukas couldn't tell if he was alone or surrounded by a crowd.

After some time, Lukas heard a door open, and footsteps approached him. His hood was pulled off his head. His glasses sat beside him. Lukas' eyes adjusted to the light and saw a blurred figure standing above him.

As Lukas' eyes adjusted, a distorted, disturbing

image came into focus. It was a clown's face.

****

Taylor paced nervously in his hotel room. It was evening, and Lukas had been gone several hours by now. He called Molly. "Any luck, yet?"

"Not yet, Taylor. How are you doing?"

"I'm nervous to be honest. I didn't expect them to take Lukas. Who are these guys?"

"Not sure who they are but I'd bet money they're linked to whomever took John. I'm still trying to figure out why they took Lukas and not me," Molly responded.

Taylor paused and wondered, *why would they take Molly?*

"Taylor, may I ask you something?"

"Of course," Taylor responded hesitantly, having no idea what she wanted to know.

"Do you and Lukas have feelings for each other?" Molly paused. "You don't have to answer that if it makes you..."

"Yes, Molly, yes. Speaking for myself, of course. You'd have to ask Lukas how he feels."

"I already know. I haven't seen him light up like he does with you, well, at least for a long, long time."

"Thank you. My daughter told me something similar," Taylor responded.

"I saw you two saying goodbye. I often wondered if Lukas would ever find someone. This is a new thing for him, and seeing you not being able to express that in public, well, it just broke my heart. I just wanted you to know that I'm here for you."

Taylor swallowed, not sure how to respond. "It feels like we've known each other a long time, then I realize it hasn't been, and I feel silly for thinking such things."

"Love and relationships don't come with a user's manual. There are no set templates for how one feels after one week, one month, or ten years. Just remember that," Molly explained. "John and I had one date, and I knew I wanted to spend my life with him."

Taylor grinned. "Thanks, Molly, you're very perceptive."

Molly asserted, "We've got to be strong for him. He'll be okay. We will get John and Lukas back. See you in the lobby in ten minutes."

Molly's pep talk came out of the blue, but she was able to see right through Taylor's soul. He let himself daydream for a second that she would be a cool mother-in-law as he headed for the elevator bank. He quickly tried to put that out of his mind. He had to focus.

Tory and Diego had already joined Molly, Linda, Betty, and Donna in the lobby. The six of them stood together as Taylor joined them. "We need a private place to talk," Molly whispered. "I don't know who is behind what's going on, but it's not safe here. There may be more people watching us."

"How do they know we're here?" Tory asked.

"That's what we're trying to figure out. There are hundreds of hotels in Dubai, and they know we are in this one? Can't be a coincidence," Betty answered.

Molly continued, "We are out of our fishbowl, and we don't know who knows who or what and how all of this is interconnected."

"They must've taken his phone. He's been gone for hours, and Lukas would have let us know if he was okay," Taylor said.

"I agree with Taylor. The one thing I drilled into my kids' heads was to text their mom so she wouldn't worry. It's quite possible they are holding him, too," Molly said. Taylor's shoulders deflated.

"We need to plan for the worst and hope for the best. There's a strong chance Lukas is now a bargaining chip," Linda added. "Bargaining for what we don't know."

"I don't understand why they would want Lukas?" Taylor stated. "He's not even involved with John's company, is he?"

Molly shook her head. "No. I think they took him for another reason."

Betty nodded. "He's the eldest son."

"That, and the link between Taylor, John, and me," Molly surmised.

Taylor's blood went cold. He dreaded what she inferred. "How would they know about…"

"Lukas and you?" Tory smiled. "Someone did the math, Dad. It's pretty obvious. Maybe they wanted to make sure taking Lukas would hurt."

"Well, it worked. Message received."

Betty added, "To show us they are serious."

Molly saw the fear on Taylor's face, and she shared his concern. Lukas knew nothing about Poseidon. He was a pawn the abductors could use or eliminate to suit their needs. She shuddered at the thought, but she had a card up her sleeve. "Let's find somewhere quiet to brainstorm what we do next," Molly told them.

Chapter 20

Lukas was hungry. With no watch or phone, he estimated it had been more than five hours since he voluntarily allowed himself to be taken from the San Rafael hotel. His captors had not given him any food or water since his arrival to wherever he was. He patted the side pockets of his sport coat that he surprisingly still wore. He felt something inside and fished it out. Wrapped in a piece of cellophane was the dinner mint Betty had given him. *This will help us find you,* he remembered.

Footsteps approached the door to his detainment room. He quickly unwrapped the mint and popped it in his mouth. It started to dissolve, and he swallowed it quickly. Lukas heard the key go into the door lock, and he saw the deadbolt turn. He pretended to be asleep when he heard footsteps approach him. A hand grabbed his shoulder and shook it, attempting to awaken him. Lukas opened his eyes slowly, acting as if he had really been asleep. He looked with happy relief when he saw who had entered the room. His father, John Halloran, smiled back at him.

****

Molly, Linda, Donna, Betty, and Taylor sat at a corner table tucked toward the back of the dimly lit San Rafael bar. Each of them opted for a non-alcoholic beverage so that they could have clear heads to plan out actions. "Taylor, have you spoken to Tory about the plan?" Molly asked.

Taylor nodded as he swallowed his cola. "They are on their way to Al Maktoum to get things ready. They took all of our stuff, and they'll gas up the jet. The *Goose* will be ready to go in three hours."

Molly turned to Betty. "Any signal yet?"

"Not yet." She opened her laptop to confirm. "I hope he understood my not-so-subtle hint."

As if on cue, Betty heard a ping from the laptop. "We got a location. Faint signal, but it's there." Betty zoomed in on the location. "He is outside of the city. I've been looking for hours. The poor guy must have gotten hungry."

"Looks like he listened to his Aunt Betty." Donna smiled.

"Can you see his exact location or just a general idea?" Linda asked.

"Within five hundred feet. That's as accurate as this thing gets."

"How do you have a location for him? I'm not following you," Taylor asked.

"I slipped a candy mint with a mini location tracker inside his jacket. It's a prototype, so I wasn't sure if it would work," Betty answered. "I'm sending you all a screenshot of his coordinates to keep on your phones."

"So this thing is inside Lukas?" Taylor asked. "Any idea how long it lasts?"

"Not long," Molly jumped in. "Forty-five minutes, an hour max. It will eventually pass out of him. The digestion process pretty much destroys the tracker. He won't even feel it."

Linda's reading glasses balanced on the tip of her

nose. "Looks like he's in an area called Al Quoz...not sure if I'm saying that right. Looks like it's a thirty-minute drive from here."

Taylor googled Al Quoz. "Wikipedia says Al Quoz is a neighborhood in western Dubai, big art scene, galleries. Used to be more an industrial area, but it's transitioning to hipster. Upscale areas and some sketchier ones."

"Anything about residential areas?" Molly asked.

"Yes, both Emirati families and expats." Taylor continued reading. "Makes sense. Also, a lot of hotels and dormitories that house foreign workers."

"It's eleven p.m. Let's go visit Al Quoz," Molly exclaimed, unaware of the person standing by the table.

Molly gasped in surprise when she saw him. "I live there, I'll show you around." Patrick Aziz smiled.

****

Lukas hugged his father. "Dad, I'm glad to see you. Did they hurt you?"

John shook his head. "How are you, Lukas?"

"Never been a hostage before, but I'm fine, considering. How do you feel, Dad?"

"Yeah, same. Sorry you got dragged into this."

"Dad, what the heck is *this* all about? Poseidon?"

"My guess is that it is. But I haven't talked to anyone about why I'm here. I'm not sure where I even am. No windows or anything, so it's been pretty disorienting."

"We're in Dubai, Dad. Not sure where, though. They brought me here from the San Rafael. I was blindfolded."

"How's Mom?"

Lukas nodded. "She's okay. I learned a lot about

her younger years in the last few hours." Lukas knew better than to say more about what he learned, not knowing who might be listening to him.

John smiled. "She's something else, isn't she? One of a kind."

"Actually, more like four."

Realization crossed John's expression. "The Herb Society?"

Lukas nodded. "Why did they take me, Dad?"

"Leverage, maybe. I don't know. Maybe they think you know something."

"Well then, they're in for a surprise when they—"

John cut Lukas off. "Someone's coming."

****

Taylor, Molly, Linda, Betty, and Donna stood outside the revolving entrance door to the San Rafael, waiting for Patrick to pick them up in the van.

"I'm not sure why you are suspicious about Patrick," Linda stated.

"Not sure? I've told you he rubs me the wrong way, plus how long was he listening to our conversation in the bar?" Molly asked.

"Well, God help anyone who rubs Molly Halloran the wrong way. Jeez, why are you so hard on him? He seems like a nice kid to me. He's polite, attentive, helpful," Linda added.

"I've been asking myself the same question. John thinks the world of him, but Patrick seems guarded, like he never shares anything about his personal life. Have you ever met someone who immediately just grates on you, and you can't explain why?"

Donna jumped in. "Yes. You."

Molly was taken aback.

"Yes, Molly, I didn't like you when I first met you. You were kind of a know-it-all and kind of a snob."

Molly reacted. "Really? A snob? You never told me this before, Donna."

"I know," Donna replied. "Because I gave you a chance, and very soon, I found out what a cool lady you actually were. You were none of the things I initially thought. And we became friends, didn't we?"

"Can I say something?" Linda asked.

"You're going to anyway, so have at it." Molly tried not to sound defensive. "I trust each of you, no matter what."

Linda continued, "You're cold to him. Sometimes even mean. I've never heard you say one nice thing to him. And you wonder why he acts guarded around you? But do you even know him? Have you asked him anything about his life?"

Molly thought about what Linda told her. "Thank you for telling me that. You're right. I have been kind of a bitch to him. I feel like he looks down on me because I'm a woman. Maybe because I'm old."

"Maybe you're making assumptions, which isn't fair to the kid."

"Maybe not," Molly said.

"Think about how you would feel in a similar situation. In a big job, in a new city, your boss is thousands of miles away, then he's kidnapped. I wonder how I would act at his age; probably intimidated, afraid I did something wrong, scared, and anxious to please," Linda explained.

Molly sighed. "Thank you. That makes me feel a bit ashamed actually."

Linda and Donna gave her a side hug.

"Try to be nice to him," Donna interjected, "even a little bit, and he'll forget you were once the Ice Queen."

"Ouch! Now who's being the bitch?" Molly laughed. "But seriously. Thank you."

Linda smiled. "That's what the Herb Society is for. Keeping each of us in line and real."

"Taylor," Molly called out, suddenly changing the subject. "I need a bag from the plane, but I don't want to make a big deal about it. Can you call Tory and see if she can bring it out to me when we get to the airport?"

"Of course. What color and how large is it?"

"It's a Prada bag, Papaya orange. Can't miss it."

Taylor nodded and dialed his phone. As he spoke to Tory, he gave Molly the thumbs up that the bag would be ready for her. "She said it's a beautiful bag."

In a few minutes, Patrick pulled up to the hotel entrance, driving a black Mercedes Sprinter van. Taylor held the door while Molly, Linda, Donna, and Betty got in the back, and he sat himself in the passenger seat. "First stop is Al Maktoum," Taylor announced. "Molly, I mean Mrs. Halloran needs something from the plane. My daughter will bring it out to us."

"Al Maktoum is close to the Al Quoz area." Patrick nodded as he accelerated out of the hotel driveway and into the busy Dubai traffic.

"You're a very calm driver, Patrick. I would be a nervous wreck in this traffic," Molly complimented him. Linda winked at her for trying.

"Thank you, ma'am. I drove a taxi during my university days."

"Here in Dubai?" Molly asked, surprised by this information.

"In London, ma'am, mostly. Sometimes I drive

people around here on weekends or if I can't sleep. Just to make some extra money."

"And how is it living in Dubai, Patrick?"

"It's very nice, Mrs. Halloran. I enjoy working for Phoenix Equities, and I appreciate the trust you and Mr. Halloran have put in me. Otherwise, I do miss my family at home."

"How often do you get to see your parents?" Molly asked him.

"I see them when I go back to Britain to see my wife and daughter. They are the ones I miss most, and usually why I can't sleep."

He has a wife and daughter? He's so young, Molly thought.

"Many people working in Dubai come from somewhere else," Patrick explained. "And many of us live in the area of Al Quoz. There are two societies here, the Emirati and those who serve them, plus expats like me who are here temporarily. It's okay for now, but not where I want to raise Bella, my daughter. She's five. I want her to be empowered to be anything she wants to be…like her mother."

The motorway around Dubai was quiet, unlike the commuting hours. Patrick pointed at the airport sign, knowing his guests could not read Arabic. He glided the van off the exit ramp and toward the Al Maktoum private jet terminal, where the *Goose* was being fueled.

"It feels like we've been here a week," Betty said.

"I was thinking the same thing," Donna seconded. "It's been a little over twenty-four hours."

Patrick parked the van, and both Taylor and Molly ran out to meet Tory, who was already standing outside with an orange duffel bag. Taylor kissed her on the cheek. "Thanks, honey. I hope we're back here soon and get the hell out of here. Where's Diego?"

"He had to make a few phone calls." Tory shrugged. "But I'll be ready for you, Dad."

Taylor and Molly ran back to the van. "What is the address in Al Quoz?" Patrick asked.

"I don't have one, actually. Betty is handling the navigation from her laptop, but I have a screenshot from earlier. You can see Lukas' signal there, but I can't read any of the Arabic."

Patrick studied the map. "I'm not familiar with this area of Al Quoz." He zoomed in. "I believe this is an area of art galleries from some of the shop names. Why would Lukas be here?"

"There has to be something in the area—a basement or a secluded apartment, somewhere he is being held, and probably John, too." Molly paused for a minute. "Gosh, I hope they're together."

Molly tensed her shoulders. She had no idea of what she was walking into. What if there were crowds around or if there would be gunfire? She was out of surveillance practice, and this was personal for her with her son and husband as hostages.

"I'm going to drive to the general area, and we can go from there." Patrick accelerated the van in the direction of Al Quoz. Betty sat in the back row, her face lit by the laptop screen as she monitored where they were heading relative to Lukas' location.

****

John and Lukas continued to talk about banal things, knowing they were probably being monitored. They had been in the room together for nearly an hour when they heard the door lock turn. Both men sat up straight. Clown Face entered the room and pulled up a chair directly across from them. He sat down, crossed his legs, and rested a hand on his knee. Nobody said a word. He removed his mask, revealing his actual face. John was not surprised, but Lukas didn't recognize him. "Oh my gosh, I never would have guessed. It's Malik," John said with deadpan sarcasm. "I suspected you may be involved in this. Your subtle ambush on Palm Jumeirah was my first clue."

"John, my friend. Good to see you. Again." He extended his hand to Lukas. "And I see you've brought your son along."

"I don't believe we've had the pleasure of meeting," Lukas said coldly to his father's abductor.

"Malik Bawadi is my name. Your father knows me. I've been pestering to get on to Phoenix's board, but alas, no success."

"Kidnapping the CEO is probably not the way I'd go about it," Lukas responded.

Malik laughed like Lukas' comment was the funniest thing he'd heard all day. "Your son is quick, John."

Malik Bawadi was a Syrian national born to immigrant parents who fled Afghanistan in the 1970s. Fluent in Arabic, English, Pashto, and Farsi, he was charming and clever and had a reputation for resourcefulness, as he called it. This often meant he used what he had to—theft, bribery, kidnapping, and murder—to get what he wanted. The whole Middle East was Malik's playground, but he also worked with secretive countries like Russia and North Korea if the prize was tempting enough. He was always on the move, carefully slipping in and out of a country before any of his enemies knew where he was.

Malik did not divulge much about his past. His father, also named Malik, was a crafty businessman who learned how to buy and sell what people wanted. Malik Sr. started by selling simple things like cigarettes and phone cards. His business grew when he arranged sales of assault rifles and bullets for small militant groups growing in the area and leveraged his old contacts in Afghanistan as both customers and suppliers. He brokered sales of opium to countries around the world, which brought him huge amounts of money and helped fund the Taliban in their fight against the Soviet Union. The family lived comfortably from the opium profits, until one day, he was assassinated by a sniper while walking to his mosque.

After the funeral, the Syrian government confiscated what little his family had, claiming that it was acquired with drug money, which was true. Malik was ten years old, leaving his mother to raise him and his older sister by herself. They struggled, had little money, and often went hungry. They slept on the streets, sold trinkets to tourists, and begged.

When Malik was sixteen, he found work doing manual jobs for the wealthier residents of Damascus. While walking home from work one night, he stumbled upon a couple having sex in a dark side street. It was an older man taking a younger woman from behind, and in an instant, he recognized the woman was his sister.

He learned both his mother and his sister had turned to prostitution in order to survive. Single women had few options to them, but the thought sickened him, and he vowed he would support his family in a legitimate way. By the time Malik was twenty, he was

167

already a millionaire several times over, but his family was falling apart. His mother was murdered by one of her clients and left dead in the street. His sister became pregnant by an unknown father and was jailed for adultery—a charge that was never proven. She gave birth and died shortly after in prison.

Malik was now forty-eight, unmarried, and consumed with his business dealings. Ashamed of his childhood of poverty and desperation, Malik invented a back story of intrigue, wealth, fine education, and legitimacy as a member of the exiled Afghan royal family. This gave him a mystery and veneer of respectability while he built his business on the back of a fake resume. Malik had met John Halloran several years prior at an investment conference in Riyadh and had been pursuing him ever since, attracted by John's reputation and the stellar record that Phoenix Equities maintained as an ethical business. Malik was a strategist who played the long game, and he hoped his association with Phoenix would give him the respectable business pedigree he craved.

Malik directed his comments at Lukas. "You know your father is an icon in the private equity world. He is a tough negotiator but also a visionary. Trusted implicitly, which is why I wanted to be associated with his board." Malik cleared his throat. "It would do well for my reputation."

Lukas wanted to spit at him. "I'm sure it would," was all he could say.

Lukas and Malik glared at each other for almost a minute, Malik breaking eye contact. "So, Lukas, what do you think of all this? Poseidon and all. Did your father tell you I outbid him for the Poseidon technology?"

"No, he did not. We don't usually talk about business."

"What?" Malik feigned shock. "Father and son not collaborating? How strange." He looked at John with accusing eyes. "I wonder why that is? Maybe it's your different, shall we say, lifestyles?"

Neither John nor Lukas took the bait. Malik paused for one to speak or argue with him.

"Poseidon. It's true; I was willing to pay four times what your father paid, but the technology developers trusted your father and apparently not me."

Shocking, Lukas thought. "So is this your attempt to steal it? I'm not sure why I'm here other than to pay the ransom you requested."

"Ahh yes, Lukas. The ransom." Malik paused and walked around Lukas and John. "What a good son you are for wanting to save your father, despite his obvious embarrassment about you, the oldest of his three…well, whatever you call yourself, Lukas?"

John's face started to redden with rage. Lukas gave his father a reassuring look that he was not playing into Malik's mind games. "Yes, Malik. I got the ransom together to save my father so that he would accept me and love me for who I am." Lukas' sarcasm escaped Malik, and his barely noticeable smile let his dad know he was messing with the guy.

"Get to the point, Malik!" John growled.

"Well, Lukas, I have some news for you. What would you say if I told you there is no ransom?"

What? Lukas thought. He looked at his father, who was equally surprised. "I'm not sure I follow you. We were given instructions to bring five million d—"

"And the bitcoin, yada yada, I know. It was my way of getting you here. To let you know this was serious. It obviously worked."

Malik walked over to a small, wheeled table, on top of which sat a large, overturned cardboard box. "I'd like to show you something." He wheeled the table and stopped in front of John and Lukas. Malik lifted the box. Underneath, a small machine was unveiled. John's eyes went wide. "Voila!" Malik said.

"How did you…?" John questioned him, alarmed.

"Not everyone is altruistic, John. Everybody has a price, my friend. Five million dollars in ransom is a pittance compared to what this machine will bring me, or whoever I decide to sell it to." He turned to Lukas. "Know what this is, Lukas?"

"Let me guess…an air fryer?"

"It's a prototype of Poseidon, built by the inventor. I've tried to have it reverse engineered, but to no avail. The programming is hard coded into the unit, so I can't extract that, either."

Malik pointed to the machine, explaining its various parts. "You see, we have tanks of hydrogen and oxygen. The reaction happens in a small, controlled explosion within this unit. We have the basic formula; you may have heard about it."

"In first grade. Two hydrogen atoms and one oxygen, right?" Lukas said sarcastically.

"Correct, but the magic is how we split the two oxygen atoms and join the two hydrogen atoms. That's the part we can't figure out, and I'd rather be safe than blowing us all to oblivion. The programming is encrypted, and I need the key to decipher it so I can reprogram this lovely machine."

"And how do you intend to do that?" Lukas asked, thinking back to the project he and Betty worked on during the flight over.

Malik smiled, "That's where you come in, Lukas."

Chapter 21

Lukas' location details were beginning to fade, a factor of the tracker's battery and casing breakdown due to the harsh chemicals in the human digestive system. Molly kept the orange Prada bag close to her feet so its contents could be retrieved quickly.

Patrick piloted the Sprinter van carefully through the streets of the Al Quoz neighborhood. He pointed to a row of high-rise apartment buildings in the distance and informed his passengers that was where he lived. "The rent is cheap, and it's close to public transportation. It's just me, so forty square meters is sufficient, but when my wife and daughter visit, it can be a bit crowded," he explained.

"What kind of work does your wife do?" Donna asked.

"Evelyn is a physician. She's brilliant, but she somehow found me. She specializes in orthopedics. She can't practice outside of the UK, so we can't move here."

Betty continued to monitor their position relative to where Lukas supposedly was located.

"We need to turn back. We're moving away from him. Turn right and turn right again in one block." Betty called out instructions while focusing on the laptop and trying not to get carsick.

Molly took a screenshot of Lukas' location,

knowing she would eventually lose his signal. Taylor watched traffic to assist Patrick and Donna. Linda and Betty combed each side of the road, on the off chance that Lukas or John might be on the street. It was now past midnight, and the temperature had dropped to the mid-eighties, which was significantly cooler than when the sun was shining during the day.

Couples walked together, some pushing baby prams to get some fresh air. Public displays of affection were not allowed by anyone, married or not, while out in public. Depending upon the Emirate, punishment for this infraction could range from a fine to jail time. The same-sex punishment for the same infraction could range from jail time to the death penalty.

They searched for the dark blue Bentley that had taken Lukas from the San Rafael. It was the only thing they had to go on, and Taylor was pretty sure that the car wasn't the only dark blue Bentley in Dubai. Patrick cruised up and down each street and cross-street, driving slowly enough that the group could watch for signs of Lukas or the car, but not so slowly that he attracted suspicion. Dubai had a very low crime rate overall, largely due to cultural and punitive norms that deterred many would-be criminals. But as Dubai continued to grow, so did the wealth gap between the foreign workers and Emirati citizens. A suspiciously slow-driving van would attract more attention today than in years past.

Taylor was the first person to see the long, distinct shape of a Bentley pulling out from an underground parking garage that sat below what appeared to be a multi-use residential, commercial, or light industrial building. "I think I saw the car. It just passed us,"

Taylor told the group. "It was dark blue. Should we follow it?"

"Betty, do you still have Lukas' location?" Molly asked. "I'd like to see if Lukas was in the car."

"Sometimes these smaller beacons take a while to register a location change," Betty replied.

"Lights out inside," Donna exclaimed. The van had dark tinted windows for the privacy of VIPs, but at night, anyone who was watching would be able to see the ambient lighting inside the Sprinter. Patrick cut the lights, and the van's interior went dark, except for the shielded light of Betty's laptop.

"I got a ping. Location has not changed." Betty pointed at the building adjacent, above the ramp leading to the parking garage. "He's still in there somewhere."

Two anonymous dark figures stood outside the building. The ends of their cigarettes glowed whenever one of the figures inhaled.

"Might be two guys standing guard," Taylor added. "Or two guys out for a smoke."

All of this was conjecture as nobody in the van had actually seen the abductors, nor a close view of the Bentley. For all they knew, they could be chasing a phantom vehicle.

"We should park and walk back in this direction," Taylor suggested. "This van will stick out in this neighborhood."

Patrick parked the van about three streets over. "We can walk from here. I'll go with you in case anyone needs to know who you are."

"I think we may need some backup, just in case," Molly whispered to her Herb Society mates. She discreetly opened the orange leather duffel bag, and the four women looked inside. On top of three coils of rope, headphones, and a package of zip ties lay four Glock 34 handguns.

Patrick's eyes widened in surprise. *His boss came equipped with firearms?* "Oh, you can't have those. Private guns are illegal in the UAE without a permit," he informed them.

"Hopefully we won't need to use them," Molly responded. "But I'll bet money that whoever has John and Lukas also has a gun, or several. I'll take the risk. Paying a fine is better than being dead."

Patrick went quiet. "I'm sorry, ma'am. I only thought you should know."

Molly had started to feel more comfortable with Patrick, and here he was, combing the streets with them, looking for her husband and son. She softened her tone. "Thank you for letting me know, Patrick. I appreciate you looking out for us." Patrick smiled and acknowledged her comment with a nod.

Molly walked back to sit beside Betty. "I need to show you where the Poseidon files are. We may need you to act as a call center for us should it come to that. The formula is in that folder. I might need you to stop up the drain."

Betty nodded in understanding. "In what program is the formula written?"

"Don't laugh," Molly told her. "It's in FORTRAN."

"FORTRAN? Who the hell uses FORTRAN? It's like the cave paintings of coding software," Betty exclaimed. "You are sure dating yourself using that."

"You're only a year younger than I, so don't give me any of that. FORTRAN works. It's simple, and it's…"

"Ancient," Betty interjected.

"That doesn't mean it's bad," Molly said. "Do you think you can make a copy of this and maybe add a surprise ending to the copy?"

"Lukas and I already worked on the surprise ending. That kid's a whiz, Molly. Like a real genius," Betty told her. "I may have some distant memory of FORTRAN, so we should have plenty to stop up the drain."

"Good," Molly told her. "I'll let you know if we need it sent over to us. Just sound like a call center if I call you."

Betty rolled her eyes. "I won't even touch the racial implications of that comment."

"Time to get the Herb Society back together, ladies." Molly smiled as the five of them exited the van and walked into the dark neighborhood.

****

Malik continued his explanation of how the Poseidon machine would work. John pretended to sound interested, as did Lukas, having had a thorough explanation of the technology from his mother on the plane trip. "Now, let me show you how this amazing technology works," Malik said proudly, as if he had invented it himself. One of the guards, who Lukas called the Zip-Tie guy, walked over to assist. Malik flipped the on switch. "It needs to prepare itself."

"So tell me what we are going to see," Lukas stalled. "I haven't seen how this works."

"The reaction happens in this chamber." Malik pointed to a drum shaped cylinder upon which the rest of the machine was built. "The reaction creates water vapor, which is then pumped into this condenser. Once the water is liquefied, it will dispense here."

"Kind of a cross between an espresso maker and a distillery?" Lukas asked.

The sarcasm didn't register with Malik. "For the condensing part, there is a similarity, at least in design. The magic is in the reaction, which rearranges the atoms to form new molecules. Let me show you."

Malik touched a red illuminated button to start the process, the machine began to hum softly, and after a few seconds, faint popping sounds came from inside the machine. "That is the beginning of the reaction. It will be just a few moments more," Malik told them. The Poseidon machine hummed like a pump was engaged. Malik watched proudly as the popping sounds got louder. "Almost complete." Suddenly, about five drops of water dripped out of the small spigot and into a container the size of a shot glass.

Malik held the glass for John and Lukas to see. "Introducing man-made water and an answer to so many possibilities from farming to providing safe drinking water on the spot."

"I think you're going to need a bigger machine for that task," Lukas commented.

"This was an early prototype machine, and it does make synthetic water," John explained. "The inventors patented the physics and continued to build upon it. The intellectual property Phoenix bought came about twenty years after this machine was built. Malik is interested in the turn-key system."

"Which is why you are here, gentlemen," Malik explained. "I am backed by an investor who is prepared to pay huge sums of money for licensing rights. You can retain the intellectual property."

"And how does that help you, or your investor?"

Malik appeared to debate how much to tell them about the investor.

John jumped in. "The new Poseidon technology can make vastly larger amounts of water than what you just saw. I'm talking enough to refill lakes and aquifers. Sixty-nine percent of all the freshwater on earth is locked in glaciers, and we all know what is happening to those. The new Poseidon technology can assist with filling the gap."

"Is that all?" Lukas asked his father, already having a sense of where this was going.

"Poseidon could be used to make water on other planets. Human colonization of potentially livable planets is highly likely. Having water present is essential for this possibility, just as essential as it is on Earth. The implications for humanity are huge if the technology is used in the proper way," John responded.

"And what's the improper way?" Lukas asked, already knowing the answer from his mom.

"The opposite, of course. Using the technology to destroy water by reversing the process, as you may have guessed. So to prevent that, we have a safeguard security feature built into the new version, and I'm guessing that's what Malik wants and why we're here."

Malik's silence indicated that John's theory had merit. "My investor client is willing to pay an eleven-figure sum for this technology, gentlemen. It's only a matter of time before we figure out how to get around the security features in the programming."

Lukas thought about the horrifying implications of this technology, as his mother described during their time in the jet. But something wasn't adding up in Lukas' mind. The attempt to reverse engineer a larger Poseidon unit would have been relatively simple, but the end result would be a larger unit with no brains. The secrets were in the programming. Lukas calculated that Malik's client investor was willing to pay over a billion dollars for this technology. Why couldn't they spend half as much developing their own version? *What am I missing?* Lukas thought.

Lukas had a bad feeling he couldn't explain. He unraveled the last two weeks; his dad was first missing and then found to be kidnapped, then there was a ransom, Mom took over the company, and they flew to Dubai, then he was also kidnapped, if you want to call it that. Then Malik said there was not really a ransom, so why was his father held captive in the first place?

Neither John nor Lukas was harmed, beaten, or starved. They didn't have body parts cut off and sent as evidence to loved ones. And even his own situation— he gets a phone call and is then taken in a three-hundred-thousand-dollar Bentley on a bullshit ride that brought him here, to a mockup of a kidnapper's lair in a Dubai suburb. Even Malik's pathetic clown mask. It was all theater, but bad theater, complete with poor actors and plot lines. Everything felt contrived.

He looked over at his father, who had a strange expression on his face, one of both sadness and resignation that they had been played. Lukas suddenly had a terrifying thought. "Malik, how old is the original Poseidon machine?"

"Over thirty years old. The physics theory was created a decade before we had the technology to actually use it," Malik explained.

"And who came up with the physics?" Lukas asked. No answer.

Lukas felt a lump in his stomach. "Dad, do you know where this technology was invented? I'm not talking about the machine. I mean the physics of it—how to convert gas components into an essential element necessary for all life on earth."

"Lukas," John started, "the physics of Poseidon were created in the United States, back in the '70s."

"Didn't your parents tell you this? I'm so surprised." Malik pulled out a large bound document and handed it to Lukas. He flipped it over and read the cover.

"It's a US Patent filing," Lukas read.

"Yes, now read down to the bottom," Malik suggested. Lukas flipped the page.

Project Poseidon
1972
Halloran, Eastman, Rivero, Bao
Argonne National Laboratory.

Suddenly, Lukas was filled with rage at Malik, his parents, the Herb Society. "You used us as bait!" Lukas accused Malik. "It makes sense now. How did I not see it? You're after my mother."

"I knew your mother would eventually get here," Malik told them. "She's a scientist but also a human being who loves her children. It's a good trade; she has what I want, and I have what she wants. It should be a fast transaction. Plus, I have a bone to pick with her."

"You don't know my mother," Lukas told him. *And I guess that makes two of us,* he thought to himself. "What bone do you have to pick with her?"

"Your mother and her friends invented the

Poseidon technology, and she refused to sell it to me, which I found to be quite rude, considering."

"Considering what?" Lukas asked.

"She's played a pivotable role in my life. Let's leave it at that. They are on their way here to find you, no doubt," Malik informed them. "I have guards outsi—"

Malik's statement was interrupted by the unmistakable sound of gunfire.

****

Molly, Taylor, Donna, Linda, and Patrick found themselves in the center of a darkened courtyard, not sure where to go next. Lukas' location was no longer visible and had likely stopped transmitting, but Betty remained in the van, a mobile mission control point, and she had confidence the rescue team was in the right place. Molly suggested they split into two groups; Taylor, Donna, and Linda would search laterally on the ground floor, while Molly and Patrick would take the basement area.

It was two in the morning, and the normal bustle of Al Quoz became hushed and quiet. People slept, and businesses were shuttered until the morning, so finding some activity should be relatively fast and simple. Patrick and Molly searched for a staircase or some way to get to the subterranean floor below them. The hallway had no lights, so when they found the staircase, it looked as if it descended into a gaping black void.

"I'll go first," Patrick told Molly as he began walking down the stairs. He used his smartphone flashlight to see each step. He crept down gingerly, both for stability and to make as little noise as possible. He reached the bottom floor. "There are ten steps.

181

Make sure you count them on the way down," Patrick whispered. "We can't afford for you to fall."

"I hope you aren't saying that because I'm old," Molly half-teased him.

Patrick whispered back, "I'm saying that because you're our CEO."

Molly followed, her Glock loaded and gripped in her left hand, her right hand holding the handrail as she descended into the blackness. They began to walk slowly and quietly down the hall, searching for any sign of activity. Suddenly, the overhead lights flickered on, and Molly had to shield her eyes while her pupils adjusted. Big Man charged at them angrily, pointing his gun and yelling something in Arabic. Patrick jumped between the man and Molly, yelling back at the man in his same language. Molly quickly assumed this was a security guard or an angry neighbor defending his turf. Big Man raised his gun and pointed it at Patrick. Within seconds, she heard loud popping sounds and saw Patrick drop lifelessly to the floor. The man shot at Molly and missed. Instinctively, she raised her Glock, aimed, and fired back at Big Man.

A spray of blood erupted from his forehead as he tumbled backward and dropped. There was no doubt he was dead. She turned to Patrick, who was bleeding, his white shirt splattered with his blood, but his fear-filled eyes were open. He was alive.

****

Taylor heard the gunshots first. They sounded like they came from the floor below. *Molly and Patrick,* he thought as he ran toward the direction of the sound. Donna and Linda followed him. They found a staircase, and Taylor ran down, not knowing what to expect. He

saw a man sprawled out on the floor. *Shit, what the fu...*
His thought was interrupted by a searing pain on the
side of his abdomen, and for a second, he thought he
had been hit by lightning. Another pain ripped through
his upper body. He stumbled to his knees, disoriented
and confused. Taylor looked up and saw two men, one
holding Molly, the other holding the gun that just shot
him. They were the last things he saw before everything
went dark.

Chapter 22

Malik held the gun that shot Taylor. "I'm sorry about your friend," Malik said to Lukas. "I know you two were close," he sneered. Taylor lay stretched out on a table, unconscious but breathing. He had been shot twice, one bullet through his shoulder and one that grazed his obliques on the side of his abdomen. Lukas sat next to him, keeping a red-stained white rag pressed up against the bullet wound in his shoulder. He had wedged a towel between Taylor's arm and the side of his abdomen to help stop the bleeding from his side.

Patrick fared better, with a single shot to his upper chest, just missing his collarbone. Both were in shock. Malik's remaining henchman, who Lukas referred to as Zip-Tie, had confiscated the Glock pistols carried in by Molly, Linda, and Donna. Big Man lay dead in a pool of his blood until Zip-Tie grabbed his feet and dragged him out of the hallway. A long red stain trailed from the hole in the back of Big Man's head.

Donna remembered seeing four pistols in Molly's papaya-colored bag. *Where was the fourth gun?* she thought. And then she remembered. *Betty. They don't know about Betty.*

Betty Bao had stayed behind to monitor their location and to work on some software modifications for Poseidon. *Molly must have left the fourth gun with her.*

"Mrs. Halloran," Malik started. "I am getting impatient with you and your husband. I've gone to a lot of trouble to get you to Dubai."

"Actually, you did nothing to get me to Dubai," Molly corrected him. "I got here myself. I don't owe you anything, and don't speak to me with such disrespect, you little toad. I'm old enough to be your mother!"

Lukas almost gasped when he heard his mother's tone of voice and the dressing down she gave Malik.

"I didn't mean to sound uncivilized." Malik gritted his teeth to maintain his veneer of calmness and polish. He struggled against anger, a thin smile cloaking cards he wasn't ready to reveal. Not yet. "My apologies, ma'am."

"So tell me what you want. Why did you have to kidnap my husband and then my son? Why did you feel the need to shoot my best employee, and then my pilot, who also is my son's boyfriend, as your conniving little mind has undoubtedly figured out? Tell me what you want."

Either Molly was playing the bad cop extremely well, or she had a dangerously extreme case of jet lag and low blood sugar. Again, Malik was taken aback. "My client has offered a handsome price for your technology."

"How much?"

"Ten billion dollars, US, of course."

Molly's heart raced as she continued her charade. "Fifteen billion."

Malik coolly stiffened his lip. *This was above my negotiating point, he thought.* "Ma'am, I am authorized to pay up to thirteen billion dollars."

"Fine, sold," Molly said without emotion. "What do we have to do?"

Molly sweated beneath her clothes. *Thirteen billion dollars! Holy shit.*

"I can immediately arrange for a transfer of one-third of the price to—"

"Half," Molly said bluntly.

Lukas watched his mom in disbelief. *Mom, what are you doing?*

"Fine, we will go with half. I will need some bank details and can get the money transferred immediately."

****

"Patrick," Molly asked, "I assume you have our bank details here in Dubai."

Patrick held up his smartphone with his good hand. "Right here, ma'am." He walked over to Malik and entered the bank details into the bank account field to receive the deposit from the account Malik had pulled up on his screen. He pushed enter.

"Well that was comically easy," said Molly. "I assume we now need to discuss what you want with regard to the technology."

"Yes, Mrs. Halloran. We need the new programming software and the security key."

"The software, including the security key, was written in a programming language older than you are, Malik. We would need to wipe the Poseidon unit completely and reinstall the newer version of the programming to make the requests you seek."

"How do you do that?" Malik asked.

"First, I need to make a call to my Chief Information Officer. Second, I'll need to wipe the hard drive of this unit, and third, we will need to somehow get the new programming installed remotely—which I've never tried before since this unit was built long before the internet was created, let alone Wi-Fi. Everything back then was done in floppy drives."

Malik's face registered confusion. *What's a floppy drive?*

Molly believed he had no idea what she was talking about. *Perfect,* she thought.

Molly punched a phone number into her smartphone and waited for the call to connect.

"I'm calling the Philippines," she told Malik. Betty answered the phone from the van parked three blocks away. "Yes?"

"Good morning, ma'am. I need to discuss the transfer of the programming we discussed yesterday for Project Poseidon. Is the product ready to transmit?"

"Affirmative, ma'am. I just need the address of where to send it."

"Where would you like to receive this information?" she asked Malik.

"Where would you suggest?" Malik answered, not sure of how this all worked.

Back on the phone with Betty, Molly said, "Can you suggest the best way to transmit this information? The purchaser is looking for some suggestions."

"You're shitting me," Betty whispered. "He doesn't know what the hell he's doing. Tell him we can send it in one of three ways—email, cloud, file share. Suggest file share."

Lukas decided to insert himself, just to add to Malik's confusion. "Mom, you do realize that the programming software can be sent via email or Dropbox to a personal computer but not directly to the

Poseidon unit."

A slight smile formed on Molly's lips. "Son, I know this is what you do every day, but can you clarify what you mean by that?"

"The software can be sent by your Chief Information Officer either by wired internet or Wi-Fi pretty easily. The problem is getting it to upload on the Poseidon unit. We will need a hard connection between the computer and Poseidon."

"Good point, Lukas. Can you find a cable that would work for this? Malik, do you have any spare parts lying around?"

Malik ordered Zip-Tie to go look for a cable somewhere.

"Malik, here are your options. We can email it to you, but that will take several hours. If you have a cloud account, you can have it sent there, or there's another way."

"And that is?" Malik inquired.

"Dropbox," Molly told him.

Lukas stifled a laugh. *Brilliant, Mom.*

Zip-Tie returned with a coaxial cable he found and showed it to Lukas, who nodded, indicating that it should work. Malik next ordered Zip-Tie to fetch his laptop.

Betty was listening in on their conversation, and even though she knew Molly had written some of the original software, she gave instructions anyway. "First thing you will need to do is erase the existing program and clear out the hard disk," Betty explained.

Molly repeated this to Malik and explained how to clear the hard drive. Malik struggled to understand how to do this. After a minute, Molly offered to help.

"Malik, maybe I should do this part as I built the machine."

"Thank you, ma'am." Malik stood aside while Molly wiped the hard drive with what they used to call the doomsday command—a complete removal of all information, programming, and memory, with the exception of the operating system. Molly then switched off the Poseidon unit and restarted it. "Still have to reboot to make sure it's all clean," Molly said.

"Good job, Madam CEO," Betty whispered. "You removed the critical information on Poseidon. Now let's feed it a fucked up new brain."

Molly maintained a straight face. "Malik, we are ready to upload the new software with an unscrambled security key. Your IT person can always add one later."

Malik looked on with excitement. "Thank you. This is perfect."

It was obvious to Molly that Malik was his own IT person. "What is your Dropbox account address and password?" she asked him.

Malik fumbled. "I know my email but not the password."

Molly got an idea. "Malik, would you like me to use my Dropbox account on your laptop? I can receive the programming software, Lukas can upload it to your new machine, and I will delete my account off your laptop. Might be faster and easier."

"You are fucking brilliant," Betty whispered.

"Um, okay. That makes sense." Malik asked, "What do you need me to do?"

"Just give me your screen lock password. Lukas and I can take care of the rest."

Chapter 23

"The new program has been sent," Molly told Malik.

Malik waited patiently until he got an alert that there was information in Molly's Dropbox. When the alert came, Molly swore Malik almost started dancing.

Betty told Molly, "Tell him to look at the graphic on his computer screen, and it will show the status of the download."

Molly repeated this to Malik.

"While it's downloading, have Lukas fit the cable from the laptop to Poseidon."

"Roger," Molly responded. Molly indicated to Betty that the download to her Dropbox was complete.

"Now you need to transfer from the laptop to the unit. Can Lukas do that?"

"You have so little faith," Molly whispered to Betty.

Lukas hooked up the old cable to Poseidon and, with the help of some cable adapters, was able to connect to the laptop.

Lukas hit the *Download* command to transfer the files. Within a minute, the transfer was complete, so Lukas installed it and rebooted Poseidon again to make sure the new programming was ready to go.

"Shall we try it?" Molly asked him. Malik nodded. "Let's fire up Poseidon."

Malik pressed the red button to start the synthetic water generation process. The machine made the familiar sounds, and after twenty seconds, significantly less time than the first time Lukas saw Poseidon operate, synthetic water began dripping into the cup.

"Excellent to see it work," Malik said excitedly. "And much faster."

"Now let's see if we can do the reverse, just for fun." Molly preempted what she knew Malik was already wondering. John and Lukas looked at Molly like she was crazy, handing Malik's clients a potentially deadly weapon. But Molly needed to see if it worked. Molly pointed to the shot glass half filled with the synthetic water. "We'll just turn this back into hydrogen and oxygen. Sound good, everybody?" She winked at Donna and Linda. They had been busy caring for Taylor, who was now awake but groggy. "Oh, but wait," Molly paused. "I'm not sure how to get the water back into the machine's reactor."

"How can we put the pump in reverse? There's a pump in there pushing the water out, so can we reverse it to pull it into the reactor?" John said.

Linda interjected, "I can try and do this. Shouldn't be too hard." Linda fiddled with some buttons and switches, removed the motor covering, and did some knocking around with a screwdriver. "Try it now."

Malik stared at Linda before asking her, "How do you know how to do that?"

"I'm an engineer," Linda exclaimed. "I knew that degree would come in handy eventually. Let's fire it up."

Molly offered Malik a front-row seat. "It's all yours."

Poseidon did what was asked and slurped the water into the machine. "Get a bigger cup of water in there," Donna shouted.

"Let's see how it handles a bigger cup." Malik watched with excitement as the process reversed, drawing water into the Poseidon machine and returning the water back to its elements.

"Very well," Molly said. "It looks like the software works."

"Indeed," Malik replied. "But I need to try it on a larger scale."

"Larger scale? Like how large? This machine can't handle much more than a cup."

Malik chuckled. "I'm not talking about this machine. I'm talking about a bigger one."

"What do you mean, you have a bigger machine?" John asked.

"My friend, I told you we reverse-engineered this little one, and we built a bigger one with what we learned from that exercise. Plus, now that I have the security key on my laptop. Thank you, Mrs. Halloran, for that. I can upload the programming to it much easier than our antiquated first try." Malik closed the laptop and handed it to Zip-Tie for safekeeping.

Molly paced the room. What Malik was telling them was next to impossible. Whatever this larger Poseidon machine did, it surely had not been tested since Malik didn't have the security key. But now he did. "So where is this machine, and how do you know it works?" Molly asked.

"It's inside my vehicle out back. We will download the new programming software to it and try it out. Mrs. Halloran, you and your friends invented a way to make synthetic water almost four decades ago. Your intellectual property and the patent have expired, so replicating that was not difficult. It's probably on the internet now, for all I know."

"Then why go to all these lengths to get the security key?" Lukas asked.

"Lukas, my friend, it's all about supply and demand. My investor client intends to make billions of dollars on a system that reduces the supply, thereby increasing the demand."

"And the price," Linda stated.

"Of course. Who would pay thirteen billion dollars for something purely humanitarian or a future space colonization need? Imagine how this technology will change things. Even petroleum can be replaced by other types of fuel, both fossil and renewable. But water? It's the one common substance for all life on this planet—from humans, to plants, to every animal we eat. People will pay anything for this simple everyday liquid we will purposely make scarce with this technology."

Taylor had already been awake for some time and had heard the plans Malik laid out. His pain had subsided, and he was able to think clearly. Malik's idea sounded outrageous, but the more he thought about it, the more he understood the gravity of what Malik proposed.

"Would you like to see it?" Nobody answered, but Malik started out the door and into the hallway. "Follow me."

The group followed Malik and Zip-Tie up the stairs and into a parking lot behind the complex they had been inside. Malik pointed to a small Iveco delivery box truck parked in the corner. "It's in there." Malik pointed. Zip-Tie opened the padlock on the truck's rolling door and opened it. Inside sat a large blue machine, about the size of two large refrigerators side by side.

Lukas noticed the name of the machine graphically depicted on the side panel. *Demeter.* "Clever, Malik," was all Lukas could say.

"I thought so, as well. Demeter, the Greek goddess of agriculture," Malik stated proudly.

"That she was," Lukas continued, "until her daughter Persephone was kidnapped by Hades and taken to the Underworld. Demeter searched frantically for Persephone to the point where she neglected her duties as Goddess of Agriculture. Because of that, Earth was thrown into a state of drought and, ultimately, famine and death of all living beings."

"So you know your Greek history, Lukas. Impressive." Malik applauded him. "I thought it was time for some remarketing of the technology, and Demeter is the Goddess of Drought and Famine—until Persephone was returned to her mother. Then all was good."

"Thank you, Malik, for the big reveal. Now what?" Lukas asked.

"I need to try the Demeter unit in a large-scale experiment to make sure it actually does what it is supposed to do," Malik stated.

Taylor stirred and attempted to sit up straight. "Where were you thinking of doing this test?"

"Ah, Mr. Pastore. Good to see you are awake, and I'm glad you've been paying attention. To answer your question, I envisioned testing the unit in a fountain."

"A fountain?" Donna questioned.
"Yes, and I know exactly the one I want to use."

Chapter 24

Zip-Tie, after disposing of Big Man's body in a dumpster, piloted the box truck out of the parking lot and into the streets of Al Quoz. The large Poseidon, now Demeter, unit remained strapped in the cargo area of the truck. Malik and Molly sat in the front seat while Lukas squeezed into the small area behind the seats—his six-foot frame having to sit sideways in order to fit. Donna, Taylor, Linda, John, and Patrick followed. Betty, posing as their Uber driver who just happened to be in the neighborhood, drove the Sprinter van as the small convoy headed toward downtown Dubai.

Lukas texted Betty from behind them.

—*Hope this works! Didn't expect a test run.*—

—*That software has more viruses than a sailor in Herpesville. It'll work, you worry too much*—Betty responded.

It was almost four thirty a.m., and downtown Dubai was quiet. The massive buildings that defined Dubai remained illuminated even at this hour. The two vehicles snaked through some back streets, with the imposing Burj Khalifa looming overhead like a sentinel. "That building looks huge no matter where you are," Lukas commented.

They crossed the Dubai Canal, meandered through a large urban park, and parked alongside the road. Less than one hundred meters away was Malik's target—the world-famous Dubai Fountain, housed in a thirty-acre lake at the base of the Burj Khalifa skyscraper. When the fountains performed their choreographed water show, they extended nearly one thousand feet wide and could shoot water fifty stories high. They were the largest fountains in the world, barely eclipsing the famous Bellagio Fountains in Las Vegas.

"Why are you testing this in such a potentially crowded spot?" Molly asked. "There are thousands of visitors here every day."

"Yes, the famous fountains, where an obnoxious amount of water is used to entertain the adoring, wasteful public. Do you know that almost twenty percent of the water is lost due to evaporation every single day?" Malik explained. "It's obscene. But when water becomes as scarce as gold, people may think differently. I'll be performing the actual test over there, as a sort of rehearsal." Malik pointed toward the large Dubai Mall complex.

"Rehearsal for what?" Donna questioned.

"When I unveil it at the New Year's Eve celebration later this year," Malik told them. "Millions of viewers will watch in astonishment as the fountain's water suddenly disappears."

"And…what is that supposed to prove? I mean, it's a great gimmick, but—" Linda asked.

"People need to see scarcity," Malik interrupted. "The water used in this fountain could save thousands of people every day, yet it's here for entertainment, in the blazing heat of the desert."

"It's true, Malik. Water is wasted everywhere around the world, but it sounds like you're planning for a Vegas-style magic show. Not sure if a carnival performance is the way to send folks a critical message," Molly commented.

Malik shook his head. "Mrs. Halloran, I'm not trying to send any message, but I am going to get rich off of people's ignorance. Once people see that water can be destroyed in seconds, they may value it more. And pay for it."

Not far from where they had parked was a huge man-made lake that skirted the entrance area to the Burj Khalifa. Zip-Tie had backed the box van closer toward the water and parked by a small inlet of the man-made lake, which was less than an acre in size, adjacent to the massive Dubai Mall. It was still dark outside, but the eastern horizon began to come alive with a sliver of daylight coloring the pre-dawn sky. Malik checked his watch. They had to get moving with the test.

Lukas had meanwhile exited the truck and rushed to the Sprinter van to check on Taylor. When he opened the van's door, he saw Taylor sitting and conscious in one of the passenger seats. Lukas climbed inside and put his arms around Taylor, being careful not to aggravate Taylor's injuries. "I'm glad to see you sitting up and awake."

Donna responded, "He's probably not a big fan of mine at the moment, Lukas. I kind of made him do it, despite his pain. He needs to keep changing position."

Taylor smiled. "Your mom's not the only warrior in the group. Donna gave me some water and a pep talk. I'll be okay."

Lukas sat beside Taylor and held his hand. Taylor's eyes were closed, but he smiled at the physical contact as he drifted in and out of consciousness.

John noticed the concern etched on his son's face

but was at a loss of what to do or say. John felt he never knew what to do or say to Lukas, but he decided to try. "I think he'll be okay. He stopped bleeding and is drinking water, which is a good sign," John said to Lukas.

Lukas acknowledged his father's comment with a tired, thin smile as he softly rubbed his fingers through Taylor's hair. "Thanks, Dad."

"He seems like a good guy, Lukas," John spoke to his son. Lukas had a painful, worried look but silently acknowledged his father's comment. "You really like him, don't you?"

Lukas nodded. "Yeah, Dad. I really do."

"Lukas," John said and then paused, reaching for the words he wanted to convey. "I'm so proud of you and the man you've become. He's gonna be okay."

"He doesn't seem to have a fever, which is good." Lukas nervously tried to deflect his father's compliment.

John fumbled again for words. "You know, sometimes I look at you, and I can't believe that you came from me. You've made me so proud, and I admire you so much for your bravery and perseverance." Lukas, uncomfortable with the intimacy of his father's comments, did not respond. It was uncharacteristically personal, not something John often said. "Almost forty years ago, I married someone I was proud of and admired. I had no idea what I was doing, as most people don't. But I took the leap and never looked back. And now look at us." John chuckled. "She's still trying to stop the bad guys and change the world, while I just watch in wonder. I've never gotten bored with her."

"Ma's pretty badass, Dad."

John nodded and pointed to Taylor. "So's he."

"I use logic all day to solve problems and manage emotions. But I haven't felt like this in, like…well, ever. I'm afraid that feeling will go away. I'm a mess inside."

John nodded. "That's actually a wonderful sign that you're on the right path."

Lukas bent to kiss Taylor's forehead. "Thanks, Dad."

"Thanks, Mr. Halloran," Taylor mumbled.

"You weren't supposed to hear that," Lukas chided him.

"Well, I did, and I feel the same way."

John tapped Lukas on his knee and stood to leave. "Take care of each other." He turned and jumped from the van to meet up with his wife. The Demeter unit was too large to move next to the water, so after Zip-Tie parked the truck, he unrolled what looked like a long hose and connected it to the dispensing spigot on the machine. In theory, Malik hoped, the new programming software would essentially turn the dispensing unit into an intake, through which the fresh water would enter Demeter's reactor core and return the water molecules back to oxygen and hydrogen. John joined Molly, Donna, and Linda as they watched Malik unravel thirty feet of hose from the back of the truck to the edge of the man-made lake. Betty stayed in the Sprinter, still masquerading as an Uber driver, while the injured Patrick and Taylor stayed behind, tended by Lukas. This inlet of the man-made lake was surrounded by a U-shaped amphitheater of terraced steps. On any given evening, people would sit in this amphitheater and watch the hourly performances of the dancing Dubai

Fountains. Lukas noticed his mom, dad, and friends back away from the box truck a few steps.

"I don't have a good feeling about this. Betty, can you keep an eye on Taylor and Patrick?"

"Just thinking the same thing. Plus, I'm gonna put some distance between us and that truck. I don't know who built Demeter, so I'm not taking chances," Betty replied as she put the Sprinter in reverse and moved backward about fifty feet.

Molly noticed this immediately and texted Betty. —*Make sure you're pointed away from the truck in case we need to escape.*— Betty complied quietly as Malik and Zip-Tie were engrossed in setting up the Demeter for its first test run. Lukas gently cradled Taylor's head onto a pile of jackets he'd found earlier in the van. This repositioning woke Taylor up for a brief moment.

"I'll be right back. You've stopped bleeding, so please rest and continue to drink."

Taylor tried to stand but winced in pain. "Shit," he whispered and sat back down. He smiled at Lukas and mouthed *Be careful.* Taylor's skin color had returned somewhat; his wounds stopped bleeding so the blood could do its job.

As Lukas started to exit the van, he turned back and smiled at Taylor. He marveled at how handsome he was, even after being shot and injured. He walked back to Taylor. "Oh, fuck it," Lukas said, quickly darting his head left and right, looking for police or security cameras in the park, and gave Taylor a big, long kiss. "That's to hold you over until I get back." Taylor smiled back and nodded his head.

Patrick witnessed the moment, and Lukas saw he

had a look of puzzlement on his face. "I've never seen two men kiss before. Why does everyone make such a big deal about it? It looked perfectly normal to me."

Lukas ran over to the box truck and watched as Zip-Tie and Malik made their final preparations for the Demeter test. Malik paused and barked out an order to Zip-Tie, which nobody else could understand due to language barriers, but they watched as the large man ran toward the truck and climbed into the back. Within seconds, he wheeled out the original Poseidon machine, strapped to a dolly. Zip-Tie lowered himself and the dolly on the truck's automatic loading gate and, once on the ground, wheeled it over to the Sprinter van. Molly and Lukas heard arguing in what sounded like Arabic coming from the van before Zip-Tie opened its back doors and lifted the Poseidon unit into the back. "Insurance in case we have a failure of Demeter," Malik answered before Molly or Lukas could ask the question.

Linda and Donna glanced at each other, communicating something between them. "Well, Malik. You're here; now what?" Donna asked.

"Now we see if it works. In reverse."

"Why are you doing this, Malik?" Molly asked. "What can you possibly achieve by destroying water and turning it back into its base elements? I really don't understand."

Malik pointed to the Burj Khalifa and to the impressive skyline. "All this was built because man exploited a scarce resource. Think of the number of conflicts that have occurred over it, major wars and millions of lives lost either fighting to acquire it or defend it."

"You've made that point already," Molly snapped.

"Mrs. Halloran, I play the long game. I'm not looking for a gimmick to get rich quickly. This small machine has the power to change the game for the human race."

A light bulb went off in Donna's head. "You're going to build more of these machines, aren't you?"

Malik nodded. "We already have. At least ten thousand units now sit hidden in lakes, rivers, aquifers, ready to slowly destroy the water on the planet. We have the capability to build hundreds of thousands more. It will be decades before scientists figure out how much of the world's water has disappeared, much quicker than they even predicted."

"But wait, Poseidon is here to save the day…for one dollar per gallon," Molly stated.

"Something like that, but I was planning to charge more."

"You tricked me, Malik!" Molly shouted. "This was never part of the deal."

"Sorry, it's too late," Malik explained. "As we speak, thousands of Demeter units are being activated innocuously in the world's fresh water supplies—armed with your brand-new software transmitted globally by the Demeter queen in the back of the truck."

Lukas was slightly relieved to hear what Malik just proclaimed. If all went as planned, the software would also transmit the cyber-viruses and other malware he and Betty encoded into it. He feigned outrage and argued, "You and whatever government you're working with can't possibly have enough resources to do that."

Malik laughed. "Government? You think a government could ever devise a plan like this? Russia,

China, the United States…they spend so much time building up militaries and arms, attempting to look invincible, but no man, and they're all men, will pull the trigger because they're scared of what will happen. Waning support at home, losing votes, and angering their constituencies—not to mention destroying the world."

Malik keyed in something on his smartphone, and they heard the Demeter unit start to hum. "All controlled by my phone. Modern technology makes this so much more practical," Malik sneered sarcastically.

"So what's the big plan, Malik? Are you going to show Demeter's power, threaten to kill us, and cackle like a madman no one can stop?" Lukas asked dryly. "It's almost dawn, and people will start visiting the park, so you better make their pond disappear fast while no one's watching."

"I wouldn't expect you to understand," Malik responded. "You've grown up in wealth. Never wanted for anything. You have no idea what it feels like to be hungry."

"Okay, you've got me there," Lukas said. Malik had no answer to Lukas' comment.

"So tell me, Malik, who is your investor client and where did you get the money to pay for this little box?" John asked.

"John, you wouldn't believe me if I named names. I had you kidnapped because one of my investors is on your board and was slated to take over the company and appoint me to the board. With you out of the way, our new company would consume Phoenix Equities, become the owners of Poseidon, and all live happily ever after. Then your wife named herself CEO and castrated the board, so that plan went to hell."

"It was actually a great plan," Lukas commented. "I can't wait to find out who the board member is."

Zip-Tie placed the end of the hose into the man-made lake while the other end remained fastened to the humming Demeter unit, a green light indicating the machine was on and engaged.

Malik saw someone out of the corner of his eye. He grabbed his pistol and engaged it. He turned sideways and saw the person approaching him. It was Taylor, slowly making his way down the terraced steps. Lukas immediately ran to him. "What are you doing here? You're supposed to rest."

"Here to see the show. I flew halfway around the world, so may as well watch how this thing works," Taylor commented. He smiled at Lukas.

Betty and Patrick remained with the van.

Molly, John, Donna, and Linda sat in the amphitheater, three rows back. Lukas and Taylor sat in the first row. "Okay, let's do this!" Taylor shouted.

Malik flipped on the Demeter machine. "Prepare to be amazed."

The group stood and watched as Demeter came to life, a blue light indicating the power was engaged. The unit hummed. Lukas heard a sucking sound coming from the man-made lake and could see water entering the intake hose.

All of them were there to witness a terrifying new chapter in human history unfold. Molly, Donna, and Linda looked at each other with sullen, deflated expressions. "I never expected our invention to be used like this," Donna said.

"We did it to help the world, ladies. We had no

idea that this could ever be an outcome," Linda followed.

Molly said, "Nothing has been proven, yet. I hope Betty knows what she was doing."

"Engage!" Malik commanded as Zip-Tie opened the intake valve on Demeter. A pulsating sound, deep and resonant, thumped while the probes did their work. Malik had spray-painted a line at the water level of the man-made pond to track whether the process was working. The surface of the water swirled, forming a small whirlpool near the intake hose in the water. Within the first two minutes, the water level dropped by four inches. Malik strutted proudly. "Everything's working as planned."

"Holy shit," John commented. "This thing is fast. How can the machine keep up with splitting the water molecules into oxygen and hydrogen?"

"Oh crap," Molly yelled. "Back up away from the truck, guys," she said softly. "You might want to slow Demeter down," Molly suggested to Malik. "Are you sure you're venting the oxygen and hydrogen fast enough?"

Malik yelled something to Zip-Tie, who lumbered up the terraced steps to check on the machine, still humming in the back of the truck. He tried to slow the machine down by pushing some buttons, while Malik tried the same from his smartphone. Demeter continued to hum, oblivious to what commands were being entered to slow it down.

Malik lifted the hose out of the water, hoping to slow the intake that way, to no avail.

"Why won't it stop? Malik demanded.

"You built it! I don't know. There's a kill-switch in

the original machine!" Donna yelled.

Zip-Tie remained in the back of the truck, frantically trying to get the Demeter machine to slow down or turn off. By now, the artificial lake's surface had dropped over six inches. Demeter whirred loudly as it worked faster than it was designed to operate.

"Reboot your phone!" Molly yelled to Malik, hoping that might do the trick. Malik quickly complied and shut off his phone. After thirty seconds, the Demeter slowed down and finally stopped.

"That's something we will need to fix," Malik commented, relieved the Demeter was now quiet.

Zip-Tie stood on the deck of the truck, looking for direction from Malik on what to do next. Malik walked to the water's edge and threw the intake end of the hose back into the artificial lake.

Lukas looked over at his mother. "What are you doing?" Molly shouted at Malik as she saw him power up his phone. Simultaneously, as if on cue, a panicked Molly and Lukas focused their attention on the box truck as Zip-Tie calmly pulled out a lighter to ignite his cigarette.

Chapter 25

The explosion was deafening. A huge fireball engulfed the Iveco box truck with a force that knocked Molly, Donna, Linda, and John off their feet. Having been already seated, Lukas instinctively shielded Taylor from the force of the blast that was over one hundred feet away. The explanation of the *Hindenburg* explosion his mom had referenced two days ago flashed through his mind. The hydrogen collection tank must have had a leak or breached from being overfilled. But unlike the *Hindenburg*, there was not a zeppelin-sized supply of hydrogen on the Demeter unit, or what was left of it. The explosion was sudden, strong, and brief. The flames quickly burned through the truck's cargo area, then slowly burned the embers of what little was left. The truck was destroyed, as was Demeter. Zip-Tie's blackened remains smoldered on the ground, about ten feet from the blast.

Betty and Patrick stood at the top of the terrace waving their arms and appeared to be yelling something. Lukas could not hear much other than the ringing in his ears, and he assumed the rest of the group was partially deaf as they struggled to get to their feet. Lukas had shielded Taylor's body, and his hearing appeared to be unaffected. Taylor kissed Lukas on the cheek and mouthed *Thank you*. Or at least Lukas thought he said it silently.

Betty held the fourth Glock in her hand and ran toward the group to help them ascend the terrace. "We've gotta get out of here!" she yelled, hoping their damaged ears could hear her. She knew it was only a few minutes before the Dubai police came to investigate the source of the explosion in the city center.

"Where is Malik?" Betty asked as John, Donna, and Molly rubbed their ears, hoping to regain their hearing.

"He ran that way." Taylor pointed in the direction of the Burj Khalifa. "I saw him for an instant right after the blast."

Patrick raced toward the group. "Police are on their way. I hear the sirens. Let's go, everybody!" Patrick and Taylor, both injured, were able to shepherd the group up to the Sprinter van, get in, and buckle up for what was going to be a quick getaway.

Betty slammed on the accelerator, and the van lurched forward. She could see the flashing police lights about a quarter of a mile to her right. She turned left, hoping to avoid them. "Patrick, I need you to navigate! I don't know where I am!" Betty yelled with a tinge of panic in her voice. Patrick stood up and sat in the passenger seat to help navigate.

Taylor quickly dialed his daughter. She answered on the first ring tone. "Dad, where are you?"

"Get the *Goose* ready. We'll be there in—" He looked at Patrick, who held up his hands with fingers extended. "—ten to fifteen minutes. Please clear a take-off slot for us in twenty-five minutes from now."

"Got it, Dad. Drive safely."

Tory hung up as Betty slalomed quickly through

cars approaching the motorway onramp. "Wheels up in twenty-five minutes," Taylor told the group, whose hearing had partially returned. They confirmed their understanding with a thumbs up.

Taylor addressed the occupants of the van. "We have already loaded the luggage and documents onto the plane. All we need to do is get to it, pull the door shut, and get the hell out of here."

Donna raised her hand. "What about that?" She pointed to the original Poseidon unit that Malik had transferred to the back of the van.

"We take it with us," Molly and Linda said in unison, almost ready to make a joke but deciding it wasn't the right time.

"Tory ran our documents through the private jet concierge who stamped everything, so we're good to go," Taylor confirmed. "Let's just get on that plane."

"I don't understand why the Demeter unit exploded," John said.

Betty responded, "Me neither. Probably something with the pressure relief valves. Lukas and I wrote some bad code into the new software. Let's hope mama Demeter was able to transmit it to the network of machines around the world so she could neutralize her Demeter babies before she went up in flames."

John nodded. "What if it wasn't able to transmit the new software?"

"The viruses in the software were basically designed to act as a kill switch, relatively simple commands to euthanize each unit. It should have transmitted instantaneously through the cloud network."

A car nearly cut her off, and she slammed the brakes to slow down. "Motherfucker!"

"The explosion was due to Malik's avarice to push Demeter as far as possible. He was more concerned with the speed and quantity and didn't think about venting the hydrogen gas fast enough. He should have thought about the pressure in the tanks—but for some reason, Demeter could not power down, so it kept producing hydrogen and oxygen gas until Ma had the brilliant idea to have Malik shut off his phone and reboot," Lukas explained. "Ninety percent of computer issues can be solved by a reboot. Good thinking, Ma. Now you know my secret to being a tech wizard."

"Your secret is safe with us, Lukas," Linda teased him.

"Yeah, but by the time it rebooted, the gas was already starting to leak out of the tanks. Bad timing for our friend and his smoke break."

Betty continued speeding the Sprinter down the E11 motorway that took them south past Al Quoz and directly to Al Maktoum International Airport. Lukas pointed at the airport's control tower in the distance.

"Five minutes, everybody!" Taylor prepared everyone. He called Tory again to let her know they would be coming through the airport gates soon. After a few rings, Tory's phone went to voicemail, so Taylor hung up. *She's probably doing the pre-flight check*, he thought.

Lukas saw his mom's orange Prada bag filled with firearms. "Don't forget the bag!"

"Wouldn't think of it. This was an expensive bag, Lukas."

The van made it to Al Maktoum. The rising sun sat low in the morning sky, and Betty searched for the entrance to where the planes were. There was a security guard checking credentials. "Shit," Betty exclaimed. "We are going to need our passports to get through. My stuff is already on the plane. Patrick, I need you to drive," Betty pleaded with him.

"I don't think I can."

"Just to the guard check and then to the plane," Betty commanded. "Patrick, I need you to ask the guard for access. I don't think Taylor can walk that far."

"Give them our names," Taylor interrupted. "They should already be in the system logged for departure. And for the record, I can walk that far if we need to."

"Taylor." Molly rubbed his good shoulder. "We need you to sit in the passenger seat and show your pilot's identification."

"Good idea!" Betty jumped out of the car and ran to the passenger side to help Patrick out and over to the driver's seat. John and Lukas helped get Taylor to his feet so that he could walk three feet from the back of the van to the passenger seat.

"I'm really sorry to do this," Molly said to Taylor. "I don't know how else we can get to the plane."

"It's okay." Taylor winced, his wounds still raw. "I'll do an award-winning performance." He threw a blanket over his wounded shoulder and side to mask any blood and to not attract the guard's curiosity.

"It kind of looks like a toga. Can you arrange it differently?" John commented.

Linda wrapped the towel differently and looked at her work. "You've gone from Nero to Grandma Moses, but it'll work."

Betty did a quick check. "Everybody in position!"

Patrick couldn't move the transmission out of park and into reverse due to his injuries, making even small movements excruciating. "I got it." Donna jumped up and moved the van into reverse. Once Patrick had backed out, she moved the van into drive. Patrick smiled for her assistance and drove forward. There were two cars in front of him at the guard hut. When Patrick pulled up to the guard, he rolled his window down and showed his chauffeur's license to the guard. Taylor held up his pilot badge and handed it to the guard. Everyone in the back remained quiet.

The guard looked over the identification and said something in Arabic. Patrick laughed and then the guard joined him laughing and opened the barrier. Patrick smiled and waved as he drove into the jet parking area.

"Well, that was easy," Lukas commented.

"What were you guys laughing about?" Molly asked.

"The guard asked why the pilot had a blanket over his shoulders. I told him it's because I like the air conditioning on full blast, and the pilot doesn't."

Lukas rolled his eyes and silently pretended to laugh. "Don't quit your day job, Patrick."

Taylor's eyes grew when he saw the *Goose*, with Diego standing outside to greet them by the boarding stairs. Patrick positioned the van so that it would block anyone's view of the multiple passengers exiting the vehicle. He remotely opened the sliding passenger door, and Lukas stepped out while helping Donna, Linda, Betty, and his mother exit the van. John and Lukas carried the Poseidon unit in tandem up the stairs. Patrick called out to a parking valet to take the Sprinter van to the outside parking lot. He handed the valet the keys, wondering when he would be back to pick the vehicle back up. Taylor slowly walked up the stairs, with Patrick assisting him when needed.

When Taylor stepped into the cabin, he froze. The passengers sat together at the rear of the jet with grim expressions. *What's going on?* he thought. He suddenly felt cold steel against the back of his head. "Shut the door," a voice demanded. Taylor reached for the door and saw Malik and Diego standing defiantly by the cockpit, each holding two guns aimed at their passengers.

Chapter 26

"Where's Tory?" Diego pointed toward the cockpit. Taylor pushed past him and stuck his head inside. There, Tory sat strapped into the co-pilot's seat, her head hanging forward, unconscious or asleep. Or drugged. "What did you do to her, you bastard?" He restrained himself from punching Diego, knowing it would likely mean being shot.

"I gave her a sedative. There's a lot to talk about. I need you in the co-pilot seat for take-off. I can have Lukas and his dad carry her back to the crew rest area."

Taylor's head spun as he grasped what was happening, but his focus was on making sure his daughter was okay. He called Lukas from the back of the plane to help him and fought back tears when Lukas hugged him.

"She'll be okay, baby. She'll be okay," Lukas whispered into Taylor's ear while rubbing his back to comfort him. "Let's get her back to the bed to sleep this off."

"I swear to God, I will fucking kill them with my bare hands if they've harmed her." Taylor was furious, his face flushed with anger and powerlessness.

Normally, Taylor would have been able to carry his daughter by himself, but with a wounded shoulder and waist, his strength had dissipated. Lukas helped carry an unconscious Tory with Taylor to get her to a place where she could lie down. They placed her on the resting area, about the size of a twin bed. Taylor gave her a gentle kiss on the cheek. "What the fuck is going on?" Taylor growled at Diego. Questions flooded his mind. *Who is this guy? Does Tory know? Why did he sedate her? Why the fuck is Malik on board?*

"I've got to take off. Please join me in the cockpit." Diego's voice was cold and demanding.

"Where are we going?" Lukas asked.

"I will announce our destination when appropriate," Diego said calmly. "Now let's go."

Diego stormed toward the open cockpit door with Taylor following him closely. The vintage Poseidon machine sat on the cabin floor. Molly, Donna, Linda, and Betty sat at the same four-seat table they had on the flight to Dubai. Malik sat closest to the cockpit, facing backward, glaring at the passengers. Patrick sat alone by a window, and John was soon joined by Lukas as they readied themselves for departure.

Taylor sat in the co-pilot's seat and strapped himself in, jaw clenched and eyes narrowed as he awaited instructions from his hijackers, Diego and Malik. The intercom crackled with instructions he could barely understand, and Diego responded to the control tower in what sounded like a mix of English and Arabic. The *Goose* was pushed back and pivoted to face the taxiway, and once they began the taxi, the tower would switch to English instruction. Taylor grabbed his phone discreetly and opened Google Translate to capture whatever communications were between the tower or between Diego and Malik. Once the *Goose* was in position, the aircraft tug decoupled itself and drove off to another plane awaiting assistance. Diego fired up the engines, the whirring noise, normally a comfort, adding to Taylor's indignation on the commandeering. Diego awaited taxi instructions from the tower. "Spectrum N-4136 Alpha, you are cleared for taxiway 6E, over." Taylor clearly understood the air traffic controller's English.

Diego responded, "Roger, N-4136 Alpha confirms. Heading to 6E and awaiting instructions."

There were two jets ahead of them, one a large Atlas Air 747-400 freighter and behind it, another Spectrum. Its model type was not clear to Taylor, but it was smaller than the *Goose*. The massive Atlas Air jumbo jet lumbered slowly to the runway, turned, and paused. In less than fifteen seconds, the four massive engines roared as the monster jet slowly gained speed. Even now, Taylor watched this older plane barrel down the runway, his eyes focused on the giant's tail elevators that would tip the 747 upward. These gracious, older behemoths were known as the Queen of the Skies and had revolutionized air travel decades earlier. Taylor focused on the moment the nose lifted and the jumbo jet became airborne, its tipped wings arching upward to support the massive weight of the plane. The thrill of flight, especially takeoff and landing, was something Taylor would never tire of watching.

Shortly after, the smaller Spectrum took its trip down the runway, lifting effortlessly into the air with much efficiency and speed but not nearly the grace displayed by the 747. They were up next. The *Goose* pulled into position and awaited instructions. Taylor hoped to get a clue of their destination. "Spectrum N-4136A destination OAH, you are cleared for take-off."

Diego glared at Taylor as if daring his defiance. A resigned Taylor simultaneously accelerated the plane as it quickly sped down the runway and lifted into the air. Taylor cloaked his own fears and wished he was flying with Tory, as it was their special thing. Instead, he was stuck with this stranger, hijacker, imposter, whatever he was.

Chapter 27

They climbed out of Dubai and headed out over the Persian Gulf before circling the city. Despite the tension and uncertainty Lukas felt, the grandeur of the Burj Khalifa towering over the forest of skyscrapers beneath it grabbed his attention. Dubai's skyline reminded Lukas of shards of glass protruding from an impossibly flat desert. He sat back in his seat, confused, exhausted, and daydreamed of being tucked against Taylor's body in a comfortable bed far away from here. So much had happened in the last forty-eight hours—leaving Tucson, learning about his mom's past adventures, getting to know this beautiful man named Taylor, rescuing his father, and blowing up a potential doomsday machine. Now they were again held captive, essentially hijacked in Taylor's own plane and with no idea where they were going or why.

As the plane leveled off, Lukas noticed Taylor exit the cockpit and rush toward the rear of the plane. He knew he was going to check on Tory, and he held out his hand to touch him as he walked by. Their hands met, and Taylor dropped to his knees at eye level with Lukas.

"I feel so stupid," Taylor said. "We fell into a couple of traps."

"We are safe, and we are together...all of us. That's what matters," Lukas replied. "Even if we don't know where we're going. Let's focus on getting Tory awake and then kicking these guys' asses."

Taylor kissed Lukas on the forehead and walked over to the crew rest area. Tory lay on her side, her eyes open and staring at the wall of the fuselage. Taylor sat on the bed next to her and rubbed her arm. Tory was still coming out of the sedative, and her eyes told a story of bewilderment and betrayal. She broke into tears when she saw her father.

"Honey, it's gonna be all right," Taylor whispered, his chest tightened seeing her in such pain.

"Dad, are you okay?" She stared at Taylor's bloodstained shirt. "My God, what happened to you?" Her dad looked tired, his normally calm face etched by the pain coming from his recent wounds, both physical and mental.

"I'm okay, so don't worry. I got shot twice trying to rescue Lukas' father, and well, Lukas, too. It's been a busy night. How are you feeling?"

Tory tried to stifle her crying, but she let it all out with her father there. "I feel so stupid, Dad. I really thought he was the one. I'm sorry I got you into this mess."

"Baby, you didn't get any of us into this mess. You were the first person there to help us because that's just you. You've always been that way…worried about other people before yourself."

"Diego, or whoever he is, I just thought…" She started to cry again but quickly composed herself. "We had so much in common. He's funny and warm…I just can't understand why and how."

"How? What do you mean?" Taylor asked.

"It's too random, and there are too many

coincidences. He just happened to meet me, the daughter of a pilot who was going to fly a bunch of people to Dubai to find a kidnapped guy, then he pairs up with the kidnapper and hijacks a plane to Afghanistan."

Taylor's eyes widened. "We're going to Afghanistan? Where exactly?"

"OAH airport code. I think it's an air force base close to the Iran border."

Taylor's mind spun. *Why would they need to go to Afghanistan?* He pulled out his smartphone to track their flight. He had entered the *Goose*'s tail number into an app prior to take off. Luckily, the Wi-Fi was working, so he pulled up the image of the plane. "We've just crossed into Iran. If they don't try and shoot us down, then we know they've pre-arranged to allow us into their airspace."

Tory was silent for a moment. "Dad, I'm scared. I don't know what they want with us."

"I don't either. But we're together, so we'll figure it out."

"Dad? I really like Lukas. You glow when you're around him. I've never seen that side of you."

Taylor nodded. "I really like him, too. Tory, you've done nothing wrong, and I don't think you should stay back here by yourself."

"I'm embarrassed."

"Well, you shouldn't be. Diego's the one who lied, and he's the one who hijacked the damn plane. I didn't sense anything about him either, so you're not the only one he's fooled."

Tory sat herself upright as she dried her tears. "Okay, Dad. I'll be right behind you."

Taylor and Tory approached the main seating area, and Molly jumped out of her chair and gave Tory a big hug, followed by Donna, Linda, and Betty. Tory intuitively figured out the older man was John but had no idea who the other man was because she had been drugged by Diego. Malik approached her and formally introduced himself as Malik Bawadi. "It's a pleasure to meet you, Tory." Malik went to shake her hand, but Tory clasped her hands behind her back to avoid any pleasantries Malik offered. "You're just in time. I was getting everyone together to have a conversation."

Just then, Diego walked out of the cockpit to get a glass of water. His eyes locked with Tory's, and she resisted the urge to punch him, and from the looks on the faces of Molly, Donna, Linda, and Lukas, she wasn't the only one. Instead, she stared back at him with utter contempt.

Malik addressed the group. "Ladies and gentlemen, I apologize for the change of plans. We are headed to Afghanistan to hand over the Poseidon machine. Unfortunately, Demeter was not as fortunate this time, so we will need to build a new one. We land in approximately ninety minutes."

"Why Afghanistan?" Lukas asked.

"One of my major investors wants to see the unit work, so I bring it to him."

"Then what?" John asked.

"You leave. Return home, whatever, I don't care. But I want to have a very special person stay behind with me and Zarak."

"Who is Zarak?" Linda asked.

Malik pointed to Diego. "I forgot you don't know my nephew's real name. But I guess, now you do."

Chapter 28

Lukas' mind was spinning at this news. The story continued to unravel, and now he learned that Malik's nephew, Zarak, had posed as Tory's boyfriend, Diego. A thousand questions ran through his mind. How did Malik know Lukas would meet Taylor, and how did he plant his nephew so that he could somehow wind up on the *Goose*?

"Lukas," Malik spoke, "I can see your confusion, so let me explain. I play the long game, as I told your mother. I set the wheels in motion for this project over a year ago. Now, let me set the record straight. I knew your mother and her friends invented the Poseidon technology. Any idiot with a library card could find the patent filing. The real prize was the engineering that eventually became Demeter. It sounds simple, Poseidon in reverse, but it's much more complicated and dangerous, as we saw with our friend at the Dubai fountain. These four women invented a great technology to help mankind, but it was another scientist who discovered how to make water disappear."

"Dr. Thomas Appleton," Molly interrupted. "He was a good friend of ours. He passed away ten years ago and hid the design formula with us."

"Right, Dr. Appleton," Malik continued. "His estate still retained financial rights to his work and, knowing its dangerous potential, held on to it, refusing to sell the intellectual property. But as life takes a turn, the oldest Appleton son died and the remaining children wanted their money, which is where Phoenix comes in, right, John?"

"Other than David, the oldest son who died, the remaining kids didn't know or care about their father's work. They were not scientists, and all they wanted was their inherited money," John explained. "Molly, Betty, Donna, Linda, and I pooled what money we had and offered it to the family, which they accepted and signed an irrevocable purchase agreement we sent them on behalf of Phoenix Equities."

"This is where I enter the picture. I offered the kids a significant amount of money. Much more than what they agreed to sell it to Phoenix, and they tried to back out of the deal, but the deal was iron-clad and already sealed. One thing that never changes is people's greed," Malik told them.

"And how did you get Diego, I mean, Zarak involved? That had to be more than just a coincidence, Malik," Lukas commented.

"Oh, it was not a coincidence at all. I researched Mrs. Halloran and her children and learned about you, Lukas. You were a successful technology executive with your own company. I also learned where you live, what you buy at the store, and your perversion with other men. As I continued to dig, I found you were a customer of Nimbus Aviation, and upon researching Taylor, found he was a discharged Air Force pilot and also a homosexual, but with an unexpected twist—he had a daughter. I knew it was only a matter of time that you two would find each other. That's what your kind does, isn't it? Sniffing each other out? Anyway, I found out Taylor's daughter's name and sent Zarak to find her and unwittingly pulled her into the plan we were building. Once that was set, I dropped the lawsuit against Phoenix, the sale went through, and Mr. Halloran was kidnapped."

"Yeah, if you call it that," John growled.

"I had a number of goals in this, but getting my revenge on your mother was an unexpected bonus." Malik directed his gaze at Lukas. "The whole room of dominoes was ready to go, and kidnapping John was the first one to fall. After that, the plan rolled out pretty much as planned."

"Malik," Lukas asked, "Can you explain how all of this is related? What do you want from us now?"

Malik gave Lukas an intimidating stare. "What do I want from you?" The group waited for Malik's response. "I want Molly Halloran, your mother.

"My plan is to land at Shindand Air Force base. It's run by the Taliban, like the rest of the country. Zarak and I will depart this aircraft along with Mrs. Halloran. Once we've deplaned, you're free to go wherever you'd like."

"And what is your plan for Molly?" John asked.

"She will be set free to live as a woman alone in a strange new country with nothing to eat and nowhere to sleep. She can use her talents and resourcefulness to find a way to survive. Just like my mother did." Malik glared at Molly. He paused as an idea came to his head as he looked at Linda, Donna, and Betty. "Actually, I changed my mind. All four of them will be removed from this plane, and I can see to it that they are properly documented and—" Malik searched for the right word. "—and processed. But you'll have to cover up, ladies.

The Taliban doesn't like their women without burqas."

Lukas and John protested this insane idea. "Why would you do that to them?" Lukas asked. "They would never survive. What's wrong with you both?"

"Do you believe in karma, Lukas?"

"You're not creating much positive karma now, if you want my opinion," Lukas shot back.

Malik answered, "I don't value your opinion nor your very existence! Do you not understand anything, Lukas?"

Lukas looked at his father and then to Taylor, both of whom seemed equally confused. He then glanced at his mother, who sat with her face resting in both of her hands. "Mom? What's he talking about?"

"Damascus, 1972. Do you remember, ladies?" Malik almost spat at them. "The four of you were there as young, pretty girls pretending to be tourists. You murdered my father and cast my family's life into the ashes of hell."

****

Lukas reflected on the stories the ladies told him and Taylor about Project Rosemary and their trips to lure terrorists out into the open, where they would be quickly neutralized. Lukas could tell by his mother's deflated posture that there was a possibility Malik's story had at least a kernel of truth to it. Why else would Malik go to all this trouble to find them?

"Malik, you are mistaken. We were never in Damascus or Syria. It wasn't us who killed your father," Molly explained.

"Do you know what happened after my father died? We were left homeless and living on the street. My mother had to sell her body for us to have food, and then my sister had to do the same, and Zarak is the product of one of her sinful unions. My mother died, and shortly after, so did my sister. She bled to death giving birth to Zarak in jail. I was the only one to survive, and I took in Zarak so that he didn't meet the same fate of being homeless or entertaining perverted men like your son and his boyfriend."

Lukas and Taylor remained quiet. There was no rationalizing with Malik as he described decades of pain and sadness. "I'm sorry for you and your family, Malik. It must have been horrible for all of you. But we were never in Syria. Never," Molly pleaded.

Taylor noticed that during the intensity of the argument, Zarak had left the cockpit and the plane on autopilot. He glanced over at Donna, who noticed the same. Their eyes communicated that they both knew what they had to do.

****

Donna stood and excused herself to use the restroom near the galley. Malik and Zarak continued to argue with the women, John, and Lukas. Tory could see what her father was planning, so she walked toward Zarak to distract him further. Molly had been watching Donna and played into the argument with Malik and Zarak. Donna suddenly exited the restroom, and then she and Taylor bolted toward the cockpit, entered it, and slammed the door, quickly locking it behind them. Since 9/11, all airplanes were fitted with reinforced cockpit doors, first in commercial aircraft and then in private planes. Taylor and Donna quickly prepared to take control of the *Goose*.

"Good distraction, Donna. Using the restroom was a great move."

"Thanks, but I really had to go to the toilet, and, well, here we are, sir."

"We all thank your bladder then," Taylor responded.

Predictably, Malik and Zarak began pounding on the cockpit door. Donna gave Taylor a look of concern, nervous the door may not hold. "Double reinforced steel and bullet-proof carbon fiber doors with six locking pins will keep them out. I'm glad I got that upgrade, now that I think of it," Taylor said. Donna sighed with relief.

"Now let's try and head back," Taylor told her as he disengaged the autopilot and weighed scenarios on how to return to Dubai. "I'm taking a long, wide turn, so hopefully they don't notice. We've got to get the hell out of Iranian air space."

"What if they do notice?" Donna asked. She interpreted Taylor's silence that he was still working on that plan.

The wide sweeping turn back toward Dubai took over fifteen minutes, and the extended maneuver seemed to be working. The pounding on the cockpit door had stopped and when Taylor could periodically check through the peephole, there seemed to be little happening, except for arguments between passengers and Molly's face etched with concern for a very wounded Patrick. Nobody seemed to notice their change of direction.

"Have you gotten through to Dubai air control yet?" Taylor asked Donna.

She shook her head. "Not yet. I'll keep trying."

Taylor's arm, shoulder, and side throbbed in pain. It hurt to breathe, and he felt fatigued, like he could fall asleep right where he was. It was normal for pilots to get tired while flying. The cabin pressure alone was equal to about seven thousand feet elevation, which made his heart beat faster and his breathing quicker than normal. Plus, there was the stress of being shot twice, hijacked, and then commandeering his own plane back from the hijackers. It was not a normal day at the office. In the distance, he could see a sliver of blue, the Persian Gulf, which meant they were getting close to exiting Iranian airspace. He estimated they would be in Dubai in about forty-five to sixty minutes.

Taylor accelerated the Goose to get out of Iran even faster. He and Donna scanned the horizon and the air around them since they were likely raising alarms with Iran air traffic control. A non-responsive fugitive plane flying on an improvised flight path would provoke a response. A deafening roar broke them out of their concentration. Four fighter jets thundered overhead. Taylor's combat experience flashed back as he glanced at the emblems on the fuselage. They were MiG-29 combat fighters from the Islamic Republic of Iran Air Force.

"Shit, we've got friends," Donna cursed.

"Iranians. Fuck, I was wondering when they'd show up. Damn it. How far until we're out of their air space?"

"I'm guessing ten minutes, sir," Donna responded.

"Let's make it five. Increase airspeed to maximum."

"Roger." Donna complied and pushed the throttle to accelerate to maximum speed. "Airspeed at max. We're at 665 mph. Aren't MiGs supersonic?"

Taylor nodded. "Our goal is to get into either

Oman or Emirati airspace. We can't outrun these guys and just pray they don't shoot us down."

The Iranian shoreline was still several miles below and Iranian airspace likely did not stop at their shores. Now it became a game of aeronautical chicken. Would the Iranians expect the American plane to surrender, or would they shoot it down and risk an international provocation?

"Reduce altitude to twenty-five-thousand feet!" Taylor shouted to Donna as he focused ahead, "Let's show them we are not aggressive." He hoped his strategy was the correct one. Within less than a minute, he breathed a sigh of relief when he saw the Strait of Hormuz and hundreds of cargo and tanker ships dotting the surface of the Persian Gulf. "Almost there," Taylor said. "Visual on the MiGs yet?"

Donna was just about to respond when she heard popping noises outside the plane. All four fighter jets unleashed a flurry of bullets from their guns. "Shit, they're strafing us!"

"Call Dubai air control!" Taylor commanded.

The quick volley of bullets stopped as swiftly as it began. Taylor jumped from his seat and checked the peephole. No injuries. The fuselage was another story. The outside sunlight dotted the interior of the plane. Bullet holes were visible in the cabin wall and ceiling. This looked bad.

"Captain," Donna called to him. "We're losing speed! Controls feel sluggish."

"Damnit, they saw our tail number as registered in America and probably hit us somewhere strategic like the engines or wings. Anything wrong on the sensors? Fluid levels? Fuel?"

"Nothing I can see, sir."

Taylor strained his neck to check for the fighters. He could not find the MiGs. They may have turned back or were hovering behind them, out of view, waiting to make their final strike. "How soon until we enter Emirati air space?" Taylor shouted.

Donna studied the controls. "I think we just did."

Chapter 29

Shortly after crossing into friendlier air space, Taylor dropped altitude to ten thousand feet to reduce the pressure inside the cabin and avert a fatal decompression. The strafing by the Iranians pierced the *Goose*'s fuselage with small holes, but like a chipped automobile windshield, it was only a matter of time before those small holes became big ones. Taylor heard two shots ring out from inside the cabin. *Shit! Now what?* He pressed the radio to call Dubai air control. "This is Spectrum N-4136A, we have gunfire in the cabin. Hijackers have not breached the cockpit, and pilots have full control of the aircraft."

"Voice recognition confirmed as Captain Taylor Pastore. Where is your co-pilot? Please have him respond."

"Dubai tower, the other pilot is one of the hijackers. His passport is registered under Diego Paul, country of Mexico." Taylor held his finger over his lips signaling Donna to not respond.

There was a long pause before the control tower answered. "Confirmed. We are sending two aircraft to escort you."

"Voice recognition? They obviously didn't use that when we took off from Dubai," Donna whispered.

Taylor opened communication again. "Dubai tower, give me five minutes. I need first to de-escalate the situation on board. The hijackers have firearms. We have a hostage situation with at least one injured on board. This is Taylor Pastore. I'm the aircraft owner and registered pilot. I'll radio when I'm ready. I'm going to de-pressurize the cabin."

There was silence for a moment. "Confirmed, and good luck," Dubai air control responded.

They remained at ten thousand feet. Taylor had an idea. Suddenly, the intercom button glowed. Someone was trying to call them. "Pastore," Taylor answered, thinking it was one of the hijackers.

"Hi, it's me." It was Lukas. "Two shots blasted into the fuselage. Malik is holding my mother hostage with a gun."

"Lukas, listen to me. Make sure everyone is belted in. Things are about to get—"

Another bullet missed Lukas' head but pierced the skin of the aircraft. The third bullet to do so, and there was no telling what else the Iranian air force had damaged in their assault.

"Can the plane hold up to bullet holes?" Lukas asked Taylor. "Are we going to have a decompression?"

"We should be okay," Taylor responded. "Make sure you have oxygen ready. Hang on!"

Zarak stormed toward the back of the plane and grabbed Lukas by the arm, dragging him to the front and forcibly pushing him down into a seat next to Molly.

"Oh good," Malik sneered. "I have both of you together. This will make things more efficient."

"Malik," Molly pleaded. "Don't hurt my family. Kill me, but not them. But it won't change anything,

Malik. You'll still be that angry little man blaming the world for all his problems."

Malik's face burned with rage when he heard this. "Shut up, bitch!" Malik slapped Molly across the face so hard her nose started to bleed. All civility left his face. "I've heard enough of you for a lifetime." Zarak held back Lukas, who struggled to defend his mom with a blow to Malik's face.

In the cockpit, Taylor ordered Donna to put on an oxygen mask. "Oh shit, I was afraid that was what you were going to do, sir."

"Did they ever teach you this maneuver in the Army? Great way to discipline unruly passengers. We called it *The Puking Porpoise*."

Donna rolled her eyes. "Shit, sir, this is kind of insane. The Army tends to stick to the tried and true. You Air Force guys are fucking crazy. With all due respect, captain."

"Guilty as charged. I'll take that as a vote of confidence." Taylor joked, "I'm gonna need your help in case I pass out, plus, I've only got one good arm, so you'll have to make sure we don't crash. You ready?" Donna nodded, a professional look of panic in her eyes.

"What if we both pass out?"

Taylor winked at her. "You can do it. Climb to twenty-five thousand feet."

Suddenly, the *Goose* pitched upward at a steep incline, enough to knock pillows and blankets in the cabin onto the floor. Malik and Zarak lost their footing, the sudden change in pitch causing them to steady themselves using the walls of the fuselage.

Lukas' eyes were wide with anxiety, not knowing what was coming next.

"Hang on. I think this is going to be bad," he whispered to the passengers near him.

"Oh shit, Dad…really?" Tory exclaimed.

Lukas checked that everyone was belted in except for Malik and Zarak, who were still standing and focused on Molly and her friends.

Molly sat nervously as Malik pointed the gun at her from the floor. She swallowed hard, her mouth dry from exhaustion and fear. She calmed herself the best she could, considering these were likely her final moments. Out of the corner of her eye, she saw Patrick leap out of his seat and onto her lap, his back facing Malik, shielding Molly.

"Sorry, ma'am, I know this is awkward," he apologized. It was the last thing he said before Malik's gun popped, and Patrick's weight slumped into her.

"Now!" Taylor commanded, having heard the gunshot in the cabin. He and Donna, both wearing supplemental oxygen masks, simultaneously pushed the yoke forward and drove the *Goose* into a steep dive. Taylor depressurized the cabin with one switch.

"Holy crap, I've never done this, sir!" Donna yelled through her mask.

"Steady dive to fifteen-thousand feet, then stabilize," Taylor commanded as he stared into the blue of the Persian Gulf directly below them.

The sudden plunge caused Malik to lose his footing as he fired the gun to kill Molly. Instead, the bullets tore through the ceiling of the plane. Disoriented, Malik continued to fire his gun, and three more bullets pierced the skin of the plane, and one went through the cabin door.

Molly could see blue sky through the holes as she

and Lukas wrestled their oxygen masks on. She continued to hold on to Patrick's motionless body. She didn't know if he was alive or dead, but she continued to share her oxygen with him. Patrick had taken bullets in his back to protect her. Again.

Linda, Betty, and John held their heads down in order to avoid stray bullets as Malik continued to fire wildly. They had also managed to get their oxygen masks on during the plane's sudden drop. Tory had fallen during the plunge and struggled to pull herself into a seat, quickly strapping the oxygen mask over her nose and mouth.

The *Goose* had descended significantly and continued downward, and Taylor commanded Donna to pitch it even steeper. The plane felt like it was plummeting vertically, which reminded Donna of the first time she and Wilma had tackled one of the steepest roller coasters in the world at Cedar Point amusement park. She had oxygen but struggled to maintain her sense of balance and reality.

Neither Malik nor Zarak were able to get oxygen and were in the early stages of hypoxia. Malik gasped for breath and started to lose his vision as he writhed on the floor, shooting at shadows and villains in his brain. He continued to shoot the gun almost as a reflex. Zarak vomited and crawled along the floor of the cabin aimlessly, gasping for breath. Malik's heart raced as he struggled to breathe.

Taylor stabilized the plane for a few seconds. "Climb to twenty-five-thousand feet!" Donna and he pulled back on the yoke, and the *Goose* started another steep climb. "Donna, can you hold the plane while I check the cabin?" Donna nodded and continued to climb another fifteen thousand feet while Taylor peered through the peephole in the cockpit door. Lukas, Tory, and the rest of the passengers were okay, and Patrick was sitting on Molly's lap for some reason. Malik lay on his back as Zarak pulled himself up the aisle by grabbing the seatbacks. He checked his watch. Two minutes until the UAE Air Force showed up. Taylor jumped into his seat and fastened himself in. "Descend to eight thousand feet!" Donna nodded and complied with Taylor's lead. They pitched the plane downward into an even steeper dive.

Inside the cabin, Zarak screamed, blood streaming from his mouth. He still held his pistol, but his eyes were glazed with disorientation and oxygen deprivation. He screamed in anger as he pointed his pistol toward the cockpit door. Suddenly, the plane plunged, and the g-forces threw him into the bullet-riddled ceiling.

Malik lay on his back, eyes wild in confusion, his oxygen-starved brain unable to perceive dream from reality. He lay motionless when suddenly, he saw a large, silhouetted figure that loomed over him like an angel. His mind hallucinated the figure was here to save him. *Father?* he thought until suddenly, the figure disappeared into the sky. A large chunk of the aircraft's bullet-pierced ceiling panel broke away from the plane. Sunlight instantly flooded the cabin. Zarak's body was sucked out of the plane and somersaulted into the heavens.

Taylor and Donna immediately felt the drag on the plane suddenly change. The nimble jet suddenly responded like a barge, plummeting out of control and falling toward the city below. Taylor yelled over to

Donna, "I think we've been hit, or part of the plane broke free. Feels like a hull breach."

Donna nodded. "Let's try and stabilize her. I still have flaps and speed controls! I'm descending to five thousand feet," Taylor yelled.

Malik crawled across the floor and pulled himself to his feet. He was furious and still a bit delirious from the depressurization.

Lukas stood by the galley, steadying himself by hanging onto a divider curtain, his eyes squinting from flying debris. Papers, utensils, glassware, and other items not secured whirled in a tornado of objects caused by the rapid descent and wind entering the cabin from the gaping hole. Everyone else remained buckled in, including Patrick, who still lay motionless, cradled in Molly's lap. Lukas noticed that despite a terrifying series of climbs, plunges, and the chance that they would crash into the water below, everyone on board was exceptionally calm.

Except for Malik, who approached him with hate in his eyes. "You have ruined everything!" He spat at Lukas. "I will not be beaten by a sodomite!"

Lukas was done with this guy and his archaic insults. "I bet you already have been beaten by one. I'm just the first openly gay sodomite you know about!" Lukas forced a laugh with the sole purpose of further enraging Malik. "Ten more minutes, Malik, and we're on the ground. Your career is over. You'll be arrested when we land, and you'll be lucky if the Emirati shoot you! I've heard their prisons are epic! My mother called you a toad, but that's an insult to toads everywhere."

Lukas glanced at the bullet-riddled cabin door and had an idea. "Put the gun down, Malik. It's probably empty anyway. You wasted bullets shooting the up the plane."

Surprisingly, Malik dropped the gun and charged at Lukas with complete hatred and fury. Lukas knew this was his chance. Malik screamed something in a language Lukas didn't understand, his hands outstretched ready to choke Lukas' throat. With a second to spare, Lukas leapt out of the way, and Malik crashed into the cabin door at full force. He fell to his knees, stunned. He attempted to pull himself back to his feet, and Lukas held onto the billowing curtain. Lukas saw what Malik grabbed to pull himself up. It was not something he should be touching. "Hang on!" was the last thing Malik heard before the cabin door swung open, and he slowly tumbled forward. Malik's brain hallucinated due to the effects of hypoxia, but now he was like a free bird, flying solo toward the blue Persian Gulf below him.

Taylor felt his plane rattling apart. "Can you hold her for a few seconds while I look through the peephole?"

Donna gave him a thumbs up. The *Goose* bounced from the turbulence caused by wind and temperature changes. Taylor unbuckled his belt and crawled out of his seat to stand next to the cockpit door. He was still moving slowly due to his injuries from the gunfight with Malik's henchmen several hours earlier. *That feels like a week ago*, he thought as he peered through the spy hole and gasped. "Oh my God," was all he could say.

The *Goose* had an enormous hole in the ceiling of the fuselage. Sunlight streamed into the cabin, which, along with the wind blowing in through the breach, gave the cabin a surreal appearance. The cabin door was flopped open, buffeted by the rushing air outside. The *Goose* was a wreck, and he had to figure out how to get it on the ground without killing everybody on board. Lukas held on to the divider curtain in the galley, eyes closed. Molly was still desperately cradling an injured or dead Patrick. John sat behind them. Tory, Linda, and Betty were buckled into their seats. Everyone had a look of disbelief, resignation, or pure exhaustion from all they had just experienced.

Where was Zarak?

Where was Malik?

Donna called out to him, "What happened, sir?"

Taylor stared in disbelief. "Lost part of the ceiling, and the cabin walls are filled with bullet holes. Looks like the cabin door was breached. We need to slow down!" Taylor climbed back into the pilot's seat and radioed Dubai air control. They no longer needed oxygen, so he left off his mask.

"Mayday, Dubai tower. This is N-4136A. We have lost cabin integrity, and we request immediate assistance to the closest airfield. Mayday! This is an emergency. I repeat, this is an emergency!"

"Confirmed, 4136A, do you have casualties?"

"There appear to be some casualties, but most passengers appear to be unharmed physically," Taylor responded. *Mentally is another story,* he thought. "Hijackers appear to be neutralized."

"I'm dropping landing gear. That'll help slow us down, sir," Donna informed him, to which he confirmed with a thumbs up.

Suddenly, Taylor saw a military jet to their port side. For a second, he thought they'd been pursued by more Iranians, but on closer look, it was an F-16. The emblem on the fuselage was a ring of olive branches surrounding a circle of green, black, and red.

"It's the Emirati Air Force!"

Donna yelled, "I've got his buddy on starboard," Another F-16 hovered about fifty yards away.

"We have sent requested escorts," the voice from Dubai air control informed them.

Taylor looked ahead. They were on a direct line to the towering Burj Khalifa and the rest of downtown Dubai. "Shit!" Taylor called out to Donna. "Escort my ass. They think we may be the hijackers headed for their buildings."

Donna yelled into the radio, "Requesting a new course, away from populated areas."

Dubai tower responded, "Confirmed. Sending you new coordinates now."

"Good thinking, Donna." Taylor smiled. "I don't need to be shot down today."

Taylor plugged in the coordinates to their new destination. Their altitude was now four thousand feet. "N-4136 Alpha, escorts reporting you are missing a winglet on port side. Also, starboard landing gear is down but does not appear to be locked. Repeat, starboard landing gear does not appear to be locked."

"The Iranians probably hit the landing gear. Can you maintain control? I'm gonna tell everyone what's going on."

"Roger," Donna stated calmly, "but, sir, our controls state the starboard landing gear is locked."

Taylor surveyed the surroundings below them. "This is gonna be a rough landing. They're diverting us away from Dubai International," Taylor said grimly.

Once out of his seat, Taylor unlocked the security deadbolts that protected the cockpit and opened the door. The first thing he felt was the cold air. He walked toward Lukas and rubbed his head. "You okay, babe?" Lukas nodded. Taylor went to check on Tory, who sat on the floor of the plane along with Betty and Linda. "What happened to Malik and Zarak?"

Linda used her thumb to point at Betty. "I shot him. His nephew got sucked out, then Malik opened the door by mistake and fell. Sorry about the holes in your plane."

Taylor knelt by Tory, her face stained by tears. "I'm sorry about Diego."

Tory looked at her dad. "Fuck him. He had it coming." She sniffled.

Taylor addressed the group. "We've requested immediate emergency landing, and we're being escorted in by the Emirati Air Force. I need you all to be prepared for a crash landing and emergency evacuation once we are stopped."

"What about Patrick? Can we put him somewhere he will be safe?" Molly asked.

Lukas looked up at Taylor. "Can we belt him into the crew bed?"

Patrick was either dead or very close to death. His coloring had become even more ashen. Lukas and Taylor carried him to the back and strapped him into the bed. "I'm gonna stay with him back here," Lukas told Taylor. "He saved my mom. He took the bullets for her."

Taylor nodded as Lukas buckled himself into the aft seat and then kissed him lightly. "This is gonna be a rough landing. Promise me you'll be safe."

"I promise, Captain," Lukas replied, trying to cloak his sheer terror behind a stoic face.

The *Goose* shook violently, and Taylor rushed back to the cockpit. Donna fought the controls as the plane was buffeted by desert winds and turbulence.

"She feels like she's gonna shake apart, sir!" she shouted to Taylor.

"I think she'll hold until we get onto the ground," Taylor responded.

They were now about thirty miles from Dubai city center and well beyond both of the international airports. The Emirati F-16 pilots saluted Taylor and Donna, giving them a thumbs up for good luck. They flew ahead of them and were soon out of sight.

"We're on our own, sir," Donna said to Taylor.

"God knows where they're landing us. They know it's gonna be messy," Taylor responded.

"Proceed to desert runway 35 northwest. Follow arrows for direction. We have police, fire, and ambulance there on standby. Runway has been foamed," Dubai air control instructed. "Handing you over to local air control. Good luck, 4136 Alpha."

They approached the airport, if you'd call it that. Five partially inflated hot air balloons stood on a tarmac. A large crowd of spectators, clearly visible from their altitude of fifteen hundred feet, stood by with a morbid interest. "What kind of airport is that?" Donna asked.

"It's a damned skydiving and balloon tourist center. I wouldn't exactly call it an airport, but let's not give the plane spotters a show, okay?"

"Roger," Donna responded. She could see the emergency vehicles and the narrow runway, glistening white with foam.

Taylor called the airport tower on his radio. "N-4136 Alpha ready for final approach."

"This is the SDD Tower. Confirming final approach."

Donna asked, "Have you heard of SDD airport code, sir?"

Taylor shook his head and pointed to the logo painted on the tarmac. *Sky Diving Dubai,* it read. "Donna, you don't need to keep calling me sir."

"Sorry, sir, it keeps me in professional mode to prevent me from shitting my pants."

Taylor nodded. "Okay, understood."

They looped the *Goose* in one more small circle and lined up with the runway. "I hope the landing doesn't break her apart," Taylor said to Donna as they descended rapidly. "Let's get her safely on the ground."

They lowered the jet and struggled to minimize the impact on the runway. Donna and Taylor exhaled as the wheels lightly kissed the tarmac, and Taylor prayed the rear landing gear held as he deployed the wing flaps and reverse thrusters to reduce their already too high speed and prevent the *Goose* from careening out of control. Taylor trimmed the tail elevators to stabilize the *Goose,* which he balanced as best he could on only two locked landing gear. Taylor and Donna expertly slowed the aircraft to a manageable speed and relaxed their grips. "Look like she's holding…" Taylor shouted optimistically.

Suddenly, the starboard landing gear collapsed, and the rear of the plane dropped, hitting the runway and sending off a flurry of sparks that were smothered by the fire-retardant foam. The jet plowed through the foam. The landing gear brakes were useless at this point, so their prime goal was to keep the plane from shattering apart or flipping over, which would likely cause a fatal explosion.

Donna and Taylor struggled to maintain control, blind and disoriented by the foam that covered the plane. Within a few hundred more feet, the *Goose* vibrated loudly, and Taylor felt something major dislodge from the plane. "We lost part of the starboard wing, sir!" Donna yelled, looking behind her, the broken wing fragment disappearing into the foam. Jet fuel poured out of the broken wing. Taylor had to act fast. The next thing to likely break apart was the fuselage, weakened by the bullets and the gaping hole on the top of the plane.

"Hang on!" He violently jerked the controls, sending the *Goose* into a spin. The second and third landing gear sheared off and tumbled erratically into the foamy chaos. But the jet finally came to a stop and sat sideways across the small runway on its belly. Smelling jet fuel, Taylor quickly jumped out of his seat and entered the cabin. No visible injuries had been caused by the crash landing, and Taylor manually released the cabin door and stairs.

"Okay, everybody out. Leave everything behind, please. We need to get out of this plane immediately," Taylor emphasized. Jet fuel spat out of the broken wing. He remembered from his Air Force training that fire was the main cause of fatalities in a crash, not the impact. The *Goose* still had enough fuel on board to cause a major explosion and fire. That would prove to be disastrous. He had to get people out of the plane fast.

Within minutes, paramedics were boarding the

Goose to assist the evacuation. Lukas pointed them back to the crew quarters to retrieve Patrick. Firemen rained more foam and water on the broken aircraft.

Linda, Betty, and Molly were the first off the plane, followed by John and then Tory. The second set of paramedics came with a stretcher for Taylor, his uniform tattered and splotched with dried blood. Taylor refused to leave the plane before everyone else was off. "I don't need a damned stretcher," he whispered to Lukas.

Another two paramedics carried out Patrick. His face was uncovered, his eyes half-open. Lukas saw Patrick blink once, which meant he was still alive, even if it was barely.

Lukas followed them to the exit. He turned and hugged Donna and Taylor. "Thanks for getting us here in one piece. I'm sorry about the *Goose*."

"You're a hell of a pilot, Donna," Taylor complimented her.

"You're a hell of a captain, sir. Thank you for getting us here, even after being shot up. Imagine what you could do with two good arms."

Taylor looked at his shoulder. "I think adrenaline was the ultimate painkiller."

The group walked through the foam and toward a group of 4x4 sport vehicles waiting for them. "A dune buggy ride seems kind of boring after a flight like that," Lukas said.

"Beggars can't be choosers." Taylor stopped and surveyed the wreckage of the *Goose*. He could see she was beyond repair and would most likely be retired and salvaged for scrap and spare parts. Despite being shot up in the sky and a crash landing, the *Goose* got everyone back on the ground. He turned to Lukas. "She was one hell of an aircraft, built like a tank and elegant as a dancer. I know she's just a machine, but she also felt like part of the family.

Lukas grabbed his hand and leaned on his shoulder. "She took us on quite an adventure," he said softly to Taylor.

"Yep, and she's where I met you." He kissed Lukas on the forehead.

Molly and John walked slowly, both exhausted, sore, and bewildered by the last few days. A man approached them. He was wearing a suit despite the desert temperature, which felt well over one hundred degrees. The man extended his hand to John. "Mr. Halloran, I'm Detective Abadi from the Dubai metropolitan police. I've been in charge of your case, and I'm so glad to meet you in person. We are looking for Mr. Bawadi but can't find him onboard. He's an international terrorist and is wanted in several countries."

John shook his head at the irony. "Check the Persian Gulf, about five miles offshore."

He changed the subject. "This is my wife, Molly."

Molly shook Detective Abadi's hand. "Molly Halloran. Pleased to meet you," was all she could muster.

The detective looked out over the wreckage on the runway. "I'm sorry about your plane. Will you be needing another one?"

She had to think for a minute. "We have a seriously injured passenger we need to get better first. Then, we'll think about how we get home."

"Very well," Detective Abadi responded. "I will

have my assistant book your party into the San Rafael resort on Palm Jumeirah. I believe you will find it restful. I figured Mr. Halloran would prefer that hotel over The Excelsior, considering his last experience there."

Molly and John nodded in appreciation as they walked toward the dune buggies. John looked at his wife and kissed her cheek. "Thanks for coming to rescue me!"

Molly smiled. "It was a team effort."

As they approached the buggy, John opened the canvas door to let Molly in. She thanked him, and John jumped over to the other side. He put his hand on her knee. "How did it feel being back in the international assassin saddle?"

Molly thought. "It was fun, well kind of, now that it's over. I think Lukas can take it from here."

"Don't sell yourself short, honey. You've got a lot more adventures in you." John replied.

The dune buggy bounced on their way to the SDD parking lot. Molly put her hand on John's shoulder. "Honey, if you ever go kayaking again, you're on your own."

Chapter 30

Molly sat in the lobby of the Emirates Hospital Jumeirah. She and Lukas waited for news on Taylor's surgery to remove the bullet from his body and stitch up the open wound on his side. "Taylor's going to be okay, Lukas. We're in a great hospital with the best doctors."

Lukas nodded. "I know, Mom. Thanks. Any news on Patrick?"

Suddenly, a little girl carrying a bouquet of balloons entered the lobby, followed by who Molly assumed was the girl's mother. The little girl was dressed up in a fancy dress and hummed a tune Molly couldn't identify. Her mother spoke to the receptionist. Molly heard English with a British accent. Patrick had mentioned them when they were driving around Al Quoz looking for Lukas and John.

Molly approached the woman. "Dr. Aziz?"

The woman looked confused for a second. "Hello, I'm Evelyn, may I help you?"

"Patrick's wife?"

Evelyn nodded.

"Hello, I'm Molly Halloran."

"Patrick's CEO, of course! He told me so much about you!" Molly dreaded whatever Patrick told his wife about her. "And this is Bella, our daughter. Say hello, Bella."

"Hello. Are you somebody's grandmum?" Bella

asked her.

Molly chuckled. "Yes. I have four grandchildren; the oldest one is about your age." She turned to Evelyn. "I'm sorry, do you not go by Dr. Aziz?"

"Oh, I'm sorry. I'm still a bit jet-lagged. I actually go by Dr. Randolph, using my maiden name, but please call me Evelyn."

Molly's eyes welled with tears. The exhaustion of the last several days, combined with the human toll, weighed on her. Seeing Patrick's wife and daughter reminded her of how poorly she had treated and misjudged Patrick. "Your husband saved my life. Twice, actually. I'm so sorry for what happened to him. Have you heard how he's doing?"

Evelyn cleared her throat. "He was shot multiple times, as you know. He went into septic shock due to an infection, but I think he's out of danger now. The question is whether he will be able to walk. He's still experiencing paralysis. Thank you for bringing him to this hospital. It's Dubai's best. They'll fix him up."

Molly realized she was keeping Evelyn from visiting her husband. "I'm sorry, I'm holding you up."

Evelyn smiled. "I'm glad to have met the legendary Molly Halloran. Patrick thinks the world of you. He even referred to you as—" She paused while Molly thought of the worst things Patrick deservedly could call her. "—a badass. It's such an American term, but I love it."

Molly smiled as Lukas walked back from the cafeteria. "This is my son, Lukas. Lukas, this is Evelyn, Patrick's wife, and Bella, his daughter."

"I'm honored to meet you both." He addressed Bella, "Your dad is a superhero."

Bella smiled. "I want to be a superhero when I grow up."

Lukas replied, "Your father can give you lessons, and so can your mother, so make sure you listen and learn from them. He'll be so excited to see you!"

Bella skipped toward the elevators. Evelyn said, "Please come up and visit him. Room 304."

****

An hour later, a nurse came to tell them Taylor was out of surgery and was in Room 302, right next door to Patrick. They went upstairs and found Taylor's room. He was still asleep. "Mom, I'm gonna wait here until he wakes up."

"Okay, I'll pop over to say hello to Patrick and then meet your dad for dinner at the hotel. Join us if you'd like."

Lukas smiled and nodded.

Within an hour, Taylor woke up. He was groggy, with his shoulder heavily bandaged.

"Hello, sleeping beauty." Lukas combed Taylor's hair with his fingers in an attempt to show affection and make his hair presentable.

Taylor smiled, his eyes still half closed. "Hey, baby. How are you?"

Lukas had stayed on the edge of Taylor's bed and just stared at him as he slept. Here was a man who was strong, brave, considerate, confident, and incredibly sexy. Lukas had seen Taylor in extremely difficult situations, and he always came through. He was a good dad and just a good person overall. Lukas felt he'd met his soul mate, but he'd never tell Taylor that, at least not yet. *I could love this man*, he thought, even though he was pretty sure he was already starting to. He would

251

wait awhile until he ventured into using the *L* word again so quickly.

Taylor reached for Lukas' hand. Despite where they were, Lukas interlaced his fingers through Taylor's. Taylor smiled. "So what do we do for our second date?"

Epilogue

Lukas and Taylor gazed at the stunning view of the Santa Catalina mountains as they sat together on the back terrace. So much had changed since they first met two years earlier. The start of their relationship was not typical—the two of them were thrown together in a series of events that challenged them individually and as a new couple. They did have a second date at the Delaware Room, and a third date at a pizza joint. After a couple of months, they moved in together. Lukas and Taylor watched Netflix, made popcorn, folded clothes, argued occasionally, and all the other normal things couples do together. Their physical attraction and closeness only grew, and Lukas stopped thinking about the pain he'd experienced with Drew and other men who just didn't work out. Taylor and their new life together was all that mattered.

Less than a year after the *Poseidon Project Adventure*, as it came to be called by them, Taylor visited the Halloran home for Thanksgiving. He enjoyed meeting Lukas' siblings and their significant others, as well as the grandkids. After dinner, but before dessert, Taylor proposed to Lukas in front of family and friends. "I know you're the one, Lukas. I've known that since the first time I met you."

Lukas also told his family about Taylor and when he realized he was the one. "It was here, in this house.

Dad was missing, and Taylor gave Mom and me hope. We also learned about the currents of the Persian Gulf, so I know that now, too." Lukas' family laughed. He described how sweet Taylor was to people, in general, how he made him proud, and how he wanted to help any way he could, and Lukas saw that Taylor was a man with class, empathy, character, and courage. "Plus, Taylor doesn't know that he's all these things in addition to being the hottest guy I've ever met, so don't tell him. I wouldn't want him getting an inflated ego."

****

Today was their wedding day. They planned a simple ceremony celebrating love and commitment, surrounded by family and close friends. It was a beautiful day, and the sun cast spectacular shadows on the Santa Catalina mountains. Patrick, his wife Evelyn, and their daughter Bella had flown in from London for the ceremony. Thanks to great doctors and physical therapists, Patrick recovered the use of his legs and was able to chase a soccer ball, albeit slowly, with Bella. They looked forward to welcoming baby number two in four more months.

Tory was there and brought a nice guy she'd been dating for about a year. His name was Giuseppe, and they both loved to travel. Taylor jokingly asked Tory if she had run an FBI report on Giuseppe, and to his surprise, Tory admitted she had him checked out thoroughly. "Let us know when we can start getting to know him. I don't want to get attached to anyone who won't be around." Taylor laughed.

"You can get close to him, Dad and Papa." Tory seemed happy.

Lukas and Tory developed a deep friendship, and

when he and Taylor wanted to get married, she insisted on calling Lukas Papa, saying she always wanted two parents and that she needed someone to go to when her dad told her no.

When the wedding ceremony started, Betty Bao entered as the first bridesmaid, followed by Linda, and finally, Donna, a newlywed herself. She and Wilma got married right after Donna got back from her Dubai adventure. They wanted no ceremony, but Donna had never been happier.

Wilma was much more relaxed around the Herb Society now that she was married to one of the founding members. Wilma also bought two Rhodesian Ridgeback puppies for Donna's wedding gift. "They can take down lions in Africa—so they can handle a coyote or two in Arizona," she would proudly tell people.

Taylor and Lukas appeared and held hands as they walked down the aisle. Lukas smiled and teared up, thinking of how much he loved this man and how, against so many odds, they found each other and fell in love. They wrote their own vows and recited them to each other. Taylor made a touching comment about his life since he met Lukas. "When I was about a year old in a Russian orphanage, I was adopted by my parents. All I ever wanted was to love and be loved, and look at me now. I'm surrounded by all of you, I'm a father, and I'm a husband. A family is all I ever dreamed of or wanted. Everything came true."

After the ceremony, they were announced as Mr. and Dr. Pastore-Halloran. It was a long last name, but each man wanted the other's surname, so they compromised on a combined one. By evening, the sky had turned a beautiful shade of cobalt, accented by purple and orange. People danced and celebrated under the stars. As they slowly danced to one of their favorite songs, Taylor and Lukas Pastore-Halloran held each other close. "You know," Taylor said, "it amazes me that so many crazy events conspired in order for us to cross paths, and here we are, like I've been with you forever."

"You aren't sick of me yet, are you?"

"Not even a little bit." Taylor kissed Lukas.

****

The next morning, Taylor told Lukas he had a surprise for him. They drove out to the Marana airport. "This is kind of the first place we ever really talked. I gave you my number right over there," Taylor told him. Lukas decided not to tell Taylor that he almost threw his phone number away, thinking this handsome captain only wanted a brief hookup before flying off and never seeing Lukas again. He'd maybe tell Taylor that at some point. "I've got something to show you," he said to Lukas and led him over to a gleaming new jet parked in the middle of the hangar. Taylor walked him over to the plane, and Lukas saw that it was a Spectrum 7XLR, the latest, lightest, and fastest extra-long-range business jet ever built.

"Nice jet. Is this on your Christmas wish list?" Lukas joked.

Taylor pointed to the cockpit window above. Lukas saw that *Goose 2* was painted just below the window. "Not anymore."

"You bought a new plane?"

"We bought a new plane. Adding it to the Nimbus fleet," Taylor explained. "The insurance from the original *Goose* came through, and I got a check from the UAE as a thank-you for helping them avert an international calamity." Taylor clicked a fob, and the fuselage door opened, revealing a set of stairs. Taylor encouraged Lukas to take the lead up the stairs to the interior. Once inside, Lukas surveyed the cabin. "I can't believe this is ours," he admitted to Taylor. "It's even more beautiful than the last one."

****

A dirty SUV pulled up outside the hangar. It was Tory. Giuseppe was a passenger. Both of them bounded up the stairs. "Hi, Dad." Tory kissed him. "Need a co-pilot?"

Taylor nodded. "Make sure she's ready to go. I've got a takeoff slot in seven minutes."

Within minutes, Lukas saw twenty-five more cars pull onto the tarmac. It was everyone from the wedding who had come to see them off. They applauded, cheered, and raised glasses of champagne to the new couple.

"So, baby," Taylor whispered in Lukas' ear. "Where should we go for our honeymoon?"

****

Molly, Linda, Donna, and Betty stood together, arms around each other, as they watched Taylor and Lukas depart for the runway. "I wonder where they'll go?" Donna asked.

"Well, I'd put money on it that it's not Dubai," Linda commented.

"I know Lukas has always wanted to go to Machu Picchu, so maybe that's on the agenda," Molly speculated.

Betty retorted, "Oh yeah, great place to honeymoon

when you can't even breathe."

The engines roared, and the Herb Society raised their glasses once again as *Goose 2* accelerated down the runway before it elegantly lifted into the sky.

"So what do we do next? We've saved the world and all of humanity," Molly exaggerated. "I could use some time to catch up on my reading."

Donna chimed in, "Wilma and I are looking at puppies, so we'll probably be mothers again soon!"

Linda thought. "You know? I'm going to get a massage every day this week. It'll be nice to just relax a bit."

Betty Bao stared at them incredulously. "Fuck that!" she exclaimed. "We are still young, and I'm not sitting on my ass doing nothing with a bunch of old hens."

Molly laughed. "Jeez, Betty, tell us what you really think."

"My father told me something when we fled Vietnam, and I'll never forget it," Betty added. "*We cannot change yesterday, and we can't guarantee tomorrow. All we have is today, and whatever we do today will impact tomorrow, but never yesterday. Keep looking forward, but learn from yesterday.*"

"That's a great thing to remember. Did your dad write it?" Donna asked.

"How the hell would I know?" Betty retorted. "All I'm saying is that the world has plenty of problems, and the Herb Society has plenty to keep us busy."

"I don't know about you ladies, but I had a lot of fun on our adventure," Donna remembered.

"So did I, except for the terrifying parts," Linda added.

"Yeah, and even the times we almost died," Betty emphasized.

"Well, I guess the Herb Society has spoken," Molly concluded. "In the meantime, let's go climb a mountain. Who's with me?"

****

Thousands of miles away, an old farmer and his teenage son crunched through a parched thicket of grassland and shrubbery. Following them, a small group of cows and goats, their ribs visible inside their emaciated bodies, slowly wandered through the brush, stopping occasionally to rest. The group trudged onward in search of water to fill the empty buckets carried by the two men and the cows. Most of the plant life was withered or dead. The brittle and dry grass snapped under their feet and stabbed their uncovered legs. The blackened remnants of a recent brushfire smoldered in the distance.

The old farmer stopped and pointed toward a small puddle of blue. They trudged forward until they reached the lake's edge. The water level had dropped again overnight, reducing the surface area of their lake even more. Fresh mud cracked and caked under the burning sun. The man and his son forged ahead across the newly exposed lakebed. Every step was an effort, the mud sucking at their legs and pulling them down. Dying fish flopped desperately, gulping air in their final death throes. The cows stared ahead, too tired and frightened to go any farther. It didn't matter; there was not much water left anyway.

They finally made it to what remained of the lake. From a distance, it had looked blue, reflecting the sky's brilliance, but up close, it was black and muddy. The boy gasped as he noticed water bugs skimming across what was left of the lake. Three frogs sat quietly in the shallow water, like squatters, refusing to budge. The farmer heard a humming noise in the distance, a lightly vibrating sound that sounded like it came from a machine. He surveyed the shore and noticed something in the distance, half submerged, only a few feet away from the lake's new shoreline. He shook his son by the shoulder and pointed to the object whose vibrating sound was periodically replaced by spurts of what sounded like sucking and belching. As they approached the object, the farmer noticed it appeared to be some sort of machine, its light blue casing splattered with mud and algae. Tubes ran from the machine like tentacles. A pale green light flickered and glowed like a cyclopic eye that indicated that whatever this was still had some life. He tentatively touched the machine, warm from the baking sun, and wiped some of the muck from its facing, revealing a single word he had never seen before. *DEMETER.*

A word about the author...

E. William Podojil spent his career as an international executive for Fortune 500 companies, while based in the Netherlands and United States. He earned a BFA in design and an MBA and studied screenwriting at UCLA. Podojil has traveled extensively to over sixty countries and is currently based in Northeast Ohio, where he lives with his husband and three sons. He regularly posts his stories and new projects in his blog at www.ewpodojil.com

Thank you for purchasing
this publication of The Wild Rose Press, Inc.

For questions or more information
contact us at
info@thewildrosepress.com.

The Wild Rose Press, Inc.
www.thewildrosepress.com